# RATHER A
# VICIOUS
# GENTLEMAN

Frank McAuliffe

BALLANTINE BOOKS • NEW YORK

To Mom and Dad, who did a very good job.

Copyright © 1968 by Frank McAuliffe

SBN 345–02176–2–095

All rights reserved.

First Printing: June, 1968
Second Printing: March, 1971

Cover art by Morgan Kane

Printed in the United States of America.

BALLANTINE BOOKS, INC.
101 Fifth Avenue, New York, N.Y. 10003
An Intext Publisher

# PREFATORY NOTE

Most of us, I would think, keep a history file on the people we meet in this life; even if only a mental file.

The policing establishments of the world are notorious for this sort of record keeping. Those idiots will even keep a file on chaps they have never met. Which makes it rather awkward for a gentleman in my profession.

While I am, admittedly, immune to many of the pastimes in which the average man indulges, I am not as immune, as insensitive, as some of my detractors proclaim, generally at the top of their ill-flavored voices. I have never, for instance, participated in the rape of a pregnant woman, at least not to my knowledge. Not that I am against either of these institutions: pregnant women and rape; as you shall see.

But, back to the issue of remembrances. Along with the average chap I share the need for sentimental recall. Otherwise why would I have penned this chronicle?

Memories of those I have encountered do assail me. There were the good people, the pure of heart (ah, Hope Cornflower), not very many of them to be sure. There were the impure of heart; a virtual multitude. (Where are you this day, Bertie Roche, you broken down old Spitfire pilot?)

Now, we normally do not recall those we know on the basis of when we first met them. More logically we recall the last time we met them and, if inclined, examine our memory for the last previous meeting, then the meeting prior to that, and so on.

What then more logical than to present the persons in this reminiscence in that order: the last time we met, then the time before, and on and on?

Among those you will meet in these pages is a chap named Ludwig Kelp. I have provided above the names of persons in the categories of "pure of heart" and "impure of heart." Ludwig Kelp fits neither of these. Ludwig fits in a category that keeps a business firm such as mine, Mandrell Limited, in prosperity.

You see, my firm arranges for the transfer of selected persons from this life on to the next. No, no, we are not involved in the funeral arrangements. We are on the scene rather before the undertaker.

If you will refer to the Sealed Tomb Commission which follows, you will understand. You will bear witness to the demise of Ludwig Kelp.

And you will smile.

AUGUSTUS MANDRELL

# CONTENTS

# RATHER A VICIOUS GENTLEMAN

# THE SEALED TOMB COMMISSION (1947)

THE SERGEANT SAID, "Just a minute, sir. We'll want to wait here until they unlock the other door. They won't unlock it until I have this one closed." He swung the heavy, concrete door through which we had just entered into place. The door clanged as its steel frame met the steel jamb. The sergeant rotated a lever that shot home the lock on the door.

"Even over at Nuremberg Prison we don't carry it this far," I said crossly.

"At Nuremberg," the sergeant answered, "you've a different problem, if you don't mind my saying so, sir. There, you're keeping people in. Here at Greenwood we're interested in keeping people out."

He took a telephone from the wall and spoke to somebody. "Sergeant Hawk here," he said. "Civilian Louis Proferra with me. Agent from International Military Tribunal to see Major Hammett in Complex two-two. Clearance: secret. Papers all in order."

Sergeant Hawk returned the phone to the wall. While we waited then in front of the next locked door, he said, "If you think you've seen strong security up to now, wait 'til you see what's up ahead. Particularly when it's Complex two-two you're going to."

We heard the heavy lock on the other side of the door disengage and the huge door swung toward us. "I suppose this is the only way out too," I said, my voice still childishly surly.

"It's not the only way," the sergeant said, "but it's the way you'll be coming out. It's the only exit a civilian is going to see. . . . Here he is, Henry." We were facing Henry, who had opened the second door for us. Henry was a sergeant also.

Sergeant Hawk stepped back into the tunnel through which we had entered, and closed the door, leaving me with Henry. Sergeant Hawk did not bid Louis Proferra goodby. We had not become friends during our brief acquaintance. I had seen to that.

Sergeant Henry passed me on to a Lieutenant Epstein. Epstein was a jolly sort with a good mustache. He took me to a small, six-man elevator that dropped us down what appeared to be about four storeys. Including the two flights of stairs I had descended with Sergeant Hawk, I estimated that I was then at least six storeys below ground level. Prior to boarding the elevator, Lieutenant Epstein had had to telephone someone to get the elevator door unlocked. We were then locked into the elevator for our downward journey, and had to make telephone contact with the keeper of locks and bolts once more in order to exit the elevator.

Man's mind when called upon to thwart itself will occasionally devise a labyrinth of ever diminishing circles that eventually deposit him at Absurdity. Another of those human capabilities not afforded the lower forms of life on this planet.

Lieutenant Epstein and I next boarded a small electric tram driven by an unwholesome-looking woman in uniform. The tram contained just four seats, but there was a coupling on the rear indicating that similar vehicles could be attached should the railway gain in popularity. "Watch yourself, Mr. Proferra," Lieutenant Epstein said. "These tram cars are a bit creaky. War time model. Scheduled to get the new 1947 model shortly. Perhaps for Christmas."

The major defect I noted in the electric cars was their lack of cleanliness. The seats and handrails were coated with a gritty substance that smeared instantly when touched. Inadequate air exhaust system, apparently.

"How do you like our security?" Lieutenant Epstein asked as we proceeded into a lighted tunnel. "You're in rather the same business at Nuremberg, aren't you? Holding all those

Nazi-types for trial." His voice was lubricated by a patronizing oil slick designed to keep my guilt complex inert. This diplomatic tone was in all of their voices when they mentioned Nuremberg to me. Everybody remembered Hermann Goering. Hermann had cheated our hangman with a poison pill just a month or so back. Hermann had made the International Military Tribunal Security Department quite the laughing stock.

"I'm not overly impressed with your security," I answered. "I've never been in sympathy with the theory that if one padlock brings one X-security then two locks must bring two times X. Have you ever been to see the Mona Lisa at the Louvre? You pass through but one door and there she hangs. Just one lock between the priceless lady and all the damn thieves in the world."

"She may be priceless, Mr. Proferra, but she's nothing compared to what we have here at Greenwood. There's documents in the vaults here that'll not be read by more than a handful of men for as long as they're written. You don't keep them safe by leaving the doors open."

The whine from the electric motor became more pronounced as the tram rounded a curve in the tunnel and we started upward along a rather steep incline of track. The upward travel appeared to bring us about three storeys closer to ground level.

Lieutenant Epstein nodded over his shoulder toward the receding base of the hill. "In an emergency," he said, "we can flood that whole area we just passed through. A chap bent on breaking in might get down in the elevator to the seven-one level but he'd have a time of it coming up the hill without being half fish. And all it takes is one alarm bell to open the water valves."

"What about the people at this end," I said, "how do they get out if you've flooded the exit?"

"We have our Emergency Personnel Exits, of course."

"Then there's your weak spot," I crowed. "What's to prevent an attack through your emergency exits? A bypass of this whole elaborate mechanical snare business I've already seen."

"There isn't a way in the world to break into one of the

emergency exit tunnels except with a kit of explosives," he said smiling. "And any concussion in there triggers the master alarm, which floods the tunnel in front of you. Then there's the matter of finding your way into the tunnels from outside. You absolutely can't. Best kept secret of the postwar, so to speak. Oh, we've as pretty a little cage here at Greenwood as any Pharaoh ever had in his pyramid."

The tram had reached the top of the hill. We stopped short of a steel-mesh fence that spread its twisted little tentacles completely across the railway tunnel and from floor to ceiling.

"Enough voltage in that fence to cook an elephant," Lieutenant Epstein gloated. A steel door in the side wall of the tunnel opened and an armed sergeant came out toward us. Even though the sergeant greeted Lieutenant Epstein by name he still insisted on viewing the lieutenant's identity card, in addition to scrutinizing my own entry papers. The dumpy tram driver was not asked to show any proof of her identity. Possibly on the theory that Nature, in some fit of heartless melancholy, could have produced but one such creature.

As soon as the sergeant disappeared behind his steel door again, the center section of the steel-mesh fence clicked open and our tram proceeded through. The superior smile on Lieutenant Epstein's face was rather more than I could stomach.

"It's just another locked door," I snapped. "What makes it any more valuable than the first door I got through upstairs? Look at it this way. Suppose for a minute that I don't belong in Greenwood. Suppose I knew ahead of time that an American named Louis Proferra from the International Tribunal had been cleared to visit Greenwood today. Okay, I want to get in here too, for some reason or other. I wait for Proferra, in that big parking lot upstairs, knock him over the head, and toss him into a parked car. Then I fix myself up to look like him. Even this arm business—" I flipped the empty sleeve of my overcoat "—and I walk into Visitor Security and say 'I'm Louis Proferra.' Then here I am. All the way past your locked doors. Well on my way to your very hush-hush Complex two-two."

"It's quite possible," Lieutenant Epstein said, surprisingly. "But you—if we assume you are not Louis Proferra—would never get to Complex two-two. You would be found out at Bravo Red, our next check point. You see, no one ever receives clearance to visit Greenwood unless there is some member of the Greenwood staff who can personally identify the visitor. And that means identify him from years of having known him. So somebody in here knows you, and rather well. You'll meet him at Bravo Red. Who is it, incidentally? I know most of the chaps at Bravo Red."

I chose to lapse into a peeved silence.

The tram had come to a stop at a small concrete platform. The lieutenant and I stepped out. There followed another examination of identity papers, this time at a bullet-proof window with just a slot at the bottom of the glass to permit passage of my papers inbound to a fiercely efficient young lady who retained the papers.

The young woman's voice came to us through a speaker located in the wall. "You are relieved of the visitor, Lieutenant Epstein," she said smartly.

"That's Lieutenant Goddard," Epstein said nodding at the window. "She'll let you in through that door over there as soon as I've gone." He climbed back in the tram. As the unfortunate miss at the controls drove the vehicle off, Lieutenant Epstein waved back toward my stern face.

He called, "Give my regards to Ludwig Kelp. I'm only sorry that somebody can't cop in here and kill that son of a bitch."

It occurred to me that the lieutenant's name *was* Epstein. Therefore his un-Christian solicitude for Ludwig Kelp had not only historical justification but ethnic absolution as well.

The efficient young female officer from the bullet-proof nest opened the door behind me. She glanced after the departing tram and Lieutenant Epstein. "So they know up front that we have Kelp back here," she remarked bitterly. "Some of our officers—the male officers—just can't keep their damn mouths shut at the club, can they? Here are your papers." She slapped them into my hand. "Follow me."

She led me, briskly of course, along a corridor constructed

of cement and stone. The walls had been painted but the paint did not quite restrain within the stone the dry smell of a million years.

Two uniformed women, each a few years younger than my escort, abruptly exited from a door several paces in front of us. The two were giggling and prancing about in a manner rather befitting their age. The din of their exuberance and the click of their shoes on the steel tram tracks that ran the center of the corridor left the two maids unaware of our footsteps. One of the two pinched the other thus unleashing a greater pitch of giggles.

"Carter! Grimes!" The names struck the adolescents like pistol shots. My lieutenant followed up her surprise attack with a frontal rush upon the frozen enemy. There ensued a rather predictable encounter of the type that has always embellished the armed forces' life with such enchantment for proponents of individualism.

The two ORs were quickly riddled to helplessness as the caustic shafts launched by the lieutenant tore through their thin veil of experience. Even the major defense thrown up by Privates Carter and Grimes: the fact that they had just been relieved and were on their way to a free evening in their barracks, fell before a withering salvo labeled "un-military behavior."

I maintained an icy remoteness throughout the engagement. My eye concentrated for the most part on a superb sweep of rib cage that dived like a ski trail on to a respite of flat abdomen. This shirt-covered alpine contour was the property of Private Carter. The sweet lines were impinged upon my unprotesting senses by the private's ramrod posture and by the swelling breathing cycle induced in the girl by fear.

Eventually the last bulwark maintained by the privates crumbled. Behind the redoubt was uncovered a pair of well-springs that bubbled streams of tears across the round cheeks of the two maids. The scalpel used by the sadist was washed clean in this salty torrent and then laid lovingly away behind Lieutenant Goddard's cold blue eyes. She dismissed the somewhat soggy pair of privates. They trotted off with their hands covering their faces toward a door set in an alcove further down the passageway. They were guided in their blind flight,

I suppose, by the pair of silver tram tracks that ran also to the desired door. An armed guard (male) at the door permitted the two privates immediate entry while keeping his eyes turned from their embarrassment.

As the lieutenant and I continued our stroll I asked, "Why the armed guard in front of that door?"

"That's the female barracks," she snapped. "All the rest of this area is overrun with men. Research proves that access to a women's barracks is the secret desire of every man-jack of you. I'd just like to see somebody—anybody—try it. Major O'Toole's office is just down here."

We passed into a well lighted corridor where a green tile floor kicked back the scuffing and clicking sounds made by dozens of male and female feet making their way from office door to office door. The hum of paper business being efficiently dispatched crackled throughout the Bravo Red sector. We entered Major O'Toole's office. The major's dark-haired secretary, a corporal, was inspecting the upper portion of one of her stockings. She casually drew down her skirt and greeted Lieutenant Goddard with a nod and a smile. "He'll be with you in a minute," the corporal said.

The quarter-inch of increased rigidity evident in Lieutenant Goddard's posture had been inserted, I felt certain, by the fact that the dark-haired corporal had received Lieutenant Goddard with somewhat less respect than military protocol requires. Rather a dilemma for Lieutenant Goddard. Should one upbraid the secretary of a senior officer? Or should one take the pragmatic out? To tell the truth I was somewhat disappointed as I stood there listening to Lieutenant Goddard's silence. She was an attractive woman who was obviously directing her normal lusts into a less rewarding channel: military discipline. She should have spoken up. Otherwise she was dealing in gigantic waste.

Eventually Major O'Toole called us in and signed the paper signifying that he was accepting delivery of me in his area. O'Toole was one of those short chaps. I mean, so much shorter than average height, say five-one or two, that he had to be dealt with with care. Nothing is truer than the belief that short men compensate for their stature by developing extraordinary aggressive sensibilities.

As O'Toole was signing Lieutenant Goddard's bill of delivery, I allowed my shoulders to develop a very noticeable slouch. O'Toole, with his understandable fetish for a vertebra maintained exactly perpendicular to the floor, received as a gift from me this minor triumph in posture. I shall expect your gratitude, sir.

"Won't keep you but a minute, Mr. Proferra," O'Toole said. "As soon as we have—" he glanced at a folder he had on his desk "—as soon as we have Sir Thomas Roche down here to make the face-to-face ID. So you know Sir Thomas? You do come highly recommended."

He looked at Lieutenant Goddard and said coolly, "On your way out have Corporal Pitkin get me Code 4800 on the line."

The lieutenant's "Yes, sir," was delivered with the snap of a rapier thrust. And her salute would have cracked a mason brick, had one been located in the path of her hand. Major O'Toole, I gathered, was rather high on the list of those male officers who dreamed continually of foraging in the women's barracks. The lieutenant left.

"Sit down, sit down," O'Toole said. "They'll have Sir Thomas here momentarily. He's with Staff, you know. Not much of a trip over here. Then we can pass you on to Complex two-two. So you've gotten clearance to visit Ludwig Kelp? You must be well thought of in your field. What do you do for the International Tribunal?"

His face took on the smooth intentness of a man who has just switched on a tape recorder in his head. In six months, I felt certain he would be able to repeat our conversation word for word. A few of the really good barristers have this ability; retaining on some interior wax surface every word spoken in court, frequently to the embarrassment of the Crown.

"I had the impression," I said, like a man still suffering the indignity of being "put in his place," "that I wasn't supposed to mention to anybody just why I've come to this damn place."

The major laughed a quick sterile laugh and said, "It's quite all right to talk about it now. You're in Bravo Red. With the exception of Complex two-two—and one other area that I can't even mention—you have reached the pinnacle of our security shield. Why, even the idea that the wrong person could penetrate this far is unthinkable."

He leaned back in his chair a bit and his voice was honed lovingly by the fine abrasive file of the fanatic. His eyes stared out over my head at a sight not known to lesser men. "Here at Greenwood," he said, "we have forged the tightest security ring ever known to man. Absolutely infallible. I myself, I might mention, was in on the initial development. I supervised the 'antibackout' defenses. That is, the feature of the system which ensures that even if an intruder gets past a checkpoint, he can never retrace his steps. Every barrier he passes does not put him closer to his objective. It only locks him deeper in our clutches, so to speak."

His secretary buzzed and told him she had Code 4800 on the line. She asked if he wanted to call on the "scrambler" line, referring to a second telephone on his desk. "No, no, this is internal," he told her. "I'll take it on 'channel.'"

The major asked to speak to Sir Thomas Roche at Code 4800. They told him Sir Thomas was not in the area. The major's voice took on the impatience of the hard-working perfectionist who keeps the front end of the polished machine in excellent working order and discovers suddenly that the other end of the machine, lubricated by inattention, is producing great sheets of complacency. He told Code 4800 to find Sir Thomas and be quick about it. "You people know damn well he's due in my office for face-to-face ID. Perhaps you could do with a rereading of fifty-four seventy-four down there. Face-to-face ID takes priority over any other assignment, unless waived by General Coder himself."

"There may be a few minutes delay," O'Toole said to me as he broke the telephone connection. "You understand, I can't take the responsibility of passing you on to Complex two-two until we've had face-to-face. Don't worry, they'll find Sir Thomas for us shortly."

He suggested then that I could remove my overcoat and leave it in his office for retrieval on my departure. "Bit stuffy in Complex two-two," he mentioned. I told him that I was quite accustomed to climatic absurdity. " . . . Sahara to Battle of the Bulge. . . ." My coat remained in place.

O'Toole fiddled with the folder in front of him on his desk. After a moment he said, "Ever since I saw your 'background' this morning I've been ... er ... rather intrigued. I see here you've met a man named Augustus Mandrell. Much ... er ... to your disfavor." He let his eye flick mournfully over my empty sleeve. "Evidently you met him in Teheran in '42. Had him trapped and all, and he escaped by exploding some device or other?"

"It was a damn sidearm that he'd rigged up to explode right in the hands of one of your best Colonial Intelligence people," I said. "Colonel Duncan Purdy was the Intelligence man. I was standing right next to the poor guy when the thing blew up. I lost an arm. Purdy lost a hell of a lot more."

"And you met Mandrell again in France following D-day," O'Toole said, reading from the folder. "You were CO of a prisoner of war camp at Welborn. Mandrell broke into the camp and killed a Vichy French general. You were shot by one of your own men during the confusion. Then the same Mandrell shot your ear off in the London hospital. I must say—"

"As far as I'm concerned, buddy, there's nothing you 'must say.' Read the damn file to yourself if you're so interested. Do you think I enjoy being reminded?"

"You misunderstand me," he said. "The thing is I know this fellow Mandrell. Early in the war we were worried about Jerry invading England. Their top invasion expert was a General Von Ritterdorf. I recommended to my CO—I was in Special Services then—that we get Augustus Mandrell to go into Germany and eliminate Von Ritterdorf. I'd heard about Mandrell at Scotland Yard before enlisting. Worked out rather well. Von Ritterdorf was popped off. But it looked so much like an accident that we couldn't be sure Mandrell did it. So CO and myself got together with Budget and we decided we needed the 5000 pounds more than Mandrell did. The 5000 was the remainder of his fee, you see."

"What you should have done was shot the bastard," I said.

"We might get the chance to do that yet. Our undercover network, the boys on the outside, have picked up an interesting rumor. There's whispers about that the Zionists have hired Mandrell to get Ludwig Kelp. You can imagine how the Jews would love to have a go at Kelp considering all the slaughter Kelp was responsible for in the Balkans."

"But you've got Kelp locked up in here," I said.

"We've him locked away all right. Wait until you see him. He's inside a destruct-proof boiler, or tank. We've no worry about Mandrell coming into Greenwood after Kelp. But when we take Kelp out for his trip to Nuremberg, or out for the Inquiry Board next week, there's when we might get a shot at Mandrell. That's when he'll try for Kelp."

His secretary buzzed to say Code 4800 was on the phone. O'Toole answered and listened for a few seconds. Then he said, "What in bloody hell was Sir Thomas doing at the exit? . . . All right, get him down here as quickly as possible." He rang off. "Unbelievable slip up," he said. "Sir Thomas was on his way out of Greenwood. Some accident to his wife, they tell me. Code 4800 got rattled and forgot about the face-to-face ID. Don't worry, they've caught up with Sir Thomas. They'll have him down—"

I stood up impatiently and said, "My time is not inexhaustible, Major. Can't we skip this nonsense and let me get going to Complex two-two? If I knew the way I'd just go there myself."

"They'd never let you in. I have to pass you through personally. It'll only be another fifteen minutes, Mr. Proferra." The secretary buzzed him again to inform him that Parking Area No. 2 Security was on the line.

O'Toole took the call. He listened for a second. Then he said, puzzled, "You found what man 'bound and gagged' in what auto?" After listening again, his eye fell away from mine quite deliberately. He mumbled, "One . . . one arm. . . ." He had become rather pale.

Obviously the time had arrived for cooler heads to assume command. Major O'Toole was a good man and all that but he wasn't up to the sort of shock that had been delivered to him by Parking Area No. 2 Security. As he had said himself: the idea that any unauthorized person could penetrate to Bravo Red was unthinkable.

The poor man's brain became completely absorbed in

regrouping to accept a new gospel. The brain gave away old ground grudgingly, to judge by the fixed stare that had frozen O'Toole's eyes.

I stepped to his side and dented the back of his neck with the edge of my palm.

As he collapsed to the floor, I grabbed the telephone from his sweaty grip. A male voice supported by shoddy schooling was speaking through the instrument. ". . . so I'm ready to sound the B-Zone Alarm. Unless the Major thinks I should sound the A-Zone alarm?"

"No damn alarm at all," I said to the idiot, quickly grafting O'Toole's speech pattern to my voice. "Don't go getting the whole bloody show in an uproar. The man who got past you is right here in my office. Got my pistol rammed straight in his mouth. And two sergeants are just coming in—" I directed my next speech to the wall "—Here he is, men. That's it, put those restrainers on his wrists good and tight. We're all fixed up down here," I told the Parking Area lout. "Bravo Red Security knows its business. I'm bringing the prisoner right up. Instead of being so quick to activate the alarm, you people better be getting ready to explain how this man got through." I broke off with an indignant slam of the receiver.

I examined O'Toole. His period of inactivity promised to be at least twenty minutes in length. Twenty minutes was all I could hope for, what with Sir Thomas Roche on his way down for the face-to-face ID. My Louis Proferra disguise was rather marginal, sufficiently faithful to meet the written description contained in my papers. The disguise would not mislead one who knew Proferra personally. Nor had I laid it on with that intent. Damn O'Toole.

I considered taking the necessary step for extending the Major's sleep by many years; one forceful jab into the spinal column nerve complex. The wretched man had perfomed his security assignment much more effectively than he realized. It had been O'Toole's martinet persuasion that had accelerated the search for Sir Thomas, thus causing the apprehension of Sir Thomas prior to his exit from Greenwood.

A frightful foreign ingredient had been thrown into my precision-built schedule. By plan, I should have been inside

Complex two-two and finished with Ludwig Kelp prior to any general alert attesting my presence.

I gripped O'Toole's collar and dragged him behind his desk. Happily he was a small man. I found any exertion involving the use of my one free arm rather more taxing than I had anticipated. But of course the shackling of the other arm out of sight had been a requisite since the real Louis Proferra possessed but one of these major appendages. I decided against delivering O'Toole to eternal rest. But I can hardly be blamed- if in dragging him behind the desk I did little to avoid any collision between his head and the base of his chair. Major O'Toole had been a debtor of mine for much longer than I had been aware. A man who steals 5000 pounds from another man cannot really expect civility in return for his greed.

I grabbed up O'Toole's telephone and told his secretary, Corporal Pitkin, to put me on the "scrambler" line. I was about to ring General Coder, I said.

"I can ring his office for you, Major," she said.

"No, no," I snapped. "I'm using a classified number to reach him. Just put me on the scrambler."

When I heard the line connect to the near vacuum tone of the scrambler line, I laid the telephone in the middle of the desk. Since General Coder was the Commanding Officer of Greenwood, I suspected that Corporal Pitkin would hardly dare eavesdrop. Thus she would be spared the unsettling discovery that her immediate supervisor, O'Toole, and her CO were apparently at a loss for words in their telephone conversation. Any illusions enjoyed by the ORs should not, I feel, be snatched from them too abruptly.

I then left O'Toole's office and went to sit with his secretary. I smiled with embarrassment and said to her, "The major's on a classified call. He suggested I wait out here." Her returning smile was fully sympathetic. I sat quietly for thirty seconds, thirty precious seconds, watching her dispatch several folders of papers from one basket to another. Then I said, "I suppose you've heard it many times, and it really must bore you by now, but by George the resemblance is really striking."

"The resemblance?" the poor thing said.

"It's remarkable. As though the Duchess of Alba had been reborn and is up and around again."

"I look like some duchess?" She was on the verge of snickering. That wouldn't do.

"You mean to tell me nobody's ever? ... I mean, that's an outrage. What the devil's wrong with the young guys in this country?" She sensed then that she had on her hands somewhat more than an issue of adolescent flirting.

"My dear young lady, you are the Duchess of Alba! The resemblance is more than superficial. If a guy just looked at Francisco Goya's painting of the Duchess, he'd see that you're practically identical twins. Why, your hair alone is the exact shade, not to mention the complexion." Ahhh, there my young miss, that hit home, did it not? Poor Corporal Pitkin. Hers was not a face of unblemished perfection. But, other than that, oddly enough, she was not without her credentials in the comparison I had presented. As far as I could see.

"I guess I've never seen the painting," she said. As if to prove her statement, she sat up straighter in her chair, pursuing some erroneous image of the Duchess.

"Doggone, I'm going to miss a luncheon appointment with the general if this keeps up," I said, looking at my watch. "Is the major still on the telephone?" She glanced at her telephone and said yes.

"Look," I said getting up, "I'm going to have to check with him." I had walked to Major O'Toole's door and opened it before Corporal Pitkin's protest left her lips.

With my head hidden past the edge of the door from the secretary, I called in O'Toole's voice, "Oh, Lou, I'm sorry about this delay. General Coder has just asked me to move you on to Complex two-two as quickly as possible. But he still has me on the line."

"Couldn't your secretary get me through?" I asked the unconscious gentleman on the floor. Speak up, you mutt.

"Good thinking," the voice from beyond the door said. "Corporal Pitkin, get Lou on to Complex two-two, will you. Here, Lou, here's your folder and your papers."

I walked into the room and grabbed the folder and ID papers from the desk. As I walked from O'Toole's office, he was heard to say, "Good luck, Lou. Come back anytime.

Yes, yes, General, I'm here. Yes, sir, I'll see—" The rest of his conversation was lost as I closed the door.

Corporal Pitkin had risen. She said, "We can give it a try. Usually they're pretty sticky at two-two, insist the major escort the visitors. Who are you to see?"

"A Major John Hammett," I said.

"We may be in luck then," she said, leading me into the blessed corridor. "Johnny is regular. The girls in the barracks voted him 'the officer they'd most like to have trapped in the barracks.' But don't be telling him that."

She led me to a single undistinguished-looking door. "Here's the entrance to Complex two-two," she said. It was obvious she was waiting for my reaction.

"Holy mackerel," I said. "I figured the door would be ten feet thick and have two machine guns outside." She laughed. "Everybody feels that way first time they see it." She pressed a simple buzzer set in the wall. A voice from a speaker located next to the buzzer said, "Yes?"

Corporal Pitkin explained the situation. She wielded General Coder's name with strategic application. There was some quibbling from the speaker: "Where is Major O'Toole?" Corporal Pitkin said, "Put on Major Hammett please." Hammett came on the speaker. Corporal Pitkin, using a tone of amused harassment, again explained the situation. Major Hammett said he was expecting me and would be right out to escort me into Complex two-two.

No set of regulations is immune to the manipulation of an intelligent, efficient secretary who knows how to get things done. While we waited for Major Hammett to open the door to Nirvana, Corporal Pitkin said, "I'll have to look for that painting of the Duchess."

I said, "I sure think you should. I'm telling you, if they put the two of you side by side, I'd like to be there to see it." Major Hammett arrived and took me from all that sort of contemplation.

I had arrived at Complex two-two!

"We've Ludwig Kelp back this way," Major Hammett said, leading me along a corridor of offices. "He's in a tank we rigged up. It's sealed from outside. Has bullet-proof glass windows. Self-contained sanitary facilities. His food goes in through a double-lock chamber; can't open one side until the other side is locked. Food is in small squares so there's no hiding anything in it. Twenty-four hour watch to see he doesn't bash his head against the walls. One thing we're determined here in Greenwood—nothing is going to happen to the bastard while we have him."

We were past the office section. A steel door was opened for us by an armed guard and we entered a sterile corridor of ceramic tile walls and bright blue lights caged in flush with the ceiling. The single homey touch to the corridor was the existence of a lavatory at one point.

"Has Kelp been nervous?" I asked. "Had he heard any of these rumors about the Jews trying to kill him?"

"It's strange, but I think he has. I don't know how. I suppose a man with as many atrocities on his conscience as Kelp possibly develops a sense normal people don't develop. He's been more nervous than ever these past few days."

Major Hammett was a decent sort, very friendly. Too damn friendly, as a matter of fact. In an effort to make me "feel at home" he moved us along the corridor at an infuriatingly casual pace. He mentioned that we had plenty of time. "Ludwig Kelp isn't going any place." The major could not be blamed, I suppose, for not knowing that "time" was a quantity that was being stolen from me with piercing abruptness by his unreasonable hospitality.

"It could be that Ludwig Kelp's anxiety is an awareness of the approach of the day of retribution," I said and attempted to quicken our pace.

"That could be," Hammett said and stopped dead still to think over my earthshaking analysis. "What do you want of him, Mr. Proferra? Preliminary questioning for the trials of Nuremberg?"

"Oh no, no. Plenty of time for that. I'm interested in his commercial ventures during the war." I deliberately set off again down the corridor. Hammett paused for a startled moment, then hurried to catch up with me.

"Oh, is that what the Special Inquiry Board is all about next week?" he asked.

"Yes. Kelp is known to have looted every major library in the Balkans," I said. "Most of the stuff was found but there's still a big chunk missing. The Cavarocchi paintings are a good example. Seventeen oils by the Albanian master Nicholas Cavarocchi. We know Kelp had them."

"You mean the Inquiry Board will pull Kelp out of here just to ask him about a packet of paintings? Take a chance on the Zionists killing him?"

"It's pretty serious business," I said pompously. "Three or four of the paintings have shown up on the art market. Some of the experts claim they're fakes. Other experts say they're genuine Cavarocchis. Ludwig Kelp can help straighten out the whole thing if he tells us what he did with them. I might mention that a couple of my countrymen, Americans, have bought these Cavarocchis, and paid good money too. They're pretty upset at this talk about fakes. A guy like Hank Van de Erve, the head of Uni-Coffee, doesn't want to think the two Cavarocchis he has in the lobby of his New York office building are going to make him a laughing stock. He sort of brought pressure," I said proudly, "to get the Inquiry Board on the road."

"But dammit man, don't they realize the risk they're causing?" Hammett wasn't hanging back now. He moved along smartly to keep his case close to my ear. "Here we spend all this effort and expense to ensure Kelp's safety—"

"What you don't seem to realize, Major," I said, "is that there are Allied Military people involved in this dirty business. Kelp was captured in Yugoslavia. Obviously he had his loot nearby when he was apprehended. Somebody got hold of it. Some military people. They didn't turn all of it in. Now they're trying to make a profit on it. The Inquiry Board intends to find out who these military people are."

"But Kelp was picked up by British Forces," Major Hammett said.

"Yes," I said coldly. "We are all well aware of that."

The coldness of my tone was reciprocated by Major Hammett. He muttered, "I supposed you're here and that's that. We'll have to show you Kelp. Come along." The camaraderie was happily shattered. Hammett led me smartly to a door that put us on a landing overlooking a large concrete-walled room.

The room hissed with the sounds of squirting compressed

air that leaked from various rubber hose connections. Most of the hoses ran to several box-enclosed instruments located on long tables scattered about. Two main hoses, basically black in color but wrapped with red tape to differentiate them from their other reptilian brethren, were routed to a steel house located exactly in the center of the room.

The house, about the size of a small delivery van, was the residence of Herr Ludwig Kelp. Individual privacy has never been an absorption of the Military. They had certainly not permitted their assignment as Kelp's jailers to dilute their thinking on the subject. The steel house was ringed with windows located at eye-level. Ludwig could not make a move that was not observed from outside his cozy vat.

Three junior officers were in the room. They spent their time walking about with charts and recording the information indicated on the instruments attached to the rubber hoses.

Despite Major Hammett's animosity to me, he'd have been less than human had he not felt some curiosity regarding my reaction to the sight of this achievement in the art of maximum security.

"Now that's what I call a jail," I said with enthusiasm. "What are the hoses? Some sort of sewerage system?"

"Compressed air supply," Hammett said shortly, but not without pride.

"Air supply!" I bubbled. "You mean you've actually cut him off completely from Nature's world. I'll be a son of a gun."

My enthusiasm did not go unrewarded. As Hammett led me down the narrow, spiral staircase to the floor of the room, he quoted a glib column of figures to me: input pressure, exhaust velocity, cubic centimeters of volume, all applicable to the air system. Then I heard a resumé of the other services being accorded Herr Kelp: calorie count and vitamin content of the daily food ration ("... had his breakfast about an hour ago...."); sanitary facilities, number of gallons of water per day; entertainment: hand-operated gramophone, books.

"We gave him a copy of the King James version at first," Hammett said. "Plus some volumes on Jewish history. Orders from General Coder. But Ludwig wasn't partial to that. Sat around in a funk. Wouldn't eat. He gets some decent stuff now. Thrillers for the most part. German translations of Ambler, Agatha Christie, Kip Chase. Very fond of Mary Roberts Reinhart."

The report of Herr Kelp's preference in books was evident. At the moment he was stretched on his cot with a copy of Reinhart's *The Door* in his hands. As I peered in at the man called the Balkan Butcher, his very clear blue eyes leapt from the book and staked themselves to my face. The eyes did not contain fear. Just intelligent speculation.

He had about eighty pages yet to read in Miss Reinhart's book. Ah well. . . .

"I suppose this is your communication with him," I said, pointing at a microphone and tape recorder sitting on a desk.

Hammett nodded. "Chaps from Intelligence come down and chat with him now and again. He's not much of a talker. You should see General Coder's face get red when Kelp refuses to answer him."

"Really amazing," I said, looking about at all the gadgetry in the room. My eye ran wildly seeking out the red valve with the hinged top. According to the photograph I'd seen, the valve would be about the size of a hand grenade. I finally spied the device. Some idiot had partially covered it with a paper wrapping.

"I guess your compressor is behind the wall there?" I said, walking across the maze of rubber tubing. "And this must be a moisture trap or filter of some sort?" I gave the paper wrapping a quick yank, half ripping it from the red valve.

Then I stared down in disbelief at what I had uncovered!

"Yes," Hammett said. "That's the filter. Had the lab people down just yesterday to install that wire mesh over the lid. Lieutenant Nash here sent for them. Nash felt the filter was a weak link. That anybody who wanted to pot old Kelp could do it by simply lifting the lid and dropping a few poison pellets down the pipe." Hammett smiled. "Nash, as you'll note, is young yet."

Lieutenant Nash grew quite red with embarrassment, but

still managed a bright grin. Had I been standing closer to him I'm not certain that I could have restrained myself from striking him.

I released the two soft poison pellets from my fingers and withdrew my hand from my pocket.

Too much time had passed since leaving Major O'Toole on the floor of his office. There had to be another rat hole through which Ludwig Kelp could be delivered the dietary innovation contained in my pocket.

"All of your hoses appear to be rather firmly attached," I said to Hammett.

"I wouldn't pull on them that hard, sir," the major said. "They are wired down well but there's always that one chance. Did you want me to get you an interpreter down? Kelp doesn't speak any English and I and the lads here know just enough of Jerry's language to tell Ludwig to behave."

"I speak the language," I said crossly as I moved to the microphone. "That's one reason I was assigned the interrogation. Now, what the hell, Major, why can't you pull him out for a minute so I can talk to him face to face? These electrical contraptions—"

"Not a chance, sir. Our number one order is keep him inside."

On the wall behind Kelp's cage was a board containing three lights, a red, a green, and a yellow. Each light was identified by a placard. The yellow meant ALERT. The green meant B-ZONE ALARM. The red was the A-ZONE ALARM. The lights were all extinguished.

I sat in front of the microphone and opened communication with the Balkan Butcher. Ludwig Kelp had not lost his arrogance. After my voice reached him he stared out at me for several seconds without moving. Then he slowly left the bunk and walked stiffly to the microphone located in his cage. He was tall; his balding head held in a bow to avoid the metal ceiling.

"I have some good news for you," I told him in German. "The Allies are having great difficulty locating witnesses to testify against you at Nuremberg. That is: Witnesses who have concrete knowledge of your activities in Yugoslavia. It seems many of them were eliminated during the last six weeks before the English and Marshal Tito reached Belgrade."

"Who are you?" he asked, his voice rightfully suspicious.

"It appears you cannot possibly draw a death penalty," I continued. "You might get off with as little as ten or fifteen years."

"The Nuremberg Trials are illegal," he sputtered. "A man cannot be prosecuted for obeying orders."

"You have some friends who feel the same way," I said. "They have sent me to assure you that you will not have to suffer the indignity of such a trial."

Abruptly the yellow ALERT light on the wall in back of Kelp's boiler illuminated. A buzzing alarm sounded throughout the room.

"See what that is, will you, Nash," Major Hammett said to the young lieutenant. Nash walked to the rear wall and started talking on a telephone that was mounted below the yellow light.

I forced my stomach muscles tight for a second, then slowly relaxed. I smiled sadly at Ludwig Kelp and raised my eyes as though asking him if he could hear the ominous buzzer.

"How does your air supply smell?" I said to the prisoner. "Notice any difference since I was over by the filter a minute ago? Nothing to worry about. You still have thirty seconds at least. We of the Hagannah are not without our merciful side." Kelp's eyes grew wide. A rather pretty blue.

"What are you asking him about the Hagannah?" Major Hammett said to me. "That's the Jewish terrorist group, isn't it?"

I nodded to the major and indicated I would answer him in a minute. I turned back to Ludwig, who was sniffing the air. His brow had pulled down over suspicious eyes.

I said, "The English major, who is rather a fool, has just asked me why you have become so pale. He wants to know if anything is wrong. He didn't see me drop the gas into the air supply. Goodby, Ludwig. You'll start thrashing around and screaming in a few seconds. I have to be out of here." I stood up.

"Halt!" Ludwig cried, his voice coming to us with metallic

shrillness over the intercom receiver. "Stop him!" He was up banging at the window with his fist.

From the back of the room Lieutenant Nash called, "Major, Security says they're about to throw a B-Zone Alarm. This is no drill. Major O'Toole is coming on and wants to talk to you."

Ludwig Kelp continued hammering on the window. His shirt was slowly darkening with sweat stains. "Get me out! Get me out! . . ." he screamed.

"What in God's name. . . ." Hammett sputtered, staring at Kelp. "Tell O'Toole I'm coming," he called to Lieutenant Nash.

I grabbed his arm. My voice was frightened. "Major, how long ago did you say Kelp had his breakfast? He says he has terrible cramps. His stomach is being eaten by acid!" I had to shout above the screaming of Kelp coming over the intercom, which of course, I had left open.

Kelp pushed away from his microphone and started moving around his prison, beating on the walls and staggering like a wounded beast that is intent on expiring without grace. The human imagination is Man's most entertaining companion. But it is an extremely gullible faculty.

The green B-Zone light illuminated. A harsh, clanging bell threw its ugly echoes around the room, causing Lieutenant Nash to cover one ear and bend over as he attempted to hear the conversation on the telephone.

Kelp, in his cage, in his damn protective cocoon, had his back to me and Major Hammett. "Look, we have a chance yet!" I cried, my voice aimed directly into Hammett's ear. "He's vomiting. How quickly can we get a doctor down here?"

Sweat broke out on Major Hammett's face as he flailed his mind, pleading with it to produce some neat command decision. The other two junior officers had something to do. As soon as the B-Zone Alarm had sounded they had opened a locked cabinet and were adding to their burdens the trappings of the soldier in action: belt, holster, and sidearm; gas mask kit; steel helmet; truncheon; and a yellow plastic arm band that could be seen in the dark, thus identifying friend from foe in the gloom of chaos.

Lieutenant Nash was shouting from the telephone. We couldn't hear him until he moved closer to the back end of Kelp's prison, bringing the telephone receiver with him to the limit of the electric cord.

"They say there's unauthorized personnel in Greenwood!" Nash shouted.

"They'd best search the kitchen," I shouted to Hammett. "That's where the poison came from."

C'mon, Major Hammett. Action, man. Action. The decision appears rather obvious to me.

I turned my pale stricken face directly in front of the confused major. "My God," I screeched, "another Hermann Goering scandal!"

Hammett's eyes were shocked to life. "Not while I have the duty," he cried. He pushed me out of his path and ran to the end wall of Kelp's boiler. "Here, Cottrell, Crumbaugh, give a hand here," he shouted to the two armed officers. They immediately fell to and commenced undogging the latches that secured the entrance plate of the steel prison.

Kelp, on his side of the exit, threw himself against the plate and attempted to dislodge it by the less sophisticated method of brute actuation.

That's more like it, lads!

Hammett shouted to Lieutenant Nash, "Get that ass O'Toole off the line and contact Medical."

I saw that I could be of no further assistance to the major. I withdrew discreetly up the spiral staircase to the landing by the door to the corridor. As I undid the buttons of my overcoat, I watched the frenzied retrieval of Ludwig Kelp from his boiler. The entrance plate was lifted out of place by the junior officers. Kelp collapsed, gasping for air, across the threshold of the opening, half in and half out of what he had been led to believe was his sealed tomb. The military chaps grabbed him under the arms and dragged him upright. Kelp's head pitched loosely back and forth on his neck, his face aimed at the ceiling.

Then Kelp's eyes caught sight of me on the platform overhead. His head snapped to an abrupt stop. He appeared particularly intrigued by the pistol that I held rigidly in my hand.

At that moment a shocking noise shook the whole of Greenwood. A combination of bells and sirens split the air. The A-Zone Alarm had been declared.

The explosion from my pistol was almost incidental to the great wave of clamorous sound that bounced from the concrete walls about us, causing even the metal railing under my hand to sing with vibration.

The sudden, dead weight of Ludwig Kelp very nearly pulled the two junior officers from their feet. The last memory I took with me from the room was the sight of Major Hammett's face, startled to complete smoothness, rotating slowly from the sight of Kelp's collapsed corpse to myself. He watched me with stupefied calm as I opened the corridor door and exited.

Goodby, Major. May the god of loquaciousness visit your side frequently in the next several days.

As I slammed the door on Kelp's temporary resting place, I threw back the portion of my overcoat that covered my left arm. The corridor before me, with its bluish lighting was empty, but the sounds of fast-moving boots were to be heard in adjacent corridors beneath the fantastic clamor of alarms. As I moved rapidly toward the first intersecting corridor, my escape route out of Greenwood, I struggled with the leather bindings that lashed my left forearm to the small of my back. One of the damn slip knots had become partially unanchored and was no longer a slip knot but a tightly set knot of normal configuration. A fingernail broke, adding slippery blood to the tangled mess of leather wrapping. I paused and tried to pull my left arm out to where I could view the problem.

A voice just behind me called: "Just what the hell are you doing in this area?"

An Army captain and three ORs were standing just behind me. The captain held a pistol aimed with blatant incaution at my chest cavity.

When I turned to face them the captain's eyes abruptly saw beyond the civilian overcoat that hung over my one shoulder. He saw the gleaming general's insignia on my other shoulder.

"Oh, sorry sir," he stammered, and returned his gun to its case. The men behind him popped to attention.

"Quite all right, Captain," I shouted. "Lend a hand here will you." I turned the snarled knots to his eager fingers. He had my arm free in a moment.

As I stretched the numb arm slowly, I shouted to the four of them, "Don't ever take a piece of eighty-eight shrapnel in the elbow if you can avoid it. The damn Medical will have you in a harness like this the rest of your life."

I threw my overcoat to the nearest private and said, "All right, come along. Let's see what this A-Zone Alarm is about. What have you heard? I was busy in the 'radiation' complex when the alarm sounded." I turned to the private. "Careful with that garment, lad. The synthetic lead lining is rather brittle." He blinked with confusion under my demanding stare. Then he lifted his arm head-high so as to hold the coat at full length.

As we moved briskly along the corridor, where other soldiers were being stationed at strategic intervals—at each doorway and corridor intersection—Captain Calkins explained that he was not aware of the specific cause of the A-Zone Alarm.

The captain was in charge of "Tunnel Security." When he encountered me, he had been about the task of changing the guards who were stationed at the machine guns in the tunnels. "No telling how long the alarm will last," he said. "I want at least one rested man at each gun emplacement."

I commended his action, carrying my approval even to the extent of slapping his shoulder and calling out, "Good soldier." He was so aswim in the narrow pit of momentary glory that he took no note of the odd fact that I had pulled my general's cap from my blouse and installed it on my head. Nor did he take it as anything but a compliment that I stood by with him and watched as he changed the guard at one of the tunnels.

We stopped at the steel door that led to the tunnel. Captain Calkins pressed a buzzer next to the door to alert the two soldiers inside to our presence. Through the bullet-proof glass we watched a private jump from his glass-domed gun pit and trot over to face us from his side of the entry door.

Calkins took a plastic card from his pocket and passed it through a slot located in the steel door just below the window. There was a speaker attached to the wall just above the door. The private's voice came out to us through the speaker. "Yes, sir, have it opened in a sec."

The other soldier inside the tunnel remained in the gun control booth, staring out over the barrels of the twin machine guns down the long blue-lit tunnel, his eyes aimed hypnotically at the point where the two shiny paralleled tramway rails that ran off out of sight down the tunnel appeared to come to a single point.

It was the soldier who remained at his post who received the relief. As soon as the private at the entry door had inserted the plastic card into a contraption that unlocked the door, he was sent back to the gun position accompanied by the private who had been carrying my coat. The coat went over to the man who had been relieved. A corporal in our group gave him instructions in just how to carry the garment.

The next corridor was my immediate destination. "I'll leave you here," I told the good captain. "See that the coat gets back to the 'radiation center.' Do you know where it is?"

"I'll find it, sir," he shouted, saluting smartly. He was not about to admit that he had never heard of the place.

The corridor I entered was one Major Hammett had led me through on my way to visit Ludwig Kelp. Several soldiers came through the door at the far end, the door that separated the Bravo Red section from Complex two-two. The lads passed me, maintaining a good military "eyes front" as they trotted past my array of potent brass. As soon as they disbursed out of sight, I ducked into a lavatory.

The insignia on my shoulder identified me as a general but I was not yet the "right" general. I was only Louis Proferra with a rank the real Louis had never achieved. I washed the Proferra disguise from my face. The whitish substance on my left ear (the fake ear) came away with exasperating reluctance. I pulled my kit from under my shirt and laid out the eyebrows, hairpiece and weathered complexion of a far more famous general. None other than that of Lieutenant General Keith Coder, Commanding Officer of Greenwood.

I had the hairpiece and eyebrows in place and was in the act of inserting the thin rolls of rubber between my molars and cheeks (Coder possesses the firm ruddy cheeks of a discriminating trencherman) when I heard the clatter of more soldiers in the corridor. Over the din of the alarm bells a harsh voice was calling directions. ". . . every doorway. And inspect that lavatory. . . ."

I snatched up my kit and ran into the cubicle. The door to the lavatory was slapped open. I heard the terrible sound of an Enfield bolt being actuated to push a bullet into firing position.

"All right, come on out of there," a confident voice snapped just outside my confined hiding place. "Out, or I'll put a bit of hot lead through the wall."

I exited with my hands still busy buttoning my trousers. "What the hell is this, Sergeant," I growled. "Do you think your CO can anticipate when we're going to have a damn A-Zone Alarm?"

He was properly flabbergasted. "What's the form anyway?" I asked.

"Unauthorized personnel in Greenwood, sir," he blurted. "A one-armed civilian. Last seen entering Complex two-two."

"God dammit, how did that happen?! Get me to Major O'Toole's office immediately. I want to know what's happened to security down here."

As he quickly backed out the door to clear a path for me, I said, "Hold on. I'd best take this." I pulled the yellow plastic band from his arm and installed it on my own sleeve.

"I don't want you lads shooting at me in the event the lighting system goes out. Come along."

He came along; with what thoughts in his mind I cannot say.

We exited Complex two-two and marched through Bravo Red to Major O'Toole's office. Poor Corporal Pitkin was seated at her desk sobbing with her face pressed against the blotter. Her resemblance to the Duchess of Alba was somewhat less apparent.

We were told by the sergeant standing uncomfortably on

guard over prisoner Pitkin that Major O'Toole was at the Bravo Red entrance directing security arrangements to ensure that the invader did not escape.

My sergeant and I proceeded to the Bravo Red entrance. We passed the door to the female barracks, still under guard, and arrived at the small room where the lovely, cold Lieutenant Goddard had accepted delivery of Louis Proferrra from Lieutenant Epstein less than an hour earlier.

On this occasion there was a male lieutenant on duty behind the bullet-proof window that overlooked the tram stop located out in the tunnel. A thin telephone cord ran out through the slit under the window and into the tunnel. The eye, following the black cord, found that it terminated at Major O'Toole. He and three other officers were standing in the tram tracks where Lieutenant Epstein had deposited me.

The lieutenant behind the window took note of his commanding officer's presence. He immediately pressed the buzzer that released the lock on the door leading to the tunnel. I dismissed my sergeant escort and pushed through the door to take my leave of Bravo Red. So much for Major O'Toole and his "anti-backout" defenses.

I stepped out on to the unloading platform perfectly ready to assume command of the hunt for the intruder—even if it meant tracking the churl all the way to the parking area.

I glanced about the tunnel and found myself staggered by the sight that assaulted my eyes!

Major O'Toole was shouting into a telephone, requesting that the clatter of the A-Zone Alarm be reduced in order to improve communications in the Bravo Red area. The major was obviously in contact with the people in the upper regions of Greenwood. He and the three officers with him were staring down the tunnel toward the main office building, through which I had entered Greenwood. Although that was the direction of their gaze and entreaty, they could not see very far. O'Toole was standing right where the tram tracks passed through the electrified fence and then started downward toward the lower levels.

The whole damn tunnel in front of him was flooded with water!

Would this cursed commission never end!? There had been naught but frustration throughout the day. First that idiot O'Toole had been able to catch Sir Thomas Roche, the same Sir Thomas who knew the real Louis Proferra personally, before Sir Thomas had cleared Greenwood on his way to visit his injured wife.

Then there had been that dolt Lieutenant Nash who had put the screen over the air supply filter, forcing me to find another means of dispatching Ludwig Kelp. But these offenses were as nothing compared to this latest mocking rebuttal. Some outrageously deformed mind had ordered the main tunnel flooded!

At every turn, these people had laid waste a polished schedule of exquisitely timed events. Each milestone in the schedule had been designed to permit the demise of Herr Kelp without the visiting of undue acrimony upon the agent of that demise, myself. I had planned that Sir Thomas Roche would not be available for the face to face ID. Thus Major O'Toole would have passed me on to Complex two-two without the required absolution.

Once inside Complex two-two it should have been a simple matter to visit Ludwig Kelp with Major Hammett and deposit the poison pellets in Kelp's air supply. The poison would have melted over a fifteen- to twenty-minute period and possibly I would have been completely clear of Greenwood before Major Hammett and his friends noted Kelp's indisposure.

I had even anticipated the possibility that Kelp might detect the questionable purity of his air prior to my complete exit. Had his cry of "foul" been prematurely issued, I had my General Coder identity prepared. The general was to be my passport through whichever locked doors remained between myself and the grand fruition of the Sealed Tomb Commission. I refer of course to the collecting of my fee.

What did these idiots expect me to do now—swim for my money?

I announced my presence to Major O'Toole with the following greeting: "Who in flaming hell ordered the tunnel flooded?"

My voice rang out rather effectively since O'Toole had

been successful in his demand that the decibel content of the alarm be reduced.

"I did, sir," O'Toole was man enough to admit. "The unauthorized personnel is still in this end of the plant. Our anti-backout defenses require that there be no way out for the rodent while we hunt him down."

"And do they also require that you keep your commanding officer a prisoner while you 'hunt him down?' " I snarled. You cocky little pipsqueak. "How long will it take to clear that tunnel of water?"

"Pumping time is four hours and ten minutes," O'Toole said crisply, standing straight and glaring back at his general with that strange bravery that has always been the zealot's shield.

"Well get on with it," I snapped. "You've already cancelled me out of an eleven o'clock conference at Downing Street." Four hours. Great Caesar!

O'Toole went back on his telephone. He ordered that the tunnel be pumped dry. He kept the line open and turned to me and called, "They're attempting to contact the Engineering Office topside, sir."

Somebody came on the line and spoke to O'Toole. The major listened, then sputtered, "What the hell do you mean: 'General Coder said'? I've General Coder here at my end. Listen, put the Exec on, will you. You people sound confused."

I moved quietly to the bullet-proof glass and signaled the lieutenant inside to open the door for me. There appeared little need for me to stand about a damp tunnel watching the water level recede. Not exactly the sort of pastime for a man of my rank. Besides, I was not at all intrigued by the line of inquiry O'Toole's conversation with "topside" had taken.

Once back inside Bravo Red I sent the lieutenant behind the bullet-proof glass off to find Captain Calkins for me. "I believe he's about posting watch at the machine guns," I said. "I'll take over here."

O'Toole was still at the telephone. He was shouting into it. I reached down and disconnected the jack on the end of the telephone line. Through the slot at the bottom of the window I could just hear O'Toole's voice as he continued to shout into the dead line. " ... hello? Hello? God damn. ... Hello? ..."

My next move was one that, as I understand it, is rather alien to good military procedure. I deserted my post. And locked the door behind me, to boot.

With any luck at all it would be quite a while before anyone could reach the electric buzzer that unlocked the door to the tunnel. Thus blabbermouth O'Toole and his unhealthy suspicions were momentarily sealed out of Bravo Red. Of course this fact did not improve my position to any noticeable degree. I was sealed *in* Bravo Red.

At the entrance to the women's barracks I mentioned to the guard stationed there that I wished to speak to Major O'Toole immediately. The lad was good enough to dash off to the major's office.

Behind the barracks door I found a rather serviceable lounge area containing writing tables and stuffed leather chairs. In an effort to reduce the utilitarian decor somewhat, the ladies had installed a rug over the concrete floor. The tasteful fabric even covered the silver tram tracks that ran directly through the center of the room and out under a door at the far end.

The lounge was deserted but somebody was in the act of opening the door on the far side. I scurried through a door on my left that bore the legend OFFICERS ONLY.

There were several doors on each side of the corridor I had entered. All but one were open, revealing quarters rather similar to those inhabited by male officers but emanating an unmilitary odor of perfume and sachet that one does not find in BOQ. At least, not with any regularity.

As I strode past the one closed door it abruptly popped open. Lieutenant Goddard, in the act of zipping the side of her skirt, came to a shocked halt and stared at me.

She was equal to the occasion. She left the zipper half open and saluted. As I returned the salute she said coldly, "Begging the General's pardon, but I do not consider your rank nor the A-Zone Alarm sufficient excuse for invading the female barracks. Regulation 5474 says—"

"Come off it, Lieutenant," I said. "The alarm has been actuated because there are unauthorized personnel loose in

Greenwood. We are quite certain they did not reach Bravo Red, but we must conduct a search. I felt I'd best search this area myself."

"There are female officers well qualified to conduct any such search," she said, guarding her sex with brazen firmness. She stepped past me delivering the following idiotic proposal. "Rather than have a precedent set, sir, I prefer to get a ruling on this immediately. I feel that even during an A-Zone Alarm the sanctity of the female barracks must be maintained if a responsible female officer is available. I'm certain that Regulation 5474 will bear me out—"

I grasped her arm and spun her back toward the door of her room. The arm trembled under my hand as I continued to hold her and speak my piece.

"Rubbish, my dear," I said, running my eye enthusiastically over her figure. "As CO of Greenwood I have access anywhere. Anywhere." My eye moved slowly and obviously to her bed. "It is even possible," I added, moving her further into the room, "that a strict interpretation of the military code demands that you obey your general even if he should order you to disrobe."

She backed away from me into the quiet little room where the A-Zone Alarm was barely audible. Her face was flushed; from embarrassment, anger, or something more attractive than either of these, it was hard to say. I closed the door behind me.

The only person in Greenwood who knew my exact location stood before me. The lieutenant was about to be confined to quarters. Immobilizing the senses of a woman by striking her neck with the edge of the palm is generally a delicate venture. The ladies are, despite the modern rebuttal on the subject, constructed of less durable parts than the male. They wear the identity "fragile" with legitimacy. And with pride it is hoped.

"I'm rather familiar with the regulations, General Coder," Lieutenant Goddard said. (I did not learn her first name until several days later.) "I believe I would be acting within the regs if I summoned the guard and ordered your ejection and arrest."

Her voice was a bit breathless. Her eyes abruptly widened

and she blurted, "No man is ever permitted in these quarters. Ever! There will never be a man in here. . . . Here with me. . . ."

"Ah yes . . . er . . . the A-Zone Alarm was just about to be rescinded, incidentally," I said, a bit dismayed, I must admit, by her reaction thus far. "They'll be shutting it off in a minute. So there's no need for you to report to your station. You are off duty I take it?"

"Yes," she snapped. "I'm completely available to the General. Completely at his disposal."

"What I would like you to do," I said, "is remain here in your quarters and—"

"You mean you can't bring yourself to 'order' me to do it?" she interrupted. Her voice had a quiet shrillness to it, an undertone of strange hysteria. "I understand," she added, and started unbuttoning her blouse. "You don't want me testifying that this was an order." Her tight fist snapped the last two buttons open.

By George! From the waist up she was constructed of uncommonly sound lines. I might point out also that the real General Keith Coder was not a man who would be found wanting when assessed by a feminine eye. He had a soldier's physique that had but recently been invaded by the slight paunch inherent in "desk" assignments. Lieutenant Goddard's "sacrifice," therefore, was not as blatantly duty-oriented as one might assume. Certainly not as duty-oriented as she had told herself.

As she stepped out of her petticoat she said, "Surely you are not going to just stand there looking." She stood straight, and yes, proud too. "I've felt your eyes on me at mess," she said with a nice blush. "You are not disappointed, are you?"

The answer she wanted was in my eye. I said, "A general does not commit himself to an . . . encounter without first inspecting the ground. Let me make a quick survey outside, then I'll be right back."

A small frightened surmise ran behind her eye. "There's nobody in the barracks," she said coming closer to me. "Unless some 'off duty' failed to hear the alarm."

I held out my arms. Good soldier Goddard nearly leapt

against my chest. "I really must make a quick check," I said. "Can't throw off years of military training in a wink."

I attempted to reassure her with a kiss. My generosity was almost my undoing. In her enthusiasm to impress her CO the lieutenant very nearly dislodged his nose. I managed to press the thing back in place.

"By God, I'll be back in thirty seconds!" I cried passionately as I pried her forcibly from me.

"Do hurry," she breathed. "I'll have something on I've been saving. Something a bit less 'issue.' And promise me one thing," she said gripping my sleeve. "Promise to leave your blouse on. I want to feel your insignia under my fingers while we're doing it."

Ah, my dear, would that my freedom were not so dependent on my utilizing the short period of confusion still in effect in Greenwood.

I left the lieutenant and returned to the lounge room. It was unoccupied. So was the dormitory area of double-tiered bunks located beyond the door under which ran the tram track. I was in the act of following the track to the far wall of the dormitory when the sound of quick light footsteps invaded my ear from the right. I slipped quietly behind an upright wardrobe and watched with a stern eye a young woman hurrying across the far end of the room.

She was dressed in a robe and carried in her hands a clutch of combs, hairpins, and soap dish. She paused to adjust one of her slippers that had become dislodged in her haste. As she bent over I detected a familiar contour through the open front of her robe. By George, those could belong to none but Private Carter, the poor novice soldier who, with Private Grimes, had been brutally reprimanded earlier by Lieutenant Goddard in the corridor just outside the female barracks.

Private Carter fled on and pushed through a door marked OFF DUTY QUARTERS. As I proceeded on my own way I heard Carter's voice pleading with some other resident of the room. "Peggy! Peggy! For heaven's sake wake up! Come on, you idiot. The A-Zone Alarm is ringing. I just heard it when I left the shower. We'll catch hell if God finds us here."

For the moment I was intrigued by the odd juxtaposition

in her last sentence. Then it occurred to me that it was not the imminent arrival of any major deity that had the girls unnerved. Lieutenant Goddard, of course.

The tram tracks led me to a wide steel-sheeted door at the far end of the barracks. There was a placard over the door proclaiming the portal to be a disaster exit. The door was not locked but there was a stenciled advice to the casual traveler on the frame: WARNING - DO NOT OPEN EXCEPT IN DISASTER EMERGENCY. DOOR CONNECTED TO CENTRAL SECURITY ALARM.

One additional alarm buzzing away in central security shouldn't receive any remarkable degree of consideration. I pushed open the door and walked on to a bare, empty cement-walled corridor. The passageway was narrower than the other corridors I'd been through and had an air about it of infrequent use. Around the first turn I came upon a dead-end wall. Ah, but adjacent to the terminating wall stood the door I sought. The door was locked, and contained a glass panel with wire mesh buried in the layer of glass.

Through the panel I saw two prime members of His Majesty's Forces seated in the glass-domed control station behind twin machine guns. They were staring away from me, guarding the long, blue-lit tunnel that led God-knows-where.

I pressed the buzzer, illuminating a red lamp in the control station. The corporal of the two hopped from his seat and trotted over to the door. He pressed the communication button and I heard his voice from the speaker over the door. "Yes sir?"

"Open up, Corporal," I snapped. "I want you and . . . who's that with you?" Private Remsen, he answered. "You and Private Remsen," I continued, "over in Complex two-two right away."

"Yes sir!" he responded. Then he did nothing. The idiot stood there staring at me. Eventually his embarrassed eye crept down to the small slot located under the window. "Er . . . begging the General's pardon," he stammered. "But I can't open from this side without the matrix."

"Speak up, Corporal," I said. "I can't hear you on this side. Something wrong with the speaker."

"The matrix, sir," he shouted. "I've got to have it." Damn it! There had to be some other way to open the cursed door. They wouldn't chance trapping two of their soldiers on the loss of a stupid bit of plastic card.

"Corporal!" I snapped, "there's an A-Zone Alarm on."

"But ... but, sir, I can't explode the door open until the A-Zone Alarm goes critical. Those are my orders."

Ahhh, that was more like it; an explosive circuit for opening the door.

"And what do you require, corporal, to consider the A-Zone Alarm critical?" I asked sarcastically. "There's an unauthorized civilian loose in Greenwood!"

"Sir, my instructions are as follows," he sputtered, his shoulders straight and a certain degree of righteous dignity in his youthful face. "The entry door shall be exploded open when the A-Zone Alarm goes critical as indicated by a pulsing siren which will replace the normal A-Zone Alarm bell. The entry door shall not be exploded open at any other time except when the commander of the gun emplacement determines that an emergency exists that requires opening the door or when there is an obvious need to evacuate personnel to the emergency exit."

The corporal's dedication to direction illustrated the obvious risk we accept when we permit the military to pump into their young charges a total reliance on General Staff acumen.

I recognized the enemy crouched in the corporal's eye: Indestructible adherence to the printed word. Logic and common sense were futile weapons in such an engagement. Ahh, but I had dealt with this adversary before. He could be overrun by an onslaught of well directed guile.

"Very good, Corporal," I said. "Stand by while I obtain the matrix." I spun away and left him. As soon as I passed the corner of the corridor I ran back to the female barracks. I required assistance. Military personnel are not the sort I run to quickly for support, but in this instance they were all that was available.

Privates Grimes and Carter were just trotting from the OFF DUTY quarters. They saw me suddenly and both came to an abrupt, rigid halt.

I returned their salute and said, "Better get back inside your quarters. We're facing a fiendish enemy." They followed me into the smaller dormitory.

I glanced about at the remnants of their obvious haste: crumpled robes and night dresses scattered on the unmade bunks. "Very disorderly," I muttered.

As I turned to face them they came to trembling attention. "Privates," I said, "we are faced with a military calamity beyond anything I've experienced in twenty-seven years in the Army. As you can hear we have an A-Zone Alarm on. The exact reason for the alarm is confidential but I'm going to tell you. I think perhaps you can assist your Commanding Officer where everyone else has failed thus far. Here's our problem. You are familiar with our emergency personnel exit security, are you not? Two soldiers guarding each of our tunnels?"

"Yes sir," their squeaky voices assured me.

"Very well then, I'll tell you ... er ... stand at ease."

As they gradually relaxed their stiff, somewhat touching, posture, I continued in a more informal voice. "The enemy knows that he can never break into Greenwood through the 'front door' route. So he has tried the 'back door.' The emergency personnel tunnels. He has managed, God knows how, to pipe a very effective nerve gas into all the tunnels. The men on the guns inhaled a bad dose before we discovered the plot about ten minutes ago and shut down the source of the gas. And shot the enemy agents who were feeding the damn stuff into the tunnel in short order, I can tell you that. But now we've discovered that our men on the guns will not respond to orders from their officers. Even from me! Damn bad show."

I went on to explain that my staff of officers was trying everything they could think of to get the gassed soldiers to open the main entry doors so we could get these "fine lads" to the hospital. The Medical Officer had advised me, I said, that if we could get the boys out of the tunnels and into beds for a few hours we could save their lives. "Every minute counts." (Of course.)

"Now it occurs to me," I said, pacing about in an absolute maelstrom of concentration, "that these lads may be momentarily gassed, but they still retain some of their instinctive military values. Their devotion to their Commanding Officer, for instance. If the two fellows in the local tunnel should look out their window and see their CO being physically attacked by the enemy I'm certain they will rush to his rescue—instinctively."

Since the rest of my staff was occupied at the other tunnels, I explained, I would have to ask the two privates to act as the attacking enemy. "Any questions?" I concluded.

Of course there were. How to attack? With what? For how long, etcetera? I resolved these. "Just a bit of jumping about on me. Get me to the floor and give the appearance of trying to pin me there."

We established our timetable for Operation Mousetrap. I would go alone to the entry door of the tunnel and attempt to bring the stricken soldiers to the window. Privates Carter and Grimes would wait in ambush just around the corner of the corridor. When I uttered the code words: "God only knows where it will all end," the privates would attack me in front of the tunnel door. We were ready.

"One thing more," I said as we were about to exit the small dormitory. "Obviously if the lads see you dressed in your service uniforms they are not going to think you are the enemy. I suggest you discard blouses, skirts, and shirts. Just wear whatever it is supply issues you to keep your ... er ... under areas warm. I'll go on ahead while you're preparing."

I could not quite restrain a quick, flailing glance at Private Carter's totally adequate shoulder-to-waistline installation.

As I turned to leave, I left behind my traditional rallying cry to my troop, "Let's give them a good show." Possibly a poor choice of words, for the slight blush of redness that had been on their faces suddenly deepened.

I was on my way out when Private Grimes said, "Excuse me, sir, do you happen to know which men are assigned to the local tunnel? We ... er ... know some of the lads."

"A Private Remsen," I said, "and Corporal ... ah ... dash it, can't recall his name offhand. Tall dark-haired chap. Fine even teeth. Pleasant looking. Be a shame to lose him."

"That'll be Corporal Donald Wood," Private Grimes

gasped. She and Private Carter glanced at each other in some stricken communication that generated a bit of trembling about their eyelashes.

"Don't forget now," I said, "we must get those lads to bed-rest." I fled their embarrassed enclosure.

On my way back to the tunnel entrance I debated whether or not to enlist also the services of Lieutenant Goddard. She had exhibited a talent for the sort of contest I had in mind, and she would certainly be dressed for the affair.

Ahhhh well, sorry, my dear. I believe I'd best keep this strictly a show by the ORs. See what they're made of.

I rushed to the glass-paneled door. As before, Corporal Wood responded to my pressing of the buzzer. He saluted and his voice came through the speaker. "If you'll pass me the matrix, sir, I'll have the door opened immediately."

"The matrix is the least of my worries just now, Corporal," I told him. "Get Private Remsen over here. We've got an ugly situation on our hands." Happily the speaker communication permitted me to speak in a low voice. No point in alerting the females just up the corridor to the real tragedy that had overtaken Greenwood.

When both soldiers were at the door I explained the insidious plot that had been flung against Greenwood by a ". . . desperate, Godless enemy. . . ." I explained that the enemy had somehow penetrated to the kitchen and deposited some diabolical chemical in the food being served the resident armed forces. Fortunately the high command had discovered the plot before all of our people had eaten the polluted food.

"Only the female forces ate the stuff," I said. "Whatever it is that's in it, it has driven the poor wretches mad. They're running about the whole of Greenwood acting extremely peculiar. Rather difficult to explain," I said, an embarrassed flush creeping over my face. "It seems the girls are rushing about in their underclothes attacking the male personnel. Ruddy disgusting sight. Some of the older officers are actually encouraging. . . . Well, that's neither here nor there. We've isolated most of the females, but there's still a few about. Actually Medical tells me the only healthy way to deal with those that have been infected is to do exactly what the ladies obviously want done."

I made a quick-eyed appraisal of my audience. Somehow the bright sheen on their eyes led me to sadly conclude that the gentlemen did not quite share their Commanding Officer's disgust.

I drew a deep breath and said loudly, "God only knows where it will all end."

Like two practiced troupers my female supporting cast picked up the cue and dashed on stage. They came smartly along the corridor in an energetic display of elastic garments and startingly white flesh. They were obviously possessed of some undisciplined demon, for they ignored completely the stern military demeanor with which I received their extraordinary arrival. They instead flung themselves upon me.

Great Scott, ladies, have you no respect for your Commanding Officer? It occurs to me also, young women, that you are out of uniform.

Speaking of uniform, there was decidedly something amiss in the garments worn by the maids, a lack of standardization. As they wrestled me to the floor I had occasion to note that Private Carter restrained the more mobile portions of her upper torso in an elastic contraption that was black in color with a scattering of pink figures; butterflies I believe, or some of the more frisky insects. A similar garment, worn by Private Grimes, conversely was white in color and had an aura of utilitarian plainness that was unmistakably governmental in concept.

During the ensuing gymnastics on the corridor floor, the opportunity to test the resistance factor of each garment was forced upon me. I can say only that neither device restricted a rather accurate appraisal of the contours of the encased property.

Actually the encounter between the sex-mad privates and the outraged general did contain some elements of realism. I discovered that the maids could not quite discard their instinctive coyness. Quite naturally they wanted to exhibit a certain percentage of their goods to the goggle-eyed young men at the window. Yet they were wise enough to realize that a full-bore display of all of the uncovered flesh might saturate the market. I became the coquette's fan behind which the girls attempted to shelter themselves. The realism in the encounter, therefore, resulted from my efforts to dislodge my attackers from under me and behind me; get them out in the open. (Careful there, Carter! That protuberance is forcing my hairpiece to come unhinged! Possibly you are causing the glue to melt.)

Two small but obviously destructive explosions momentarily stunned our senses. The door to the tunnel fell from its hinges. Good lad, Corporal Wood! Obviously that nerve gas did not destroy your basic military judgment.

Rarely, I suspect, has a general received such eager retrieval. The boys were upon the enemy instantly. Corporal Wood took Private Carter prisoner, which I guess was in the cards as they say.

"All right now!" I cried, the voice of irresistible command. "Hustle them off to bed. Keep them there at all cost."

The order fell on four sets of ears. Each of the combatants proceeded to carry it out. They ran off down the corridor toward the female barracks.

It was a delight to the old general to witness such dedication, such unquestioning obedience. They're a well trained command, sir. You can be proud of them.

As I had concluded, the tram tracks I'd been following were the heart of the Emergency Personnel Exits System that Lieutenant Epstein had mentioned during my arrival. In a disaster the long exit tunnels would have to be negotiated at a smart clip. Thus the system of railways had been installed.

I found one of the electric trams housed in a large white enclosure next to the machine gun emplacement. It was a simple matter to connect the batteries and be off down the long blue tunnel.

The actual exit from Greenwood was over a mile from the machine gun. I am not at liberty to mention just which part of the English countryside I encountered when I broke my way through the final exit door. I am not without an awareness of the citizens' burden in the matter of preserving state secrets, despite what you may have heard to the contrary. In this instance it is not what I encountered as I departed Greenwood that should be of lingering interest to the discriminating reader of this chronicle, but rather that which I left behind.

Three evenings later a Commander D. P. O'Keefe of the Home Office visited General Keith Coder's London residence to discuss the shocking affair at Greenwood. Coder owned a home in a good section close to Richmond Park; rather a nice large rambling place for a bachelor general. Then, he had always known how to live well.

As Commander O'Keefe was being ushered in he encountered the general seeing off two guests who were departing. The guests had heard Commander O'Keefe announced and since the two had been to a degree involved in the Greenwood affair they insisted on speaking to the rather jolly looking commander.

General Coder introduced Commander O'Keefe to the guests, with marked reluctance. The gentleman and lady were Sir Thomas Roche and his wife Mrs. Hope Roche.

"Ahhh yes, splendid," Commander O'Keefe said to Sir Thomas. "You were the chap who was to give the face-to-face ID. What happened there? The report we received at the Home Office is rather confused on the point."

It was Sir Thomas' wife who answered. She was apparently rather incensed about the whole thing. "It was awful," she told Commander O'Keefe. "Tommy was waiting to go down and identify poor Mr. Proferra at Major O'Toole's office. Then he got this ghastly phone call telling him that I'd been struck down on Oxford Street by a drunken American driving a red Bentley. Tommy knew I was in the city for the day—I was meeting Aunt Cis, you see—so the whole thing sounded logical. Particularly when you know those Americans and their autos. I'm certain whoever rang up must be in league with the murderer. Although I wouldn't quite call killing Ludwig Kelp murder."

Mrs. Hope Roche was a lovely looking woman, despite her loquaciousness.

"Of course Aunt Cis and I spent the whole morning at the

House of LeRoy," Mrs. Roche concluded, "and knew nothing of the affair until the wireless broadcast."

Commander O'Keefe turned to Sir Thomas again. "You were quite ready then to identify this American from the International Military Tribunal, or the Allied Control Council as I believe they call it now, anyway you were ready to identify Louis Proferra?"

"Yes," Sir Thomas said. "I've known Lou for several years. We were in hospital together when he was having his ear replaced."

"Ah yes," the commander said, "the war appears to have made modern man's indebtedness to the surgeon's skill an ever-accelerated flight from reality, wouldn't you say?"

General Coder looked at Commander O'Keefe coldly, then to Mrs. Roche he said, "Proferra was at your wedding, wasn't he, Hope?"

"Good God, don't remind me of that ghastly night," the lady said. Startlingly frank young woman.

"Oh, that sounds terrible, doesn't it Commander?" she said. "If you had been there you would realize what I mean."

"I'm certain Commander O'Keefe must have read about it," Sir Thomas said, and took his wife's arm. "Come along, Hope, Ira Loftwood and the lot are waiting at the theatre. We're late as is."

"In my opinion," Mrs. Roche said, "one could never be too late for a film starring Lulubelle Courage. Goodby, Commander."

As Sir Thomas was bidding the Commander goodby he asked, "By the by, who are you with over at Home? I know quite a few chaps over there."

"I'm afraid I really can't say, sir," the Commander replied, his icy mask of security-consciousness looking a bit ludicrous on so jolly a face.

Sir Thomas evidently didn't see the humor. He snapped, "Don't be an ass. Just because I'm leaving the service doesn't mean I'm not informed. I know as much about what happened at Greenwood as anybody. I know bloody well it was Augustus Mandrell who got in there and out. And made idiots of the lot of us."

His wife, who had been by the front door, walked back to the tense scene. "Who in heaven's name is Augustus Mandrell?" she asked. "I've never heard of him."

General Coder stepped in. Glancing at Mrs. Roche he said, "Let's discuss it another time, shall we, Sir Thomas. I'll see you out."

When the guests had departed, the general walked back to Commander O'Keefe. He was not in a pleasant mood.

General Coder said, "You really have an art for getting people up off their heels, don't you, Mandrell? Come along and collect your damn blood money."

The general asked if I would mind conducting business in his sleeping quarters while he changed. "It's more private," he remarked.

As he led me upstairs he said, "Seeing Thomas Roche reminds me. I've meant to ask what you know about the disappearance of his brother Bert Roche."

"Bert Roche?" I said, recalling the name with difficulty. "Didn't I hear that he had gone into the religion field? Gave up the title to his brother Thomas and took to the monastic life?"

"That's what the record says," Coder said grimly. "Bert Roche served this country well. One of the best damn fighter pilots we had. I want to be certain he got exactly what he was looking for."

"Oh I imagine Bert got what was coming to him," I remarked. General Coder snapped his eyes around to me, but said nothing. We entered his bedroom suite. Coder went on to his bedroom to change clothes. I remained in the sitting room reading the titles of the books scattered about the room.

"You gave me a few bad moments the other day," Coder called through the open bedroom door. "When I heard you were still down in Bravo Red after the tunnel was flooded, I thought they had you."

"Your parking area security detail was more alert than you had led me to believe," I said. "I had not anticipated that they would find Proferra lying in the parked auto."

"That was your fault," Coder said. "They wouldn't have

found Proferra if you hadn't been so careless dumping him in the vehicle. Parking Area Patrol was driving by and happened to see the finger lying on the ground."

"Whose finger?"

"Proferras'," Coder said. "When you slammed the door on him his hand must have been lying near the edge. You. . . ."

A door on the opposite side of the sitting room slowly opened distracting my attention from Coder. A very pretty young woman in a dressing gown stuck her head past the edge of the door. Her eyes widened when she saw me.

She said, "Oh I thought General Coder was. . . ." Her head pulled back and the door closed. The last time I had seen her she had been in the women's barracks at Greenwood awaiting the return of the man she assumed to be General Coder. The general had not returned, but that had not stopped her. Lieutenant Goddard, exhibiting the determination of a good soldier, properly motivated, had gone after her objective.

I picked up Coder's voice again. ". . . I'm sorry it was Proferra the International Tribunal sent over to question Kelp. His background is too closely connected with yours. Notice how quickly Tom Roche came up with the name Augustus Mandrell? I'm afraid the Inquiry Board is going to stumble on the same conclusion."

"That's more desirable than having them stumble on the name of the chap who has been selling the Nicholas Cavarocchi paintings."

"There's not much chance of that," Coder said coming into the sitting room. "It's a big operation, with the top man's identity rather well hidden." He had on his dressing gown and smelled of shaving lotion.

In one hand he carried a packet of bank notes and had a leather pouch under his arm. He walked directly to the door on the other side of the room and opened it far enough to stick his head in. He murmured a few words to somebody in the adjacent room. The only word I overheard was the name " . . . Ruth . . ."

"I have a bit of a sporting proposition for you, Mandrell," Coder said turning from the door. He placed the packet of money on a small table. "A hell of a lot of money," he muttered. "I remember the time you did a job for me for a thousand pounds."

"Depends on how you look at it," I said. "The sum is only about half of what you will realize from the sale of but one of the Cavarocchi paintings. If Kelp had told his story to the Inquiry Board, you wouldn't be around to sell the Cavarocchis. Hank Van de Erve at Uni-Coffee might take all the paintings you have left if he's convinced they're not forgeries."

Coder didn't answer. He laid the leather pouch on the table next to the money. The pouch had a small padlock holding it closed. There was a wax seal, with a vaguely familiar imprint in the wax, poured over the keyhole of the padlock.

"This is a packet of papers left with me by Bertie Roche last year, shortly before he disappeared," Coder said coldly. "That's the Bullrusher crest on the seal. Bert asked me to forward them to Scotland Yard if anything violent happened to him. He didn't say so but I believe he was dealing with you at the time. I know he frequently had your name in his newspaper articles about then. Take your choice, Mandrell. The money or Bert's papers. I'm pretty certain there's an account in there of how Bert commissioned you to kill his father. And possibly something about the death of Scotland Yard Super Sir Bruce Peak. I think you were in on the Sir Bruce thing no matter what the report reads. Take your choice."

"Has it also occurred to you that your name is mentioned in there?" I asked the swine. I am not partial to people who tamper with my fee. "As I recall it was you who fed Bert my name when the need to retire Sir Robert Roche became apparent. You and I had just concluded that affair involving your American mistress."

"I'll take my chances," Coder said. "The only reason I haven't forwarded the papers is I'm not quite certain what's happened to Bert. All that damn monastery will say is that no such person by that name is with them. Which doesn't mean a thing."

"You may retain your dilemma, sir," I said grabbing up the irresistible bank notes. "What you do with Bert Roche's papers, the raving of a very undisciplined mind, is of little interest to me."

(It was not until several years later that my choice in Coder's house that night came back to haunt me: *The Fighter Pilot's Ghost Commission*.)

"Bert Roche's undisciplined mind functioned damn well in the skies over England," Coder snapped. "Saving the likes of you from German bombers."

"Your concern for those who have served well is bloody touching," I retorted, a surprising anger invading my judgement. "Your own record would lead one to believe that honorable service is the least of your preoccupations."

His hand leaped out and took my jacket in a fierce grip. "Out with it, you jackal!" he hissed. "What are you talking about?"

"Your association with Ludwig Kelp," I said, glaring into his military eyes. "You were parachuted into Yugoslavia when Kelp was Hitler's chief administrator in the area. You sent back the startlingly detailed reports on German activity in the Balkans, including accounts of Kelp's looting of the museums. But you were not in Yugoslavia with the British forces that captured Kelp in '44; the group that retrieved the stolen treasure. Yet it is you who ended up with the stolen Nicholas Cavarocchi paintings. It's as though you and Kelp were joint owners in a mutual business venture. He hid the paintings and told you where to find them. But why you? Because he knew you from the 'old days.' Your underground success in the Balkans, one might conclude, may have been due to information provided you by Kelp. A gesture on Kelp's part that must have involved some reciprocal action on your part. And you commissioned me to dissolve the partnership before Kelp reported it to the Inquiry Board."

Coder released my jacket and pushed me from him. "If any other man said those things to me I'd kill him," Coder said, in a surprisingly mild tone. He sat down and lit a cigarette taken from his dressing gown. He stared at me with intelligent, speculating eyes.

"A man would have a time of it trying to kill you, wouldn't he?" he commented. "You're the true expert on killing on a man-to-man basis. All I've been taught for the past fifteen years, ever since I got my captaincy, is killing on a mass basis. I missed out on that nasty trench-warfare business of World War One. Too young. I didn't actually kill a man until '32. Potted an Uzbek Dragoon in a dark alley in Negbit Dag one night. A single bullet. He had a sword as long as your leg and was out to skewer my CO. . . ."

I kept half an ear to Coder and bent my major attention to a far more exhilarating preoccupation—counting the neat packet of money. Gnawing at my mind also was a further grotesque distraction. The frightening rumor that the Crown was considering devaluation of the pound still poisoned the land. A chap in my position, a true entrepreneur with a startling hoard of unreported cash, had to be constantly alert to such fiscal shenanigans.

" . . . The next time I actually took a man's life within arm's reach was in Yugoslavia," Coder continued. "Ahhh, there was an operation I could have used the likes of you on, Mandrell. My first field command. Taking eight frightened ORs by parachute into occupied Yugoslavia. 'Blow up some bridges.' 'Derail some trains.' That's all those bastards at Command could come up with by way of a plan. But that's the sort of assignment you draw when your fate falls into the hand of some idiot general who's sitting out the war in London because he couldn't handle his field assignment."

"How did you happen to meet Ludwig Kelp?" I asked.

"I never met Kelp directly," Coder said. "Never even spoke to him until he was brought into Greenwood. Now Frau Kelp, that's a different story. A sweet piece of German pastry. Part of the time in Yugoslavia I passed myself off as a civilian engineer with Red Cross. My papers said I was an Irish neutral. Robert Patrick Kelly, no less. I got to know Mrs. Kelp. Ludwig was off from Belgrade quite a bit, getting the weekly count at the concentration camps. Irma was a trusting soul. Gave me the run of the house, including Ludwig's desk. Either that or she just didn't care. Ludwig wasn't an easy man to live with, from her side of it. Quite quick to boil up a rage; break the furniture, kick the cat, and burn the drapes. Took quite a delight, I understand, in going into a museum and smashing a few statues in front of the Director and his staff."

"Frau Kelp, then, was the source of the data you sent out of Yugoslavia?"

"You'll find it all in my memoirs one day," he said smiling. "When I get around to them. She caused me some trouble though that's been hanging over me these past few years. You had all sorts of groups fighting in Yugoslavia during the war. There was Tito and his Communists. They were helping me. Then there was Colonel Mikhailovich and his troops. They represented the government-in-exile for a while. It was some of Mikhailovich's people who found out Robert Kelly was a British officer. They fed the word back to London, to King Peter and his gossipy little exile court here, that I was being seen at Kelp's house. Ever since then I occasionally run across some 'admirer' spouting the same conclusion you reached. That if Kelp helped me then I must have helped Kelp."

"And your only crime was providing comfort to the lonely wife of the enemy?" I said. "Was it Frau Kelp then who told you where the Cavarocchi paintings were hidden? Or is she a part of this organization of yours that has gotten the paintings out of Yugoslavia and into the art market?"

"Oh for God's sake, Mandrell, stop being an ass," he said, standing up and crushing out his cigarette. "There was no need to get the paintings out of Yugoslavia. Ludwig Kelp destroyed the lot of them three years ago. I saw him do it. Threw them in his own fireplace and burned them for the sport of it. That's what he was going to confess to the Inquiry Board. That's why I hired you."

# THE BULLRUSHER COMMISSION (1946)

I BOARDED THE passenger train at the first stop outside London. An unhurried search brought me to the compartment I sought. Seated in the compartment reading a copy of *They Gave Me Wings* sat a self-possessed young man. The book contained an autobiographical account of his career in the Royal Air Force. It had just been published. Portions of the story appeared to amuse him, for he smiled twice during the period in which I watched him from the passageway.

Seated across from the young man sat a heavy-jowled gentleman reading the *Times* with stern intensity through eyeglasses that appeared to be a new, and resented, addition to his face. Next to the gentleman was a woman of thirty or so who was pleasantly aware that her plump knees frequently drew the young man's eyes away from his book.

I entered the compartment drawing all three pairs of eyes momentarily. My costume was a common one in post-war England: soiled Army blouse, unpressed civilian trousers, garish pre-war tie improperly knotted about the wrinkled collar of a cheap white shirt. The veteran making a slovenly adjustment to civilian life.

My progress through the compartment was marked by an imbalance of body movement that was more pronounced than the swaying of the railway car warranted. Inebriated, more than likely.

I fell into the seat between the young man with the book

and the window. I immediately pressed upon the youth a white card bearing a handwritten message.

He pushed the card back toward me without reading it. A scowl had erupted on his handsome face and hung from his forehead with the practiced ease of a frequent visitor.

"Can't say I blame you, lad," I said loudly. "Nobody wants to be burdened with us poor wretches that's back from the war with 'orrible diseases. But give a look here, lad." I held the card in front of the young man's face.

He absorbed the complete message with one flick of his cold impatient eyes. The shock that slammed through his body, and drew his eyes back to the card, was nearly imperceptible. At any rate, it went unnoticed by the jowly gentleman and the handsome young woman across the compartment. The lad was a cool one.

The handwriting on the white card formed the following intelligence: I AM AUGUSTUS MANDRELL. ONE MOMENT WHILE I SECURE US A BIT OF PRIVACY.

"Yes," I said loudly, "the damn medical chaps said the climate here at home would kill off the beri-beri. But I find everything I touch still turns a slimy green." A racking terrible cough erupted from my chest cavity. My hand tore at my pocket and pulled forth an incredibly dirty handkerchief.

The man and woman across from the disease-riddled war veteran watched with reluctant fascination as the invalid poured what sounded like half the lining of his breathing complex into the rag in his hand.

"Just come from visiting Ralph," I managed to gasp between hacks. "A bit of a time he has when he gets to coughing now that his nose is dropped off. Can't hardly find a hankie big enough," I giggled.

The laughing fit that clutched me triggered another explosion from my lungs, one of such proportions that it tore the handkerchief from my hand. The offensive cloth fell on the well-shaped foot of the young lady.

With a strangled scream she jumped from her seat and beat at the handkerchief with her magazine, knocking the verminous rag into the lap of the young man seated next to me. Then the maid threw her magazine and fled the compartment for more sanitary quarters.

"My God, man," the jowled gentleman addressed me, "you shouldn't be about in public conveyances in your condition." He still retained his seat and with an entrenchment of body that indicated a decision on his part to stand fast, defend his ruddy perimeter.

"Aye, sir," I conceded. "But the leper colony is at capacity. I'm on the list and they'll give me a cell as soon as. . . ." Another coughing attack absorbed my full attention. A thoughtful volume of my forcefully exhaled breath took the jowled gentleman full in the face, fogging his glasses.

He bounded to his feet, snatching off the eyepiece. His arm drew back and he very nearly unleashed upon me the railway commuter's most outspoken challenge, a slap in the face with a folded *Times*. Some last-ditch reservoir of sense took command however, and restrained his arm. Perhaps it was the sight of the red fluid leaking from the corner of my mouth that sobered him. Anyway he turned about and exited the compartment.

I wiped the red dye from my mouth and seated myself opposite the young man. He smiled and said, "So you changed your mind about seeing me, eh Mr. Mandrell? My oh-so-very-exclusive Mandrell?"

His eyes ran from one corner of my face to the other. He did not restrain his curiosity. We had met before and he was looking for familiar landmarks. Although he possessed a pair of extraordinarily acute eyes (he was one of the best Spitfire pilots developed by England during the war) he saw no reassurance that the Augustus Mandrell seated across from him in that swaying railway compartment in the year 1946 was the same Augustus Mandrell who had negotiated the Captain Robert Roche Commission with him in 1943. Nor did he see the Augustus Mandrell who had discussed the Scotland Yard Commission with him in a small hotel room in Bloomsbury in 1944. The disguises I employ are not designed to trigger recognition, obviously.

"Mr. Roche," I said, "why is it that I find the name Augustus Mandrell appearing so frequently in your newspaper articles?"

"Column, old boy, newspaper column," he answered. "And I as the writer am the columnist. An occupational title provided by the Yanks, so I hear. God bless their commercial little hearts. You'd be surprised how much power goes with the thing. There's not a restaurant or club in London that'll charge me for dinner and drink. They're afraid I'll not mention them if they do. And the young actresses about, what they won't do to get their names in print. Ah, but it's a lovely life."

"That is rather the point, sir," I said. "I have no wish to see my name in the periodicals. Yet it appears in "Rochey's Roundup" with unexplainable frequency."

"Come, come, Mandrell," he said. "Surely you have a normal appetite for fame? I have decided to make you famous. A legend in your own time. Everytime your name appears in 'Rochey's Roundup'—terrible title that but I couldn't convince them otherwise. I suggested 'Rochey's Thundermug.' As ever, more plebian heads prevailed. Anyway, every time your name appears, more people will say: 'Did you see where Augustus Mandrell has done it again?' Fame, old man."

"But I have not requested that you mention my name."

"Of course not," he said. "That's what I like about you. You're not pushy." Oh, but he was having a great spot of fun.

I noticed that his neck that had once been thickly muscled from its daily rotation to left side of cockpit to right side of cockpit in search of Jerry, the strong neck that grows a full two shirt-collar sizes during the period when a fighter pilot progresses from a fledgling to a veteran survivor of air battles, this good neck of Bertie Roche had become overlaid with a fatty tissue derived from rich sauces and expensive wines.

"Have you no supervision at your newspaper?" I asked. "No person who insists on authenticity in your column? The several items in which my name was mentioned were totally untrue. I, for instance, do not have a machine entered in the next Grand Prix. And even if I had, I should never contemplate piloting it myself. I am a wretched driver. Did no one question that item when it appeared in your column?"

"Ahhh, I see the trouble," he said. "You just don't have a grasp for post-war reporting techniques. Truth, old boy, is the least ingredient required. There are still a few old-fashioned readers about, so we do make some concession to veracity. Thus, as you may recall, my mention of you and your Grand Prix entry was predicated by the phrase, 'This reporter hears that none other than Augustus Mandrell has the auto to watch entered in the et cetera, et cetera.' You see? Of course what the reader, that slovenly hausfrau with her adolescent hunger to keep up on the International Set, what she is not told is that it was myself who stole up to me in a smoke-filled Shrewsbury saloon and whispered the secret in my ever receptive ear."

"But the readers do not know Augustus Mandrell," I protested. "How can his activity, earsay or otherwise, be of interest to them?"

"They didn't know your name six weeks ago," he gloated. "Now they do, thanks to 'Rochey's Roundup.' When I first started mentioning you I had to identify you as 'the mysterious Augustus Mandrell.' Do you recall the one that went: 'Who is the international mystery financier who owns half of the new Brazilian merchant fleet, the half not owned by Uni-Coffee? Can it be that publicity-shy international financier: Augustus Mandrell?' Gradually, using your name at least once a week, I feel I have established your identity. Thus, in yesterday's column my readers had no difficulty flashing up a mental image when they read: 'Insiders of the Green Room Set say it was a dispute over who would throw the upcoming Augustus Mandrell birthday party that caused that unholy din in the Poe Park Tavern powder room last P.M. Miss Myrna Loy of Hollywood USA is said to have ordered raw beef steak for breakfast this morning. And was it Miss Lulubelle Courage who had her knuckles bandaged on Harley Street at 3 A.M.?' A new art form, old man. Before I am finished your name will be as well known as that of Genghis Khan. I've already had several inquiries about Augustus Mandrell as a result of the column. A few from the chaps at Scotland Yard. Awfully gratifying to know they read my stuff over there."

"All right, Mr. Roche, I concede that your publicity campaign is more or less embarrassing to the firm. We do not, as a rule, run advertisements."

"I'll say!" he laughed. "They would make smashing copy though. 'Want somebody killed? See Mandrell, Limited.' Or: 'Having a spot of trouble with the missus? Anxious to sport a new, younger model? Mandrell arranges all.' By God, I'll speak to the business office people if you like?"

"Mr. Roche," I said patiently, "in response to your unauthorized use of my name I have sought you out. That was your intent, was it not?"

"You know damn well it was," he said crossly. "I tried to reach you through normal channels for better than a month. Your contact men, or whatever you call them, kept me running a bloody rat maze from one to the other of them. I saw that deviate in Mayfair so many times he must have thought we were engaged. Oh a lovely bit of fun they had with me."

"Your trial was of your own making," I said. "Was it not explained to you in the first week that I had denied your petition?"

"It was. I'm only surprised that it took you a week to learn how many creditors I have chasing me about London."

"You of all people must be aware that Mandrell, Limited is not a philanthropic institution," I said. "We do not service paupers. Firstly, their number is of course staggering. Then their one abundant resource, their gratitude, is flagrantly non-negotiable. It was indeed the report of your financial destitution that governed my decision to refuse you."

"Oh I know your love for pounds sterling right enough," he snapped. "You nipped me for 8,000 that time you did in my father—"(*The Captain Robert Roche Commission*) "— and Keith Coder tells me you've practically made a pauper of him over the years. One thing I know about Mandrell, Limited—"

I interrupted him. "You and General Coder discuss the negotiations you have had with Mandrell, Limited?" I asked. As with any small business firm, Mandrell, Limited prefers that the recipients of the service do not reminisce with each other. There are many factors involved in establishing fees. The financial security of the petitioner, for instance, comes into it. Then the accessibility of the person who is the focal point of the negotiations naturally influences the fee. The firm has accepted as little as a thousand pounds for a commission when circumstances justified such an absurd commitment. (*The Irish Monster Commission* comes to mind.) Do not misinterpret me, however. We do not grant discounts.

Therefore an unqualified comparison of fees can serve only to distort the faith of one of the patrons (he who paid the higher) in Mandrell's policy of fiscal impartiality. There is such a policy, sir, and it is inflexible. If you anticipate availing yourself of Mandrell, Limited's talent, come prepared to pay, and pay well.

"Keith and I have talked about Mandrell, Limited a good many times," Mr. Roche answered. "You were involved in that show at Cornflower a few years back weren't you? When Keith's little American lady-friend disappeared."

Ahhh, that is more comforting, my boy. Your discussions with General Coder cannot have been all that detailed if you are uninformed regarding *The American Mistress Commission.*

"Let us restrain our conversation to the present," I said. "To your lack of adequate funding and your reportorial excesses. Since the former of these appears incurable I would suggest you inhibit the latter."

He smiled; a deliberate movement of his lips, with all the warmth of a hollow fang. "There was a time I'd get a chill up my back when I thought of meeting you head-to-head, Mandrell. Not anymore. Here you are chasing me around the countryside for this meeting. And pleading to get your name taken out of the dailies, just as hard as some others plead to get into my column. Oh, but this newspaper business is a fine profession for a man with a taste for getting his own way. Would you guess that Miss Lulubelle Courage is so anxious to have her name in the London papers that she'll give a lad a nice spot of entertainment if he can put her there? Picture that? Bertie Roche, broken down Spit pilot, and the queen of the American flicks on the silk sheets. If she's half as good an actress as she is in the other, she'll. . . ."

The simile escaped him for the moment. I took the occasion to puff the lad up a bit. He was rather a fool in most things but he possessed the frightful tenacity of purpose of an instinctive gladiator. A troublesome combination: dull witted and heedless of tribulation. The combination, incidentally, that has infected most of the men who have changed our history. A susceptibleness to flattery has frequently been a companion asset shared by these gentlemen. The one trait that made them bearable to their companions.

"You do appear to have made a success of your journalistic pursuit," I said. "As I recall, your initial assignment from your employers was rather war-oriented. A report of your remarkable career in the cockpit."

"That's when we discovered a hidden talent in old Bertie," he said, settling down more comfortably in his seat, a concession possibly to the weight of his ego. "'Before my month's contract for the articles had run out, the paper received a nice bit of response in the post. A good many of the letters pointed up how interested the readers were in the post-war activity of the old Spitfire gang. How old Allen Rutherford, Mr. Wingleader as the papers called him, had gotten swacked at Lucy Belanger's party and did a dive bomber attack on Holly Cooper, only to be intercepted by Holly's hubby. And Colonel Ball's bit of a run-in with the Up Thames bobbies when they had the audacity to inquire into the Colonel's state of undress on their town mall. We suddenly discovered a covey of readers made very international-minded by the war. They have a great thirst to know just whose French underclothes were found beneath the seat of whose Ferrari following the sports car rally. I rather get around in that group, you know. What with the war record and the family name. And it seems I've the talent for that thin line between what you can print safely and what you can be sued for.'"

I complimented Mr. Roche on his promising career. I then questioned the wisdom of jeopardizing his professional position by the inclusion in his column of unreasonable fiction: the Augustus Mandrell mythology he was erecting. He said he was quite prepared to desist from this portion of his journalistic pursuits even though "it has been a damn good bit of fun." In return he wanted but one concession from me. I was to remove from the roster of living members of the Roche clan the then senior representative: Sir Hilary Roche.

Bert's preference for such a change in the family structure was quite understandable. Sir Hilary's younger brother Emerson had died recently in New Zealand in a boating accident. With Emerson deceased, Bert had become next in line to inherit the title and, more importantly, the funds and lands in the family. The acreage in question included that grand estate in the west of England, Bullrusher.

"The commission is quite feasible," I admitted. "Once you gained control of the family money you could dissolve your debts, including my fee. My reluctance to accept the commission arises from that residence dictum maintained on the family charter. That the title holder must live at Bullrusher six months out of the year or forfeit. You do not strike me as the stable sort who could meet the commitment."

"We'll discuss money later," he said with an odd smile. "First let's talk about the commission. It's changed some since I described it to your man in Mayfair."

The change he spoke of so blithely was staggering! Not only did he want the demise of Sir Hilary Roche secured by Mandrell, Limited, Mr. Roche also wanted a particular person charged by the police as being directly responsible for the demise.

"That idiot girl who's marrying my brother, I want her charged with the killing," Bert snapped. "Her name is Hope Cornflower."

Miss Cornflower it seems had been courted by both Bert Roche and his younger brother Thomas. She had chosen Thomas. It appeared that Bert was prepared to accept the decision with somewhat less grace than is common.

I did not mention to Bert that I knew Miss Cornflower. I knew the maid well enough to realize that she was not the type who would resort quickly to homicide.

"Now is the ideal time to get it over with," the young man said. "The girl is in London for her trousseau at the House of LeRoy. Uncle Hilary is also in town. Most of the family is. I can tell you where they're all staying. The wedding is a week off. I want it done before then."

"I must advise you," I said, "that my experience in these matters leaves me with the conclusion that it is a violent mistake to graft inordinate complexities on to a commission.

You would be much wiser to settle for the demise of Sir Hilary only."

"No! I want that damn girl blamed."

I shrugged and said, "And of course you are prepared to assume the additional expense involved? This cannot be considered to be a normal commission. The abnormality must be compensated for. Let us say 10,000 pounds for Sir Hilary and an additional 5,000 for the manipulation of the accusation."

The additional 5,000 was a bit excessive; even I admit. Actually I was encouraging him to reconsider the Hope Cornflower portion of the assignment. My previous contacts with the young lady (*The Irish Monster Commission, The American Mistress Commission*) were of a nature that installed her in my memory with fondness. Which is of course much more than I can say for most of the people I encounter in my profession. A characteristic of the business, one assumes.

Bert waved his palm at me and said, "No, Mr. Mandrell, you are not setting the fee this time. I am. The fee for the whole business will be 1,000 pounds. And you're bloody lucky I'm giving you anything. Perhaps I'll even throw in a copy of my book here, if it's a good show. Autographed of course."

"You are an absurd young man!" I sputtered. "One thousand is not a professional fee. It is the wage one offers a menial."

"That's all you're getting from me. And if you don't do the job you'll be finding your name in 'Rochey's Roundup' every day of the week."

"You would be well advised to reconsider, Mr. Roche," I said, manfully attempting to stifle my rage. "Mandrell, Limited will not be dictated to. And recall, sir, that the firm has inherent in its structure rather an effective mechanism for discouraging abuse delivered by private citizens."

"I've taken care of that," he said, and the light in his eye was that of the old Spitfire pilot peering through his gun sight. "I've left some papers with a friend. Should anything violent happen to me, he's to post the documents. There's a complete description of the whole business about my father, including the fact that I hired you to kill him. And there's as much as I know about the murder of Scotland Yard Superintendent Sir Bruce Peak. I know damn well you did that, no matter what the police think. And I suspect that all they'd need to reopen the case is a bit of encouragement."

"A Frenchman named Paul Zardi has already been tried for Sir Bruce Peak's death," I said. "There is minimal speculation as to whether or not Zardi did do it. He was observed in the act and he has confessed."

We were speaking here of an interesting affair that I had chronicled somewhere or other under the title: *The Scotland Yard Commission*. I mention this fact, and have interspersed the rest of this journal with other such references, for the benefit of those scholars among you who are intent on publishing a credible research document.

"I don't care who confessed," Mr. Roche snapped. "I came to you and told you Sir Bruce was out to get you and all your customers. Next thing Sir Bruce is dead. I've written it all down."

"Your exposure to the typewriter has obviously been excessive," I commented. "You are more dangerous now than you ever were in your airplane."

"As long as you understand that. All right now, suppose I give you Sir Hilary's city address, and Miss Cornflower's. I'll try and learn a bit about their schedules for you. Hope Cornflower won't be hard to reach but Uncle Hilary is another story. He'll be about London in search of a nice fuzzy-cheeked young man, since that's his preference. God knows where you find them. I'll see what I can find out. Aunt Cissy will know the form."

"That will not be necessary, Mr. Roche," I said standing and unlocking the compartment door. "Mandrell, Limited does not accept your terms. They are an affront to any but the meanest chattel. Good day, sir."

I left the wretched swine. And left the railway at the next station, where an auto had been deposited for me.

In the ensuing days it was difficult to get about without being reminded of Bertie Roche and his family. I was somewhat engrossed at the time with the Ascot Commission, one of the few Mandrell, Limited commissions involving an animal other than man. In this instance, I refer to that renowned thoroughbred Chrysoberyl.

Even the superb concentration I am called upon to exercise during the final phase of a commission was penetrated by reports of the Roche family activity. For instance, as I departed the race course (the dismayed buzzing of the spectators in the grandstand still in my ear and the disassembled parts of the crossbow hitting against my shin bone inside my trouser leg) as I departed, I came upon a grubby vendor of periodicals. A sub-headline of the newspaper he thrust at me carried the following roar: HOPE AND TOM MOBBED IN PICCADILLY.

The dailies and the wireless had taken a fearsome grip on the upcoming uniting of Thomas Roche and Hope Cornflower, at the full insistence of the public. It was, as one female writer precociously identified the event, the Wedding of the Year. The young couple's pre-nuptial activities were pursued with offensive intensity.

There were certainly the normal ingredients involved in the affair to attract public attention: beautiful girl (Hope photographed smashingly); handsome war hero (Thomas Roche too had won some medals); Great Family. Added to these was the sadistic ingredient to not only attract but inflame public interest. There was the Rejected Older More Famous Brother catalyst.

Bert's fellow journalists, spurred on no doubt by the camaraderie inherent in that profession, gleefully peppered their respective newspapers with accounts of as many of the Roche family secrets as could be bribed from friends of the clan and from tradespeople who serviced the household of Bullrusher. The major fact exhumed during this journalistic digging was the intelligence that there had been quite a row at Bullrusher. When Bert, the former suitor, had been informed of the wedding he actually struck his brother Tom. According to the account, Bert had then been forcibly ejected from Bullrusher by Tom, a couple of servants, and a Captain Ira Loftwood (HMRN), a friend of the family.

The width of the fissure opened between Bert and family was not fully dimensioned for the public until several weeks later. Bert was delivered the supreme indignity. He was not

invited to the wedding. The reading public gasped with hor-
rified pleasure. Not invite the national hero? The man in line
for the title? How terrible. How titillatingly terrible.

Bert was still the renowned outcast when my name first
appeared in his column, that unsupervised sewer disposal
pipe: "Rochey's Roundup."

The mob activity in Piccadilly mentioned in the newspaper
headline had become the public's normal response to any
appearance made by Thomas Roche and his fiancée on the
streets of London. They had become the darlings of the shop
girls. They were Cinderella and her prince and were pursued
everywhere by giggling well-wishers. This subservient pursuit
was generally harmless, but occasionally a few of the more
zealous of the shop girls would dart at the handsome pair and
attempt to remove a portion of their dress. This was recognized as a public display of devotion similar to that brought to
fruition during the war years by a group of American mop-
pets wearing low-cut white socks who served a deity known
as "Frankie."

So, as I said, one was rarely in a position of indifferent
isolation regarding the Roche family during this period. And
each time the name fell upon my senses I was reminded of
Bert and his insulting offer. One thousand pounds! The ass.

Ahhh, but a dangerous ass.

Two days prior to the wedding the following item appeared in "Rochey's Roundup": " . . . City Sights: Sir Hilary
Roche mincing across the lobby of Claridge's arm-in-arm
with Augustus Mandrell. Beautiful women throughout lobby,
awaiting the opportunity to become involved in the Mandrell
mystique, turning away in confusion. . . ."

Contrary to the general concept retained by law enforcing
agencies regarding Augustus Mandrell, I am totally human. I
cannot, as some of my more hysterical adversaries contend,
pass through stone walls. Thus, having my name brazenly
linked (arm-in-arm) with Sir Hilary Roche and his strange
passions drew from me a reaction rather similar to what
your own would be, it is hoped. I am not without my prudish
side, you see.

Mention of my name did not appear in the following day's
issue of "Rochey's Roundup." I could only hope that the

young man had been delivered of his madness. He had, I must admit, achieved one of the objectives of his employment: increased readership for his periodical. I became one of the earliest, and least objective, readers of the rag. (Not the *Times*.)

The poison typewriter was not silenced for long, however. One day only. The next morning the following excerpt from the column smote my eye: " . . . Rumor has it that the expected post-war boom in big game hunting has faded from so-so to ho-hum. Hardest hit is Augustus Mandrell, who will cut fees in order to survive. . . ."

How dare he! You choose to tamper with the price structure, the very gauge of quality of an honorable firm, do you sir?

I had hoped that my tastefully worded notification to Bert of the consequences of any continued penetration into my privacy had restrained his adventures in fiction. Obviously not. The caution would have to be delivered in a more strident format.

I rang up the offensive scrivener and announced my displeasure. As soon as he recognized me he said, "Stand by a sec." He was silent for a moment, then came back on at the same moment that my finely attuned ear detected a minute click in the telephone line at his end.

"There appears to be no bottom to your perfidy," I said. "I presume that is a recording device you have invited into our conversation? You are not only imprudent, but also a fool, Mr. Roche."

"We'll see who the fool is, Mandrell. I had another visit from the Scotland Yard lads after today's column. They appear to think I must know you personally, know where you are. At least I'm certain that the red-faced gentleman with the continuous eyebrows thinks I know where you are. He's taken to following me about London. Rather an inordinate expense to the Crown when you consider the places I visit of an evening."

"All right, Mr. Roche," I said patiently, "you shall have your way. The firm is accepting the commission."

"On my terms," he said sharply.

"On your terms," I conceded. "You shall have the demise

of your Uncle Hilary. And the police shall charge Hope Cornflower with the deed."

"There's some satisfaction in hearing you give up," Bert said nastily. "But you're too damn late. You didn't do the job, so now you can bloody well get ready to see your name in 'Rochey's Roundup' every day. And I think it's time I started hinting about what it is Mandrell, Limited really does for its livelihood."

"Yes, I had thought that would be your reaction," I said. "That's one factor that caused me to concede. Now, when you say 'it is too late,' Mr. Roche, what exactly do you mean? Has your Uncle Hilary expired of his own reluctant will?"

"No, I mean that girl and my brother are being married this very minute in Salisbury."

"You confuse me, sir. I had thought that securing for yourself the Roche title and lands was your objective. I do not see that the marital status of your brother becomes a factor."

"I also wanted the girl blamed," he shouted at me. "Now, that's impossible. Tom and she will be off to America in a few days on their honeymoon. You've botched it. Your one chance to get at Uncle Hilary and blame the girl was when he and Hope Cornflower were in London."

"That is not quite accurate," I said. "Isn't the wedding party, including your uncle and the bride, scheduled to spend this evening and tomorrow at Bullrusher?"

"Don't be an idiot," Bert said. "The only persons who will be allowed into Bullrusher are those with wedding invitations. The gates and grounds are guarded, what with all this asinine adulation exhibited by the damn public."

"Let's not accept defeat so readily," I said. "Let's not exclude the possibility that a gentleman, one exhibiting a spot of imagination, could get himself invited to the wedding. Some might succeed where others have failed," I added maliciously.

"What do you mean by that?" he snapped. When I did not answer, he said, "All right, suppose you could sneak past the guards—I'd guess you're quite accustomed to jumping over fences and skulking in hedgerows and the like—what then?

You couldn't spend ten minutes in the house without being discovered by one of the staff."

"The details you must leave to me," I said. "Are we agreed then? I shall ensure Sir Hilary Roche's release from his dreary day to day preoccupations. Miss Cornflower, or I'd guess it is Mrs. Thomas Roche by now, will be identified as the agent of Sir Hilary's demise. You will cease the use of my name in your column. And, finally, you will deposit in my hand the sum of—" (finally I forced myself to mumble the words) "1,000 pounds."

"Agreed!" he snapped. "But I don't believe you can bring it off. I think I'll be using the name Mandrell in the column for quite a while. At least until the gentleman with the straight eyebrows who's been following me about sees fit to put the name in headlines. I'm not one to forget anyone who does me dirt."

Nor am I, my boy. Nor am I.


There had appeared to be no necessity to mention to Bert Roche that I was located somewhat closer to the scene of his brother's wedding than Bert imagined. In fact the event had taken place but a few miles from where I stood as I spoke to Mr. Roche on the telephone. I left the shelter of my hotel room in Salisbury and proceeded to Bellinggame's Restaurant.

The newlyweds and guests had arrived at Bellinggame's an hour previous for early dinner. Only fifty or so of the two hundred people invited to the wedding had been invited also to Bullrusher. To compensate the one hundred fifty "outsiders" for the logistic endeavors associated with the trip to Salisbury, a wedding feast had been laid for all two hundred. And of course if one wished to serve two hundred people at one sitting in Salisbury, one turned instinctively to Bellinggames. Then, if one had given proper notice, a minimum of sixty days, and one had the proper credentials (the Roches' had), why then Bellinggames would open their kitchen to you.

When I arrived at the ancient building that housed the restaurant I found the bordering streets mobilized by obsessed shop girls. Their number was so great they had

spawned a traffic snarl that defied the talents of the two
constables who were attempting to dislodge the inundated
taxis, autos and vans. The girls, exhibiting a wisdom beyond
their years, paid little heed to the police. Each maid squealed
her vicarious participation in the wedding party taking place
in the restaurant. Their upraised, waving arms kept a bank of
toilet water scent in a constant stew above their pretty,
empty little heads.

I plowed into the skirted pack and bulled toward the front
portal of Bellinggames, vividly conscious of my physical contact with the shapely mass. "Pardon-a. Pardon-a," I was
quick to blurt when a young miss here and there in my path
reacted with startled anger at the vigor of my passage. I
carried a valise, you see, and it was of a size that did not
glide neatly through a crowd. In fact, held waist-high in front
of me, the luggage led several of the maids to a premature
conclusion regarding my intentions.

Then too, my general appearance, as each young woman
spun on me with protest on her lips, was not totally reassur-
ing. I was wearing a soiled white trenchcoat, purple beret,
and rope sandals; a costume less in use in that time than
today. For the most part, though, my eyes stifled the unjust
words before they could escape the rouged lips. I was wearing a pair of black horn-rimmed spectacles the lenses of which
magnified my eyes to five times their normal size. Thus I
successfully traversed the milling herd without suffering any
but mental lacerations.

Two gaudy doormen and a constable of some twelve stone
of heft comprised the final barrier between myself and entry
to Bellinggames. As I broke through the ring of ladies to the
front steps of the restaurant, one of the doormen rushed
forward to tend me the establishment's traditional welcome
for uninvited diners. He grasped my biceps and attempted to
throw me across the road.

I cried out in great Italian outrage. "Aside! Aside! Do not
touch-a me, you pail-a garbage. Arresta dis man," I demanded of the bobby, as I flung the doorman to the ground.

The constable, taking note of my aplomb, tried to find his
footing. He asked who I might be.

"The House of LeRoy," I declared. "You do not recognize-a the House of LeRoy?" I held up my valise and cried, "Dese rabble—" I swept my arm indicating the squealing females—"take-a dem from-a my sight."

The valise on the end of my swinging arm struck the other doorman straight across the chest. The impact drove the man down the steps and into the wall of women, whom he had been holding at bay with his supercilious demeanor. The man was quickly passed to the rear of the female ranks by eager hands. Swallowed alive. His fellow doorman and the constable plunged down the steps to retrieve him. I entered Bellinggames.

In the foyer of the restaurant, a grand Renaissance hall with gaily rotting tapestries hung about the walls, I encountered an adversary worthy of my steel. The maitre d'.

The man stopped dead still at the sight of me. His lackeys, including a pair of waiters of water buffalo proportions, froze about him, a step to his rear. All gazed at the incredible invader with ferocious disdain.

"Ah-hah!" I shouted. "Where is des Signor Bellinggame? Des proprietor of the dung heap." My voice caressed the fragile music drifting from the main dining hall with a steel claw. "Bellinggame, hez-a stand in the path of the artist? Hez lock-a hez door to the artist?"

The maitre d', a superb professional, accepted the challenge. His staff drew its strength, its discipline, from their chieftain. He could not permit a mocking of the name Bellinggame from any source. In particular he could not permit it from such a disreputable source.

He flicked a yellow silk handkerchief from his sleeve and moved toward me holding the cloth not quite to his nose but close enough. The coolies smirked. Their leader had drawn first blood.

The maitre d' paused in front of me and leaned forward as though to remove some grime from my face with the handkerchief. Then, he quickly drew back, as though having discovered that what lay beneath the dirt was an even more repellent disfigurement. A formidable thrust, on most occasions. In this instance it proved only that he had yet to realize that he was hopelessly outclassed.

The maitre d' drew himself to his full Olympian posture.

His holy voice informed the wall behind me of the following: "Mr. Bellingame, the founder of Bellinggames, expired on Dec. 3, 1722 at 3:47 in the afternoon. He is not available."

"Then who's-a lock-a dis door between the poor bride who's-a eat at you table—the Mrs. Roche—and-a her trousseau? Who?" I cried. My voice had lost none of its former vigor, a point not unnoticed by my opponent.

"Bellinggames," the pontifical voice commented, "was not aware that Mrs. Roche required her complete trousseau at the wedding feast. The meal will last but two hours and twenty minutes."

He tried manfully to restrain his aesthetic eyes from the heavy run of beady sweat that bubbled across my forehead and down my great hawk-like nose. (Difficult bit of business, the unleashing of conspicuous perspiration, but not impossible with a spot of practice.)

"In-a two hour," I answered my opponent, "the Mrs. Roche she will be dead from-a shame right atta you table. The House of LeRoy will not letta this thing happen. I— Signor Orlando himself—have come. Bring-a the woman to me."

I threw back my head and stared at him across the bridge of my magnificent beak. The maitre d' found that he could not hold my oversized eyeballs with his own eyes without suffering a flow of fluid that forced him to blink. Behind the thick lenses of my spectacles my eyes looked the size of fried eggs with black pupils.

"You are from the House of LeRoy?" he asked, genuinely afraid now that my credentials might be in order.

"FROM?" I thundered. "I'm-a not from. I AM the House of LeRoy!" The ancient tapestries on the walls fluttered and the music from the dining hall lost a beat.

"Without Signor Orlando," I raved on, "deez woman, deez Mrs. Roche, NAKED she will go on-a her honeymoon." I believe the maitre d' staggered a bit at this point.

"Months and-a months I'm-a work on des trousseau—" I dropped to knees and commenced fighting with the lid of my valise "—my whole life I'm-a give deez garments. The UNDERDRAWERS alone—" He shivered and one leg buckled "—they would restrain a regiment. Then today dis is-a happen. De lasta day. Is it my masterpiece that's-a delivered? *No!* Dis . . . dis CORRUPTION is delivered."

I flung from the valise several dresses purchased that morning from a gypsy peddler.

The maitre d' possessed at least the soul to appreciate good cloth. He stared at the scattered dresses and gasped, "That . . . that is Mrs. Roche's trousseau?"

I bowed my head. Then, like a sob one hears from a great wounded animal, I moaned, "Deeze, they are only the formal gowns."

The battle was over. "Perhaps, perhaps I'd best summon Mrs. Roche," he mumbled and fled, now utilizing his yellow handkerchief to some legitimate purpose. A general with an empty scabbard.

I stuffed the rags back in the valise. A moment later my late adversary returned leading several notables from the wedding party: Hope Roche (née Cornflower); her new husband Thomas; her new mother-in-law, a woman somewhat glaze-eyed from the over ambitious consumption of alcohol; and a scattering of others, including the redheaded bridesmaid Miss Angela Millins.

"My gowns," Hope cried, stricken. "What's the matter? Madame LeRoy said they would be ready in time for my honeymoon."

"Ah-hah, I would recognize you in a street of a thousand female bodies," I said. I grabbed the dear girl's hand and kissed it. "At-a the House of LeRoy I'm-a work only with the dress-form, the dummy. But these eyes, the eyes of the artist, they see-a the real body. Quickly—" I addressed the maitre d' "—there is a room available for Mrs. Roche final fitting? Des catastrophe, it must be undone."

"Yes, yes, of course. There is a lounge upstairs," the poor idiot replied.

"Just a minute now, old man," Thomas Roche said. "The ruddy wedding feast is in progress."

"A matter of a minute. A matter of a minute," I said. I had not relinquished Hope's hand. I attempted to pull her toward the staircase.

"Sorry, old man. Damned impossible. The guests, the dinner, the whole ruddy show. I'm sorry."

His mother's watery voice floated to the surface. "Who ever is it?" she asked, attempting to peer through the distillery mist. "Was he on the list? Not from our side, I'm sure."

Several of the guests commenced mumbling a growing protest in support of their host. That would never do. I drew a great breath, preparing to discipline them. Then my eye was invaded by a terrible sight. Through the archway leading to the dining area a haunting figure propelled itself, gliding forward like a vindictive shade out of my past.

It was Louis Proferra, sitting upright in a wheel chair and rolling along the edge of the rebellious crowd. Good Lord, why had I never thought to glance at the guest list?

I tore my eye from Proferra with difficulty and turned back to the elegant mob that thought to place itself athwart my ambitions.

"What-sa dis?" I cried, my voice rising hand over hand, along the rope of my indignity to the enemy plateau. "You would deny-a des woman the most important part of-a her honeymoon—her clothes!"

A sufficient volume of liquor roiled within the guests to induce a round of smirking. Hope attempted to twist her hand away from me. I was forced to distract her by secretly working my fingers about in an effort to dislodge her opulent engagement ring. Her husband came forward to claim her. He said, "As I told you, old man, this is neither the time nor place—"

"I'm-a see it now!" I raged, gesturing with a vigorous arm movement, a waving of my limb that was not only picturesque in appearance but also somewhat lethal. "I'm-a see it now. It-sa get back at-a Mussolini you do dis. The war, she's-a not finish for Italy. She never be finish. Never will Italian man be free from the mockery in-a dis country. You CRUCIFY me to get atta *Il Duce*."

My resonant voice had already garroted the music from the dining hall and was at this point laying to waste the chatter of the two hundred guests. Many of the dears had taken to pouring into the foyer for an eye witness look at the "incident" at the Roche wedding.

Among the late arrivals, striding forth with majestic dignity, had come Mrs. Cecelia Roche, proud and capable matriarch of Bullrusher.

"I'm-a to pay forever for the sin of-a my dead FASCIST papa!" I was heard to scream.

"Who invited the Italian person?" Thomas Roche's fogbound mother inquired with delightful timing. "Somebody get me the list. . . ."

"Mr. Roche, something has to be done," the maitre d' gasped to Thomas. "I'm afraid I really must insist."

"Tommy. I must know what has happened to my gowns," Hope said. She had abandoned her efforts to free her hand from mine.

"Yes, yes, I quite understand," the buffeted groom stammered. "I say, old man, can't you hold your voice down? After all—"

"It wasn't like-a dis in 16-a-37," I shouted on. "Oh ho-ho, no. Den you English you plenty glad to see-a de Italians. And 1702, whosa say den SPIT on-a de Italian people? And-a 17-a-23 when-a you have de DIARRHEA War—"

"Mr. Roche, this is Bellinggames. I must insist. . . ."

"Oh, Tommy, my gowns. . . ."

"Somebody bring me that list. And a glass of port too. A large glass."

"Then inna 18-a-42. . . ."

"Will you all kindly cease this bloody racket!" Thomas cried. "All right, get on with it. Go ahead, Hope. Hop upstairs and have it done with." He turned away muttering. "Why these things go until the last minute. . . ."

Success! I clutched my prize and started urging her toward the staircase. Abruptly a voice of militant intensity was heard, casting the ugly aura of sanity into the situation.

"One moment please, Signor," the voice commanded. "The bride has her duties here at the wedding feast. She is not available for wardrobe adjustments. Come along, child," Aunt Cis said to Hope. "And the rest of you kindly return to the table."

Confounded woman! Was there none who would challenge

the matriarch of Bullrusher? None who would question this position she had assumed? She was, after all, but a cousin to Sir Hilary Roche, the actual titled head of the family. But she was also one of those fearsome shrews who had the capacity to step into command when the male lineage faltered.

Let us face it. Where would England have gotten without them?

And there were indications that the Roche family would continue to produce such women. For beside me a clear firm voice said, "Aunt Cis, excuse me, but I intend learning what has happened to my gowns." Stout girl, Hope!

The dowager's eyes snapped about to pounce upon the newest member of the family, a Roche of barely eight hours of seniority. A mutiny of questionable authority and no doubt of it.

Ahhh, but Aunt Cis was equal to the revolt. The harridan instinctively recognized the need here for negotiation. Give in a little, but still get your own way.

Aunt Cis said, "All right, dear, but there is no need for you to be involved at this time. Angela Millins can accompany the Signor. She was kind enough to assist during the fittings in London, so she knows the requirements. Come along now. And the rest of you—shoo, shoo. Back to the table."

The assembly turned and was herded to the dining hall by the implacable shepherd. I too gave ground gracefully. I released Hope's hand, permitting her to depart with her husband.

Angela Millins, her practiced eye assessing my masculine potential to the nearest gram, walked to my side. "Yes, Aunt Cis," she muttered through clenched teeth. "Anything you say, oh Potentate Extraordinary."

I turned to assist the lovely Miss Millins up the staircase. She was, possibly, an adequate substitute. I would have to investigate. Up we go, my dear.

Abruptly my oversized eyeballs discovered that Aunt Cis's influence was not quite trans-Atlantic in scope. A misshapen man in an American Army uniform had not responded to the dowager's dictum. Lieutenant Colonel Louis Proferra continued to sit silently in his wheel chair, staring with thought-ful concentration at ... Angela Millins? No, I fear it was the boisterous Italian who was the target of the one-armed man's disquieting curiosity. Do you have the impression that you have met Signor Orlando before, Colonel Proferra?

I noted that Proferra had two ears. When I last saw him he had but the left ear. I had just shot the right one from his head, you see. A justifiable bit of impromptu surgery, as any of you who are familiar with *The Scotland Yard Commission* can attest. The replacement of the appendage appeared rather extraordinary testimony to the gentleman's recuperative pow-ers. The American ingenuity that one hears so much about, I suppose.

Proferra turned his wheel chair and rolled silently out of the foyer.

"Come," I said to Angela, as I bustled her up the stairs, "des disgrace to my talent, it must be undone."

We were directed to a room on the third floor by a flustered lackey of the restaurant. Once closeted in the room Angela turned to me for direction. "Remove-a. Remove-a," I said to the girl, waving my hand casually at her dress. As she complied, I absorbed myself with the contents of my valise.

My original intent had been to isolate myself with Hope, the new Mrs. Roche, and express to her, in anguished termi-nology, the many mutilations that had befallen her wardrobe while my back was turned. ("The satin ... how you say? ... insert, ina you riding suit. The imbecile seamstress, she is pleat this.") That sort of thing. I had at my command a complete description of the trousseau as published in the *Times*.

The obvious solution to the catastrophe, a solution subtly suggested by myself to Hope if the maid proved dense, would be my taking up residence immediately at Bullrusher with my needle and thread. ("I am sacrifice-a my schedule. Let-a the wife of Premier de P—— wait for her maternity gowns. ... Ahhh, yes, she is finally been-a caught. You didn't-a hear? They say the father is the Irish Ambassador to Paris, but whosa know. We can discuss dis further ata Bullrusher. ...")

But Aunt Cis had placed her resounding foot into the plot. I was saddled with Miss Millins, a person with but tenuous authority regarding the housing of strangers at Bullrusher. Angela could hardly be expected to defy the " . . . Potentate Extraordinary . . ." just to ensure adherence to design in another woman's trousseau.

Angela had to be fused with a much more personal motivation before she would insist, regardless of objection, that Signor Orlando be provided shelter at the great estate.

My eyes wandered up casually from my valise and anchored with unsavory intensity on the collation of pink flesh emerging from Miss Millins' bridesmaid gown. As Angela disrobed she uttered pitiful little cries concerning Hope's trousseau; what a shame it would be if such a beautiful wardrobe were not exactly to the specifications agreed upon in London.

I glanced about at the room. The door locked from the inside. Aside from the overhead light there was but one floor lamp, located next to the full length sofa and emitting only timorous rays. Perfect. (Ah, Bellinggame, you old rake!)

"Remove-a, remove-a," I said to Angela, indicating the body wrap of elastic and satin that enclosed her from thigh to shoulder joint. "I'm-a you dress designer, not-a you dentist."

I stood staring openly at her as she continued shedding. My foot tapped on the rug and my fingers nervously kneaded a yellow measuring tape. The impatience exuding from my huge eyes established me as master, she as the delightful cork to be tossed about on the broiling sea of my unleashed appetite.

Eventually she was peeled to a scant degree of charming cover. She could go no further without completely invalidating any claim to modesty. Her body, I am forced to record, represented a classic justification of all of this nutrition mumbo-jumbo one endures regarding the importance of vitamins and calories and the like. A delightful structure.

I stepped into the arena, my cape and muletta at the ready.

There ensued then a period during which a true artist exposed to a layman the secret ingredients of his artistry. The layman was obviously absorbed in the process and also puzzled. She said, "I . . . I've never been measured in that . . . ah . . . section before."

"Then-a it is a butcher whosa measure you," the artist said scornfully.

The search for dimensional data continued; a more or less heavy-handed procedure in this instance. I collected several intriguing but, even I admit, somewhat useless statistics pertinent to Miss Millins' torso. A measure of my diligence is evidenced by the fact that I was forced eventually to remove my glasses. They were becoming fogged.

Ahhh, but once again there came verification of one of Man's oldest truths: He who labors with distinction shall be rewarded. The artist eventually found that the material beneath his talented hand was vibrating with fine trembling here and there. Also, Angela's breathing rhythm had accelerated.

The young lady recalled, with a bit of a stammer, that she had never seen me at the House LeRoy, had never been fitted by me.

"Am I the sausage maker?" I growled. "No. I'm not paid enough to stuff-a fat ladies ina my creations. The dressmaker's manikin, made from-a the body of-a the customer is enough insult to my hands. Breath-a deep . . . ahhh. In a lifetime of gown design I'm-a never work with a body like-a dis. So pale as the marble. So much dis inner heat that's-a come out to my palm. Such—"

"Signor . . . Signor, you shouldn't put your hand—Signor!"

"Orlando, Signor Orlando. So kind-a to hold very still now. Dis isa delicate dimension. Move-a the leg over here."

Slowly, slowly the stem bent. The flower moved closer to the consuming insect, to the great, hairy, lumbering bee. The slender stem bent . . . and bent. . . .

Many minutes passed. The wedding feast two floors below came to its end. The absence of the red-haired bridesmaid was noted by the official photographer. An emissary was dispatched to retrieve her. He was Mr. Luke Lawless, an American Army Captain, who was considered to be Angela Millins' escort for the wedding.

The sound of his pounding fist on the locked door of the

third floor of Bellinggames came too late to preserve the delicate flower from the trampling of the ravenous Italian bee. As the staccato of the intruding fist increased to distracting proportions, I wrung from the semi-coherent Miss Millins a vehement guarantee that she would obtain accommodations for me at Bullrusher for the following day. "They'll bloody well allow you in, darling, even if I have to kill the old harridan. And we'll do this measuring thing all over again, right from the beginning."

To show my gratitude I assisted the charming maid from the sofa and into her clothes. Meanwhile I unleashed a series of Neapolitan curses that intimidated the fist wielder to silence until such time as I was prepared to pass to him his lady friend.

Bullrusher is rather a pleasant estate, if your taste runs to the open moor, nude hillside sort of place. Mine does not. On the afternoon of the day following my appearance at Bellinggames I arrived at Bullrusher.

I encountered a predictable period of delay at the main gate. First, I had to squirm through the gathering of shop girls standing outside. Their number had diminished. Only the truly loyal remained.

Then one had to break past the ring of constables. Their sergeant eventually accepted me as a legitimate guest. Next came the stuffy gateman. He never quite believed that any person as disreputable in appearance as Signor Orlando could have been invited to Bullrusher. His faith in the Roche family suffered some slight constriction as he watched the auto sent down from the house carry off the outlandish figure in the beret and dirty trench coat.

I was welcomed at the front entrance by a radiant Angela Millins. "My God, I thought you'd never get here," she greeted me. "Come along, we'll get up to my bedroom."

The dear girl's impatience was to suffer further whetting. She led me through the grand entrance hall and along a side corridor to the active side of the huge house; the portion of the house containing the main sitting room that overlooked the gardens and the terrace where guests and members of the resident family most generally congregated during clement weather. The rest of the house was given over to guest suites, family bedrooms, servant facilities, and of course the great dining hall (adjacent to the chapel) used on an average of once a year.

At the entrance to the sitting room we encountered the newlyweds, Thomas and Hope. They were dressed for tennis and on their way to the courts. Angela and I were urged to join them.

"I am not play des bourgeoisie game," I said, priggishly. "These hands of the artist, they are not-a made to squeeze sweaty tennis racket. Only the woman's body they squeeze."

"I say, you are very quick with picturesque terminology, aren't you, old boy?" Thomas Roche said. He was not amused. With a distressed glance at Angela, he marched off saying, "Come along, Hope." His triumph over his bride's flesh the night before had sharpened his tone of authority. Which was as it should be.

Hope squeezed a confused smile at Angela and followed her new master.

Angela took possession of my arm again, pressing it to her delightful chest, and moved us onward deeper into the house. "All the bloody staircases are down this way in this stupid place," she muttered. "I swear, there's less privacy in these corridors than Waterloo station. Look up there—" We were passing through the main sitting room where several of the wedding guests were chatting or reading. Angela's interest though was for an architectural oddity located on the room's inside wall, the wall opposite the French doors that led to the terrace. Angela pointed at the balcony located on the wall.

"That was put in by Sir Winthrop Roche in 1890," she whispered. "Some say so he could watch that his wife had gone down that hall to the Lord Nelson wing, where their bedroom was located. It's the only way into the wing. Then when she was off, Sir Winthrop would slip over to the servants' quarters where he had several favorites among the maids."

"Dese Englishmen, they confound me," I muttered.

We turned a corridor and found ourselves in the path of a young pair who were trotting along the hall toward us. The lovely female of the pair was emitting a laugh known throughout the civilized world. She was Miss Lulubelle Courage of Hollywood, USA. Or: Queen of Sophisticate Comedy, as her studio unhesitatingly identified her. Miss Courage too, on this occasion, was dressed for tennis.

"My God," Angela gasped, "she has nothing under her blouse." A total inaccuracy. Miss Courage had a masterpiece under her blouse. Quite obviously too, since the actress' energetic progress along the corridor left little doubt in the issue.

"I still don't know how she got herself invited," Angela added as we stepped aside for the running pair. "Probably through Ira Loftwood. And she'll have paid well for it too," Angela giggled pleasantly, "if I know Uncle Ira."

"Dese man with Miss Courage," I asked, "he is you Uncle Ira? The famous Cap-e-tan of Royal Navy?" Obviously the man had not been Ira Loftwood, being a good twenty years younger than the naval hero. He was the same man who had reclaimed Angela from Signor Orlando at the upstairs room at Bellinggames the previous evening. I had met him before, prior to the Bullrusher Commission, but could not recall where.

"Uncle Ira is an admiral now," Angela said with proper family pride.

"And that wasn't he with Miss Courage. That was that idiot American baseball player, Luke Lawless. You may have read about him." (Ah yes, Mr. Lawless. The man had certainly put on a bit of weight since I last saw him—*The American Mistress Commission.*) "He's a ball-thrower, or 'pitcher' I think they call them. Very good at it, whatever it is. He'll tell you so himself if you give him half a minute of time."

As a matter of fact, my dear, Mr. Luke Lawless, prior to the War was the best practitioner of the questionable art of throwing baseballs since the prime playing days of a gentleman with the delightful name of Dizzy Dean. I was to encounter Mr. Lawless again following the Bullrusher Commission. He was to a degree involved in a picturesque incident that took place in a year not long after the War; Augustus Mandrell's introduction to the kinetic world of baseball. Picture if you will the sight of myself standing at "Homeplate" as the Americans call it, with a length of wood in my hand and a mean-tempered gentleman standing sixty feet away throwing baseballs at me, as forty thousand spectators roared their approval. This unique event took place within the confines of a structure called, oddity upon oddity, the Polo Grounds; a temple of the American pastime since discarded. The whole affair is recorded somewhere or other under the apt title: *The Baseball Commission.*

But, let's get on to Angela Millins' boudoir.

We eventually located the proper staircase and ascended to the upper halls. "It's just down here," my redheaded miss breathed, grasping my hand and actually tugging me.

"An-gel-ah!"

A steel-tipped voice penetrated our rising passion. Striding toward us from an open door further up the corridor came the grand dame of the Bullrusher household: Cecelia Roche. Aunt Cis to those who loved and feared her. Behind the dowager, trotting in his own peculiar gait, came her cousin, the Lord of Bullrusher, Sir Hilary Roche.

"Oh damn!" Angela muttered beside me.

Aunt Cis ran her painfully cold eyes over my figure and asked Angela where we might be bound. Angela, her voice a bit testy, replied that we were off for her bedroom to continue the fitting of Hope's trousseau that had begun at Bellinggames. We were to concentrate, Angela reported, on the gown that Hope would be wearing that evening at the ball, the last major assemblage of the family prior to the honeymoon. And, more than incidentally, the last time that Hope and Sir Hilary Roche would be under the same roof for some time.

"You're the one who ordered me to see to the fittings," Angela concluded to the stern empress.

"That can wait for now," Aunt Cis said. "Hope's gown appeared in no need of change in London. I want you to come along and assist me with the floral arrangements." She took Angela's arm with an authority that stilled protest. Over her shoulder, the grand dame left an order to the figurehead ruler of Bullrusher. She said, "Hilary, see to Signor Orlando's quarters. Have Prichart put him in a room in the east wing." Angela's bedroom, as you may have surmised, was in the west wing. The ladies departed.

Sir Hilary and I were alone, an arrangement that would have to be duplicated later the same day if I was to bring the commission to an acceptable conclusion. As he led me to the hands of "Prichart," Sir Hilary chatted on about his own career as an amateur couturier.

"The wife of the French Premier, Madam de P——, wore one of my gowns once," he told me. "But of course she's such a . . . a physical person—all those men constantly about her—the dress never really looked right on her. There's just a chance, by the by, that it was my dress she was wearing the night the Premier discovered her on the golfing green at the Tulon Racquet Club with that Communist chap Paul Zardi. You've heard about it, of course? They say the Premier actually took after her with the flag pin. It was the 16th hole. Quite a run to the clubhouse. I've inspected the gown since, and while I can't say positively that the stains are actually blood, there is no doubt in my mind that . . . well, the less said the better probably. The Germans were the only ones who really knew how to handle Communists like Zardi. Just the way they handled those frightful Jews. I say, is there anything at all one can do with makeup stains on one's collars? I must have a dozen shirts that are absolutely uninhabitable. . . ." Eventually we located Prichart.

That evening the grand dining hall was activated for a formal supper. Signor Orlando was not invited. Prichart informed me that a few of the wedding party, those who were without dinner dress, were being served at a small dining room in the east wing. I chose not to partake.

I reconnoitered instead the sleeping quarters of the wedding party. The suite in use by the newlyweds was surprisingly orderly: no brushes, lotions or other toilet articles laid out. But, in rummaging the closet, I did locate a pair of pink pumps that were constructed with tall, pointed heels. Obviously they were not the property of the groom. I stuffed the shoes in my pocket.

Descending to the main floor I encountered another dieter. Mr. Luke Lawless of the baseball world was just leaving the bar with two potent highballs in his hands. He looked at me and said, "Hi, pal. So you're another guy that won't put on a monkey suit just to eat a little grub. They're never going to get me into one of those things. Besides I've gotta get rid of this pot." He nudged his abdomen. "Can't report to the baseball scene like this. C'mon into the pool room. That's where the outcasts are. We got a game going."

I had little to occupy me until the diners moved on to the ballroom, except appear conspicuous to the servants. I accepted the ballplayer's invitation; and thus very nearly induced calamity in the Bullrusher Commission.

The other "outcast" in the billiard room was Louis Proferra.

He sat rigidly upright in his wheel chair as he moved efficiently around the table accomplishing excellent billiard shots with one hand. His concentration on the game was so rigid that he could spare us but one striking snake-like flick of his eyes as we entered. And the one look was sufficient to imprint our identities boldly on his brain. Proferra was a man-hunter.

"Hell, I'll never beat this guy," Luke Lawless exclaimed as the cue rebounded from three cushions and came to rest only after striking both reds. "And me with two of the best hands ever stuffed into a baseball uniform. I hold the fielding record for left-handed pitchers. Something people don't generally remember. Say do you two guys know each other?" A rather intriguing question, fraught with metaphysical overtones. Do you ever get to know a man if each time you meet, he attempts to persuade you that he is somebody else?

Louis Proferra announced that he did not know me. I said, "I'm-a not know men. I'm-a know women."

"Lou here," the baseball player said, "is skipping dinner because half his stomach is missing. Got shot up in a prisoner of war camp, of all places. One of our own camps, I mean."

Luke Lawless appeared to be quite proud of his fellow American's collection of infirmities. I was told that Proferra had lost his arm in a unique explosion in Teheran in 1942. "Then the same guy that blew his arm off," Lawless said, with amazed delight, "goes and shoots his ear off a while back. That's a fake ear he's wearing."

"Did you want another game?" Proferra asked Lawless abruptly.

"What's the matter," asked the armadillo-skinned baseball man, "got no stomach for your own medical history? Ha, ha. Get it? Got no stomach?"

"You sense of humor," I said, "it is escape-a my attention."

Mr. Lawless just smiled. A rather cruel smile.

"How about you, Orlando?" Proferra said. "Do you play?"

"Deze hands, dey are the hands of the artist," I said. "Dey are not for to be crushed between-a billiard balls." I had no wish to protrude my face into the strong light emanating from the lamp over the table.

"You got a pretty good pair of meat hooks there for a dress designer," Mr. Lawless was kind enough to note. "Here, let's see them compared to mine." He held up his left hand inviting me to lay my hand against his. "You need a good pair of mitts in my game," he continued. "And I got the best. Put it up there.'"

"I'm-a no touch-a you rough hand," I protested. "Mine isa hand for woman's body."

"Your hand looks pretty tough to me," the insidiously alert Proferra commented.

Before Proferra could move on to a logical development of this anomaly, Mr. Lawless, who was not without his addiction to the spotlight, blurted, "Yeah, how about it, Signor, you need another couple of hands to measure that Millins babe? Here they are, dad. Any time any place. Man, would I like to. . . ." And so on for the next five minutes.

Mr. Lawless eventually delivered to Lieutenant Colonel Proferra and myself, free of all charges including even a casual request, Mr. Lawless' estimate of the sexual potential of the several physically qualified young women housed at that moment in Bullrusher. " . . . I guess I'll go along with the majority opinion of the boys in the foxholes," Lawless said. "Lulubelle Courage would give you the best roll in the hay. But I'll surprise you in my second choice. I'd take Hope Cornflower. Tommy Roche has gotten himself a real hunk of dame there. Did you ever hear how their romance started? I was there, so I know the story. It was at Cornflower, Hope's home. She was in a boating accident but was lucky enough to get back to shore. It was Thomas Roche who found her, exhausted and unconscious on the beach. He'd been in love with her for years and never had the guts to say so. But the kicker is that when he found her she didn't have a stitch of clothes on. I guess what he saw when he found her made him decide it was time to speak up. Boy I really missed out on that one."

While Mr. Lawless' resume was of reasonable interest to me I reserved a degree of my attention for the man in the wheel chair. Lieutenant Colonel Proferra continued rolling about the edge of the table performing casual billiard shots. And he did not permit Luke Lawless' soliloquy in lechery to command his full attention either. Several times during Lawless' discussion, Proferra's eyes slid sideways and rooted vulture-like on my hands. On my Achilles' heel. The hands, you see, are the most difficult of the body's features to disguise.

I must chart an inroad on your patience here for a moment. I am possessed of a grievance that requires promulgation and no more auspicious forum than this chronicle is available to me.

A measure of Mandrell, Limited's success is attributable to the skill of the founder (myself) in ensuring that his back-trail is perpetually awash in a lack of information or in a deluge of misinformation. The most useful tool in this endeavor is the disguise. The authorities are not so quick to name Augustus Mandrell as the pivotal figure in one of my commissions if the man associated with the commission is obviously not Augustus Mandrell. Is Signor Orlando, for instance? Or Commander D.P. O'Keefe (*The Faming Dog Commission*)?

I have, therefore, expended considerable research into this little-known art: disguise. There are four major areas in a good disguise: the face (head), the overall figure (posture, walk, height, and bulk), the personality, and the hands.

By far the most important of these is the personality. A well manufactured personality will permit you to triumph even when you have not mastered the other major areas of the disguise. Your audience will note with much greater intensity your braggard's voice ("I told His Majesty a thing or two about how to police India, believe me") than they will remember that your moustache appeared to be rather infirmly anchored.

And as the personality is the strongest ingredient, the hands are the weakest. They, like the face, are always on display. Yet, their movements are much less at our command than the overall movements of the face. The hands, to a degree, act for themselves. Over the years they build their own pattern of action, one the owner is much less conscious of than he is of the image projected by his face.

Then too the hands lend themselves to disguise, physical change, with tenacious reluctance. A palm, some knuckles, and five fingers. What can one do with them? The coward's way out is the glove; also the fool's. Our present Anglo-Saxon society has discarded the male glove for other than inclement weather and pagan ritual (prize fighting and undertaking). Thus only a fool will attempt to disguise his hands with gloves unless he is supported by the weather.

The problem of the tell-tale hand has forced me on occasion to the extreme of manufacturing false hands. (*The Dr. Sherrock Commission* and *The Maltese Falcon Commission* come to mind.) A solution both time-consuming and awkward in utilization.

But the grievance I mentioned at the beginning of this aside has little to do with the problem of the hands. (Incidentally, ask a professional actor sometime which provides him the greater indecision in a role: what to do with his face, or what do with those two huge pieces of meat hanging from the ends of his arms.) My grievance has more to do with the lack of recognition paid to the artists of illicit disguise.

A Frenchman I know of, whose name would mean little to you unless you are entrenched in police activity, was using tinted eye pieces to change the color of his eyes back in 1927. Is he ever mentioned when the history of contact lenses is recorded? No.

I recall too the story of the man, a Mr. Lennox, who was faced with the task of hiding several surgical scars that had been indelibly woven into one side of his neck. His solution was simplicity itself. He had corresponding scars scored into the other side of the neck. The original marks were lost in a profusion of symmetry. Yet where is the modern plastic surgeon who will credit Mr. Lennox with exploration in this now commonly accepted procedure?

God knows how many more good lads, inventive men all, have gone unsung. The chap, for instance, who determined the exact length of adhesive tape that must be wound from the instep to the ankle to produce a perfect limp regardless of the unevenness of the walking surface. I have yet to hear any actor who had used the same device to sustain his portrayal of Richard III give billing to the originator.

There is even a measure of credit that must be given to the gentleman who first wandered the streets of London with a tin cup in his hand and a carefully printed (by himself) placard on his chest proclaiming the message: I AM BLIND.

Tawdry yes, but inventive.

Then there was the elusive gentleman who closed a distinctive gap in his teeth by filling it with raw potato. Have the men of the dental industry ever paid homage to this craftsman who converted their profession from a collection of ham-fisted harvesters of decayed ivory to the ubiquitous regiment of oral plumbers we know today? (I once had a steel filling intruded into one of my molars—with, as I recall, a jackhammer.)

We have come a long way, my friends, from the disguise composed of a swath of cloth with two eye holes cut in its center. The gifted men who brought us this distance are unworthy of the inattention that has befallen them.

Excellence in any field deserves recognition. Ergo: this journal.

I remained in the billiard room with Mr. Proferra and Mr. Lawless until they had resumed their match. The baseball player revealed that behind his braggart's façade there was housed a sensitive coordination of hand, eye, and will. He was very nearly Proferra's equal in the demanding game of billiards.

Their conversation gradually encompassed only the game before them and their private lives. They forgot Signor Orlando. Mr. Lawless mentioned that he had several friends who were remaining in Europe rather than returning to " . . . the

good old U.S. and A. . . ." He said, "They've gotten themselves jobs with this International Military Tribunal that's
going to put the Nazi bigwigs on trial. If you're serious about
staying over here after your discharge, Lou, maybe I could
put in a word for you?"

"I want to get out of this damn wheel chair first," Proferra
said. "Then I'll make plans."

Their concentration had apparently reached a safe level of
self-absorption. I slipped through the door leaving them. In
the ballroom I encountered the orchestra members tuning
their instruments. A trickle of guests entered the ballroom
from the dining area next door. The ladies were picturesque
all in their fine gowns.

Several hours were due to elapse before I could maneuver
the new Mrs. Thomas Roche and Sir Hilary Roche into the
proper geographic locations, the locations that would permit
me to conclude the Bullrusher Commission. Meanwhile Signor Orlando was a conspicuous and painful thorn in the
family's social paw. I did not fit in. I am certain that the
reluctant permission obtained by dear Angela, permission to
invite the seedy couturier to Bullrusher, had not included the
prospect of having the Italian person mingling with the other
guests. Yet it was essential that I remain in the ballroom.

How does one go about hiding a large irresponsibly garbed
(I had refused all efforts by the household staff to remove my
purple beret) loudmouth in a hall filled with tastefully
dressed and socially nimble people? I will tell you. One hides
such a figure in an explosion of conspicuousness. Had I
skulked about the corners and pillars in obvious awareness of
my social inferiority, Aunt Cis would certainly have seen to
my removal. Instead I elected to put the family on notice
that any effort to eject me would induce a protest of crude
proportions.

I strode, stamped actually, about the room in a posture of
pugnacious authority. Occasionally I paused beside some female and examined her dress with my magnified eyeballs. By
judiciously dispensing my craftsman's judgement, a nod of
approval over some stitch, a grunt of disgust at some fold, I
gradually built a following of sorts. The ladies in the room
were stupefied by my credentials. The House of LeRoy, with

salons in London, Paris, and Rome prior to the War, was *the* institution in what Madam LeRoy herself identifies as " ... the blood bath of dress design. ..."

Thus, within an hour, every woman in the room kept an apprehensive eye on my progress. "What does the Signor think of my gown?" was the silent, trembling question in every female mind. Naturally my nods of approval were reserved for the older, obviously influential women I encountered. There was even heard an occasional delightful cry of: "Bravo! Bravo!" from the Italian as he inspected the dress of some dowager with a bit of steel in her eye.

The grunts of disgust were lavished on the younger maids, particularly on those for whom the older ladies exhibited a degree of rancor. The members of this younger set were rather easy to identify. They were the young things who exposed to the male eyes in the room a pair of exciting shoulders or a gaping cleavage. Miss Angela Millins was one of these. I peered into her dress and emitted a completely foundless grunt of disappointment. At the same time I managed to whisper her a message. "Twelve-a midnight. Ina you room. Have-a the champagne cold pleese."

Naturally Miss Lulubelle Courage, the Hollywood product, received from me the most humiliating judgment. I lifted the hem of her gown up to my eye for inspection. The sight of her stunning legs did not go unrecorded by the gentlemen in the room, nor by myself. I then threw the hem from me shouting, "Take-a dis rag back-a to United States and de-mand-a the head of the designer on-a platter!"

Following that exercise in impartial judgment, the Roche relatives would have voted me into the family had I requested it.

My support from the old guard was such by this time, that when I ordered the orchestra leader to perform a particular piece his initial objection was driven back into his teeth by several kind ladies. Nor did I encounter any difficulty getting the floor cleared of dancers. Then, when I had completed my twirling tarantella, the patter of applause about the room came primarily from the gloved and jeweled hands of my elderly sheep.

I was securely entrenched. As I circulated about the room

following my dance a number of ladies came to me with intricate questions regarding dress design. As I spoke to each, my speech and my eye would freeze at one point in the discussion and I would ask, "Why is it that this Sir Hilary Roche is always follow the bride around the room? His eye, it never leave-a her?"

Invariably the first response would be a dismayed: "Hilary? Oh, I wouldn't think so." But each dowager thus encouraged would then stare after the head of Bullrusher, a frown of genuine proportions on her face. Nor was it likely that she would forget the strange observation should it generate applicability to any of the evening's later events.

About an hour later the bride was taken suddenly ill and went off to her rooms. There was some speculation as to what had caused the minor ailment. None stumbled on the correct answer: that some unknown hand had deposited a pellet of indigestible ingredients in the poor girl's whiskey and water. The groom went off with his wife but returned shortly with the news that Hope was resting and appeared to need little more than a spot of sleep. Thomas urged all to continue the party and joined in the dancing himself to indicate his personal lack of concern.

I wandered by Sir Hilary and whispered, "The young-a man upstairs. Heez ask-a me to bring-a you up.'"

Of course Sir Hilary wished to know which young man I was talking about. I shrugged and said, "Ima no know heem. He's-a say you know."

"How deliciously mysterious," Sir Hilary bubbled. "Lead on. Lead on."

My pleasure, sir. I took him to the room next to the suite being used by the newlyweds. I preceded Sir Hilary through the door. As he came in behind me, nearly pushing me in his eagerness, I turned and brought the pink pump from my pocket. The collision of the sharp heel and his temple was the last sensation ever recorded by his brain. By the time I removed his trousers he had ceased bleeding.

The room we were in connected to the bridal suite through a door that had been locked earlier. The lock had bent to my will. I carried Sir Hilary into the suite, into Thomas Roche's bedroom.

Hope's room was on the other side of the connecting sitting room. I moved on with my perfumed burden, across the sitting room and, quietly, into Hope's dark room.

I paused a moment to ensure that the girl had not been disturbed. She made no sound. The pellet she had consumed had put her into a coma slightly more intense than normal sleep.

I eased Sir Hilary on to the foot of the bed, his head and shoulders on the bed, his legs on the floor. The posture was one a mad rapist might quite easily fall into were he abruptly immobilized during his attack.

I then carefully felt about for Hope's hand in order to place the pink shoe therein. Something was amiss! My groping hand grew a bit frantic.

The damn bed was empty!

I threw on the lights. There was no evidence of the girl in the room at all. Even the closet that had held her clothes earlier was empty. The same was true of Thomas Roche's room. Empty.

I went into the corridor and raced about looking for a servant. Eventually I saw a maid carrying linen at the far end of one hallway. As I moved toward her the wall on my right ended suddenly and was replaced by a belt-high, iron-grill fence. I discovered that I was on the balcony that overlooked the main sitting room. There were a dozen people sitting down below, taking a respite from the ball. One older woman saw me and cried, "Oh, Signor Orlando, are you going to do another dance up there?" A few of the others in the room joined in the cry urging me to perform. I scowled at the idiots and fled after the maid.

I caught her as she was turning into another corridor. "The bride," I said, "I'm have-a the medicine—" I patted my pocket "—but I'm no find her."

"Oh she's right down here, sir," she said, indicating the only door in the corridor. "But she's asleep."

"I'm no understand," I said. "I'ma told she's in other room."

"That was a little arrangement," she said smiling. "Everybody was told the bride and groom were in the Wagner Suite. You see some of the guests, the men, like to play

jokes on newlyweds the first night. You should have seen what
they did in the Wagner Suite last night. They had all sorts of
things hanging from the ceiling and under the bed covers. Oh
they were awful." She giggled and blushed. "And they had
the bath filled with gelatin. And writing on the mirrors. And
even a gramophone player under the bed, all set to start up
by itself. Very loud music."

"The bride, she is asleep then?" I asked.

"Yes sir. She's here in the Lord Nelson wing where she
won't be disturbed. Nobody can reach here without going
past the main sitting room. Mrs. Cecelia Roche sat down
there all last night to make certain nobody went near the
bride and groom. There's a balcony, you know, where you
can see who's going to the Lord Nelson wing."

But, my dear young woman, this is absurd. I have a dead
body I must deliver to the bride.

I returned to my dead body. It had not moved. I went into
Thomas Roche's room and searched the closet. Perhaps if I
dressed Sir Hilary in some costume associated with Thomas I
could sort of half-carry the body past the balcony—assistance
to an inebriated young man—leaving the impression that it
was Thomas who was proceeding to the Lord Nelson wing. A
damned clumsy device, what with the real Thomas quite
lively in the ballroom but I desperately needed a device,
clumsy or otherwise.

The only suit in the closet was a dark business suit. Hardly
distinctive.

The door to the sitting room opened! Somebody had entered the Wagner Suite from the corridor. I rushed quickly
out of Thomas' room to intercept whichever servant it might
be before he blundered upon the distinctive tableau in the
other room. It was hardly the sort of thing a member of the
staff would overlook.

I found Lieutenant Colonel Louis Proferra just inside the
door of the sitting room.

"What the hell are you doing in my rooms, Orlando?" he
said, glaring.

"Your rooms, Signor?" I said.

"Yeah, Prichart said I could use these. They're closer to

the elevator and there's no step down the way there is in the room I have now. I came over for a look."

From the edge of my eye I noticed that I had left the light on in the other bedroom. Sir Hilary's feet were visible past the open door.

"Dis Prichart, heesa ask me to help-a you move," I said. "Heeza think you an invalid in that chair and need help with-a you trunks."

"I'm no invalid," Proferra said. "Just a pinched nerve that keeps one leg dead. Happened when I fell off a ship in Belfast last year," he added casually. I was pleased to note that he did not associate the name Augustus Mandrell with his diving expedition from the deck of the S.S. *Haleakala*. Evidently I had been successful in isolating Mr. Proferra from the knowledge that it had been myself who threw him from the weather deck of *Haleakala*. (*The Hawaiian Volcano Commission.*) He continued his medical report. "The doctors say the nerve could break loose any time. I won't be in this chair forever."

"Hmmm," I said. "Just like-a General Tullocchi. And today he's-a walk around like-a new."

"What General Tullocchi?"

"Italian Air Force," I said. "He have-a pinched nerve. Right about here. I work on-a heem in hospital ina Milan. Him and all-a the others."

"What do you mean, you worked on him?"

"Deeze hands, they are free the pinched nerve. I'm-a the expert. I fly all over Italy in-a the war. Work-a on all the soldiers. The special touch. The artist hands. I do dis in-a five minute what the doctors can't do in-a year."

"You're trying to tell me you're a doctor?" he said sarcastically. "You're being palmed off around here as a dress designer. I suppose that's a disguise?"

Ahh, Louis, do not use that word. Do not even think it.

"I'm-a dress designer. I'm-a number one!" I shouted. "But ina war, the army wants-a dress designer? The hands of the artist that know so much about the body to make-a dress, dees hands know how to feel-a for a nerve. Come on, I'm-a show you." I jumped behind his wheel chair and started pushing it toward Thomas Roche's bedroom.

"Wait a minute, wait a damn minute," Proferra said, and

tried to hold the wheel of his chair with his one hand. "I wouldn't let you touch me if you had a dozen medical degrees."

I kicked the door to the bedroom closed and stopped the chair. I reached around and started unbuttoning his military blouse. "You say I'm-a no doctor." I muttered. "I'm-a say I show you."

"Get your damn hands off me!" He slapped my hand away.

"You strike-a my hands!" I screeched. "You damage the hands of-a artist! I'm-a kill-a you!"

I launched myself upon him like a great vulture from the sky, actually leaping at him with my feet off the floor. He threw up the one arm to break my attack. The arm crumpled under my weight. The wheel chair flew backwards, both of us riding it.

My voice was filled with Italian rage and my hands struck out in clumsy blows. But my brain, like a polished steel scalpel, remained coldly focused on but one objective—immobilize Proferra.

As the wheel chair struck the wall, I snaked my hand behind his head and stabbed at his spine with fingers that knew their exact mission. The wheel chair fell on its side. Proferra did not feel the impact. He was unconscious.

I snatched off his jacket and ran with the wheel chair to the other bedroom. A few minutes later I was wheeling Sir Hilary along the corridor in the chair. The man had changed loyalties. From all appearances he had become a member of the armed forces of the United States. A Lieutenant Colonel, no less. A small rug hid the fact that the gentleman wore no trousers.

As I approached the open balcony I leaned my head forward, next to the Lieutenant Colonel's head as though to better hear what he was saying. Actually my intent was to spare the viewers below the sight of a new affliction added to the Colonel's rather overloaded list of infirmities: a hole in his head.

Whatever it was the brave officer told me was evidently rather amusing for those below in the sitting room heard my masculine chuckle.

Nice chap that Signor Orlando. There he is wheeling the wounded American about. He must not know that that corridor doesn't really go anywhere.

Once in the Lord Nelson wing I slipped the wheel chair into Hope's suite and walked softly to her bedroom.

Ahhh, there she was. A lovely sight. Those delightful mounds that trembled slightly under her thin night dress with every breath were certainly the sort of objective to ignite the beast in one. Even, perhaps, in so strange a chap as Sir Hilary.

I removed the military tunic from Mr. Roche and put it on myself in place of my trench coat. Sir Hilary's trousers and jacket I threw on the floor of Hope's bedroom. I arranged the gentleman once again on the foot of the bed. He was getting a bit stiff.

I put the shoe in Hope's hand. She stirred but did not waken. A bed lamp provided the only illumination in the room. I arranged the lamp so its rays were pointed toward the foot of the bed.

Then I crouched down behind Sir Hilary and held his upper torso upright so he was facing right at the girl. His hands were already under the blanket. Under Hope's night dress too, for that matter.

The time for the actual attack had arrived.

I carefully gathered a handful of bed clothes. Then I jerked the covers from the girl. At the same moment I emitted an insane cackle and giggled, "I've got you now!"

Hope was shocked fully awake. Her scream ran through her bedroom door and the door from her sitting room to the corridor (both open) like a steel-tipped spear.

She reacted as though she had rehearsed the role. As I crawled through the shadows away from the bed toward the door, I heard the pink shoe strike again and again.

I popped into the wheel chair, the trench coat and my beret under me, and wheeled furiously back along the Lord Nelson wing corridor. The screams of the young maid under siege flew past me. I had not yet reached the intersection of the corridor that contained the balcony when I heard running footsteps and an anguished Thomas Roche calling "Hope! Hope! . . ."

I spun the wheel chair about and started back toward the girl's room. The running footsteps had nearly reached the corridor intersection behind me. I yanked my left arm from the military jacket and tucked the arm behind me. I was still absorbed with buttoning Proferra's jacket when the panicked groom and several of the spryer male guests ran past me. They sped unerringly into the nuptial suite.

As the second platoon of rescuers swerved around me, I stopped my chair and carefully maneuvered the wheels in order to propel myself backwards. In their haste to achieve the scene of all the fun, none of the guests took note of the phenomena of the retreating chair. The runners went in one direction, the chair in the other. When I reached the intersection of the corridor that contained the balcony I started asking the passers-by, "What's going on? What happened?"

No one had paused to eradicate the ignorance of the American Lieutenant Colonel. In a huff he rolled off down the corridor, away from the congregation of boors.

I returned to Louis Proferra and reinstalled him in his military garments. I propped him in his vehicle and provided his propulsion along the corridor.

There goes that nice Signor Orlando again, pushing the poor American about.

The flow of agitated personnel had reversed itself. As I steered the wheel chair into the corridor containing the balcony, I found the rescuers returning. They were all immersed in a chatter of shocked dialogue. One of the gentlemen stopped my forward progress.

"I wouldn't go down there just now, Signor," he said. "Why don't you take Colonel Proferra to his room. Is he asleep?"

At that moment Proferra shook his head and glanced about with remarkable alertness.

"Ahhh, you have awake him," I said.

At the sound of my voice Proferra spun his head toward me. "You son of a bitch!" he cried. He jumped from the chair with the great fist of his one arm drawn back to smite me.

In mid stroke the poor man abruptly realized that he was

standing on his own two feet, as we say. He was shocked into restraint. The fist went unnoticed as he stared at his legs.

To blurt the truth, I was rather disoriented myself by the incident.

Bert Roche, or Sir Bert Roche at this point, provided me with the concluding details of the unfortunate incident at Bullrusher. I had been waiting for him at his flat. Once he accepted the inevitability of my presence ("... bloody impertinent of you breaking in. But as long as you're here. ...") we settled for a chat.

"I suppose you've come for your thousand," Bert said, snarled actually. "You've as much chance as any of my other creditors. Less in fact. You didn't get the thing done. The girl isn't in jail."

"Do not distort the assignment, sir," I said. "You never requested that Mrs. Hope Roche go to jail. You specified only that she be charged with Sir Hilary's demise. Officially she has been. That completes the commission."

"That won't do, Mandrell. You knew what I meant."

"Were I able to read your mind," I said, "I would certainly occupy myself with determining where you have cached the incriminating information that is to be posted to the authorities should you meet a violent end. Surely you see the unfairness of such an arrangement? You could be the victim of any one of a number of legitimate accidents, Sir Bert."

"Don't be subtle, Mandrell. I realize you got me my title. It's about time the thing was passed on. Sir Hilary wasn't exactly the sort one enjoyed identifying as head of the family."

"There has been no question regarding his strange end?" I asked. "The fact that he was somewhat out of place in a lady's boudoir."

"You mean by the authorities? They wouldn't dare. Aunt Cis wouldn't let them. The whole thing was pretty self-evident anyway. Except for the Italian dress designer business."

"The Italian dress designer?"

"Ha!" Bert exploded. "I bet myself a quid you wouldn't own up to it. Signor Orlando had to be you. The police didn't like it much that you walked out of Bullrusher just after the killing. I understand Prichart told the police that you came to him right in the middle of the uproar and demanded transportation to town to get you out of 'all dis terrible racket.' Ho, ho, wish I'd seen that."

"So the Roche family is back to normal," I said. "With a new lord at the helm."

"Actually the family came off rather well," Bert said, ignoring my nag. "We all feel that Hilary did the honorable thing there at the end. Sort of made up for the rest of his life by Going Out Like A Man. A hundred years from now that's all they'll remember about him. He was killed in a lady's bedchamber. Colorful chap."

"And what shall they remember about you? Hopefully that you gave up a promising journalistic career to take over Bullrusher."

He laughed. "Give up my column? Not on your life. Too much fun. Maybe they'll remember me as the Roche who had a hired assassin on a leash. A man skilled in the art of killing who had to kill any person I pointed a finger at."

"I assure you, sir, the situation you describe will not be a successful relationship if you are not prepared to pay the firm's fee. Surely your present access to the Roche fortune leaves you in a position to honor your fiscal obligations?"

"There may be a spot of trouble laying hold of the family gold," he said smiling. He threw his leg over the arm of his easy chair and swung his foot about while we continued our conversation. "I have no intention of spending six months out of the year at Bullrusher as the family charter requires. Nor am I going to give up the title. I'll let the legal chaps have a go at breaking the charter. Shouldn't take more than five or six years to settle the thing. This whole family tradition business is a bore. Aunt Cis may look on it as some sort of divine responsibility, but then she's too old to see the other side of life."

"Meanwhile," I said. "You will have no resources with which to pay my fee?"

"Afraid not, old boy."

I stood up and retrieved my hat. "Let us hope," I said

bitterly, "that the friars at the Holytree Monastery are more honorable."

"At Holytree?" he said. "Are you pulling off a little commission down there?"

I refused to answer him. Possibly I had said too much already.

He called after me as I walked to the front door. "I might be able to give you a spot of information about Holytree," he said. "Had a chap in my office the other day who knows all about what's going on down there. All about Rector Bosworth and his orgies. And the lady visitors who come in by aircraft, and run about without a stitch of clothes."

I turned back to the sitting room. "What are you talking about?" I asked. "Holytree is a complete-isolation monastery. Continual prayer and manual labor for all of the inmates. No contact with the materialistic world. In fact the friars do not even speak to each other."

"That's what they'd have us believe," he said, with surprising bitterness. "But I heard the real story. One of the friars jumped the wall and came to see me just the other morning. Name of Dan Banyai. A mad sort, but bright enough to know that what is going on at Holytree isn't right. Wanted me to print it up."

Bert then recounted the lurid details of life at Holytree as revealed by defector Daniel Banyai. According to the disillusioned friar, the contemplative life at Holytree had been replaced by nightly rounds of carnal merriment. The female participants, according to Banyai, were flown in from Europe, joined in the debauchery for a few days, and were then flown back to the continent.

"Banyai said he'd take me to the landing strip where we could obtain photographs," Bert said. "I was going to plaster the whole ugly show across page one. Unfortunately I left the idiot alone for a moment while I went to fetch the photographer. When I returned Banyai had bolted my office. Frightened to death, he was."

"And you believed that fantastic nonsense?" I asked. "Holytree has been there for centuries. The place is so steeped in legitimacy, even the Crown's tax people have ceased demanding entry. For the past seventy years there hasn't been a person permitted inside who isn't a true applicant, with several interviews with Rector Bosworth under his belt. And once you're accepted you're given a new name and you never come out. Actually, a rather pleasant life."

"Well the authorities will be pouring into the place as soon as they hear this," Bert said, jumping up and going to a cabinet by the wall. "I made a wire recording of my chat with Dan Banyai. Listen to this and tell me what you think of Holytree."

He snapped some buttons and rotated a dial or two, then stood back and we listened to the famous interview with the ex-friar of Holytree. The first voice we heard was Bert's. He gave the date, his location, mentioned that he was ". . . of sound mind and limb. . . ." and that what he was about to announce was of his own free will.

"Damn," the flesh and blood Bert muttered, "I must have had some stuff left on from a previous recording. I thought I mentioned Banyai's name right there at the beginning. Well . . . give a listen to the rest."

"As I stare out the window of my office here at the newspaper," the recorded voice continued, "all I see are these bloody fools racing about from desk to desk as though tomorrow's edition meant a pinch of snuff in God's Eternal Plan. . . ."

"I must have lost a few sentences there," Bert said puzzled. "That bit about the office I didn't say until later, after Banyai questioned my 'dedication to Christ's Eternal Plan.' And I had to play the mutt along since he was so nervous."

The voice in the recorder continued speaking. Just the one voice. Bert's. "Only my true friends know that my job here at the newspaper is a cross I bear. It gives me the opportunity to visit the sin holes of London and spread the Lord's word. . . ."

"Damn it," the real Bert snapped, "where the hell is Dan Banyai's voice? Don't tell me the mike didn't pick up the weasel." He moved toward the machine.

" . . . Oh, for the life at Holytree," the Bert on the recorder said. "The life of absolute isolation. Never to have to speak to another human being. A life dedicated to a love of God. I've spoken to Rector Bosworth. I am going to Holytree. Forever. . . ."

Bert slapped the "Off" button on the wire recorder and spun on me. "I never said those last sentences," he yelped. "By God, Mandrell, you've been at the machine, since I brought the recording home."

"That is quite true," I said softly. "But, as to your never having said those words, that is not true. Admittedly you did not say them in the sequence in which they are now presented, but you did say them. The voice is unmistakably yours. I have tested it on the same device the authorities will use to test it. Your conversation with Mr. Daniel Banyai lasted how long?"

"About a half-hour," he said, glaring at me but not yet certain just why.

"The half-hour of conversation has reduced to a very pretty four-minute statement of principles by Bertie Roche," I told him. "I particularly enjoy the part in which you mourn the passing of the German pilots you shot from the sky during the war."

"I never said that!" Bert snapped. "We talked about me shooting down the Jerry planes because Banyai asked me what I did during the war. He'd been safe in the monastery, the slacker."

"But didn't you speak of 'mourning' at some point?" I prodded.

"Just someplace in there where we talked about the poor English kids that were hit by the buzz-bombs."

"Yes, well you see there is a way of playing those wire recordings back and forth from machine to machine that permits one to change the sequence in which the words are spoken. Your apology, for instance, to your family is very tastefully handled. I even found a deep sigh early in the recording (I believe it was actually delivered as an expression of exasperation when Mr. Banyai asked you to repeat once more the names of your immediate family), anyway I located the sigh and by stretching it out a bit, it comes over very much like the cry of a melancholy soul. It now follows immediately the touching lines in which you beg your brother

Thomas to accept the family title and bring it the honor that you could never have brought it."

"All right, all right, Mandrell," Bert said. "Stop your crowing. If you doctored this recording, I presume there are more copies than the one here. What do we have now? Some sort of stand-off? I've my packet of papers telling about you. You have this silly recording telling a completely ridiculous story in my voice."

"There is only one other copy of the recording," I said. "It is sitting in the machine at your office. In your typewriter is a typed letter to your publisher requesting that he listen to the wire recorder."

"But nobody who knows me will believe that thing."

"Why not? You will not be about to discredit the message. And there will be a witness, an unimpeachable chap, who will say that he saw you climb into your machine all bundled up and drive the full distance to Holytree in the dead of night. Tonight."

"Who do you mean?" Bert snapped. "Yourself, or one of your lackeys? Not very reliable witnesses."

"No, no, I refer to the gentleman from Scotland Yard who has been following you about since you commenced using my name in 'Rochey's Roundup.' The chap with the distinctive eyebrows whom you described to me. He's still lurking about out on the road."

Bert sat down. He said, "You mean to tell me that you intend to pop me off here in my flat? Then disguise yourself to look like me? Drive all the way to Holytree? Sneak back here? Hide my body? Incidentally I understand the hiding of a dead body isn't the easiest business." His voice was remarkably cheerful, considering the discussion.

"It requires a certain good judgment," I admitted.

"You're in luck then," he said. "They've just put a monument up on the road to Croydon. A big slab of concrete with an old Spitfire, a real one, bolted to the top. Must be forty feet up. You could bundle me into the cockpit. There's no way up to the Spit so who'd ever know?"

"You are accepting your plight with remarkable equanimity," I said.

"That's the traditional RAF stiff upper lip, old man," he

said smiling. "Come off it, Mandrell. I know you're not going through with it. Too much trouble for you. And what do you gain? You only ensure, possibly, that my friend will not forward my papers to Scotland Yard, since he will assume that I am still alive and kicking. If you call life in Holytree alive and kicking."

"I will also ensure that you will make no further demand on my talent," I said. "Particularly under your medieval accounting system."

"That's what convinces me you are not serious," Bert said. "You take all the risk and you don't make a bob. That's not Mandrell, Limited's way. I'll admit you have made your point. You've proved you could put me out of the way with no one the wiser. Except maybe that idiot Dan Banyai. So—"

"Mr. Roche," I said, "use your head. I would hardly trust the role of the mad friar to anyone less competent than myself."

After a moment he said, "I should have thought of that. Anyway, you've made your point. What do you want me to do? I can get the papers back from my friend. Although I don't see how that benefits you. I can always write the thing up again."

"Do you recall the fee I quoted you on the railway a few weeks back?" I asked.

"Some ridiculous sum, as ever," Bert said. "Wasn't it ten thousand for Sir Hilary and an additional five thousand for getting Hope blamed? Then I told you the fee would be one thousand."

"You will be relieved to learn, Mr. Roche, that I was successful in negotiating a commission under the original terms. Fifteen thousand pounds in all. Ten for Sir Hilary. . . . Five, sir, for you."

For a moment he did not believe me. Then he saw the truth in my eye.

"Who? . . ." he sputtered. "By God—Thomas! You went to my brother. And he's so stuck on the title that he'd pay to have his brother killed to get it. He can't wait. The courts will probably take it away from me eventually. Then Bull-rusher can have the type of head she hasn't had in fifty years. Thomas is just the type to handle it. A hell of an improvement over Hilary. And a hell of an improvement over the old broken-down Spit pilot."

"Yes, those were not the exact words used during our negotiations," I said. "But that is the estimate of the family situation that was expressed."

"By God, Mandrell, you're still bluffing. I'm certain of it. Thomas hasn't the stomach to pull it off. It takes rather a vicious gentleman to commission the likes of you. Thomas is just a gentleman. He'd never consider it."

"How about a rather vicious gentlewoman?" I asked.

The question took him full in the mind. The logic—and the inevitability—of the situation trickled down into his senses.

"Aye," he murmured, "Aunt Cis could do it. I never thought of that." He shifted about in his chair. "You know," he said, with a sigh that was deep and somewhat false, "those were the only good times. The old days up there in the Spit. With Jerry just below and you riching the petrol mix as you rolled over and went after him."

He had shifted his youthless body. His weight was by this time more on his toes than in the chair. The misplaced fighter pilot was ready to make another attack—his last. Ahhh well, I had not expected that he would accept his demise with any marked degree of patience.

# THE AMERICAN MISTRESS
# COMMISSION (1943)

DURING A NIGHT of September 1933 two alert men prowled the alleys of Negbit Dag. They were dressed in garments indigenous to the area, and of a cut sorely associated throughout the world with the year 1933—ragged.

Both men were officers, members of His Majesty's Royal Army. Naturally they had no business prowling about Negbit Dag, a city within the borders of Soviet Russia. At least the Uzbek Dragoons patroling the streets would have considered it improper to have Britishers in the area.

One of the officers, Major Duncan Purdy of Colonial Intelligence, was in the city attempting to make contact with an underground agent he had sent into Negbit Dag two months previous. The other officer, Lieutenant Keith Coder, had no connection really with Colonial Intelligence. He was along for a spot of forced-draft indoctrination in Middle East underground theory, and enjoying every minute of it.

Abruptly, the two found an Uzbek Dragoon sitting quietly on his horse directly in front of them. The Englishmen attempted to pull the shadow about them but they were seen and challenged. Chances are the Uzbek had been sitting there in the dark watching the progress of the two disguised soldiers for several minutes before putting himself in their sight. That's the sort they are.

Anyway, Major Purdy and Lieutenant Coder ran. The dragoon unsheathed a sword as long as your leg and came galloping after them. Major Purdy blundered into a sewer ditch and pitched on his face. The dragoon turned his horse and, with a scream born in the year of Genghis Khan, he charged at Purdy, sword at the ready.

Lieutenant Coder, meanwhile, had not lost his head. He noted his superior officer's pending embarrassment and searched through the folds of his unwieldy costume until he found his pistol.

Tricky shooting that: the galloping target, the absence of depth-perception reference points, and of course the indifferent lighting.

Lieutenant Coder wisely concentrated on the horse. Two bullets were required to bring the animal skidding to her knees in the sewer ditch. The third bullet dispatched the dragoon who was crawling to his feet, sword still in hand, resolve still intact. Coder and Purdy successfully evacuated Negbit Dag and Russia.

Those three bullets changed Lieutenant Keith Coder's life almost as dramatically as they changed the Uzbek Dragoon's.

Keith Coder had received his commission just as World War One ended. He found himself a soldier without a field of battle and in professional competition with officers who had wallowed directly in the carnage of the Great War. He was a gladiator with no battle credits, and the arena was closed.

Coder had advanced to but first lieutenant by the time of the Uzbek Dragoon incident thirteen years later. He was Captain Coder by the time the lads in the officer's club at Karachi had finished buying rounds in celebration of the escapade.

During the same September of 1933, Mr. Ralph Dankers opened his second grocery in Kokomo, Indiana, U.S.A.

And in that same September '33, a young lady named Sally Hickey (age 13) was thrown to the ground behind a roadway fence in her native Liverpool by a husky Irish immigrant named Michael Bell. Michael imagined himself to be on the threshold of carnal accomplishment. He achieved only the breaking of Sally's arm. The fracture was administered to by a Dr. Sherrock who noted during the repair, and with less than professional interest, the emerging classical lines of Miss Hickey's legs. The doctor, exhibiting an extraordinary memory for a medical man, remembered Miss Hickey (one downward glance was all he needed) when she applied for a position at his offices about five years later. She was engaged.

Captain Keith Coder did not receive his majority until 1938. There was no dramatic trigger such as the Uzbek Dragoon involved in this promotion. By '38 every captain with a bit of blood in his eye was getting his major's insignia.

The jump, leap actually, from captain to major in the Royal Army is the promotion every ambitious young officer waits for in agony. The difference in the two ranks cannot be measured with any civilian gauge.

"The difference is this," I was told once by a Canadian Army colonel. "As a major, your activities are exposed to the senses of generals. The general starts to hear and see your name—for one reason or another."

This proved quite an apt description of the issue in the case of Major Keith Coder. The generals certainly heard his name very shortly after Coder's promotion. It was screamed at them.

"Started with the publication of that article written by Keith," a friend of Coder told me. "Keith called the thing: *Argument In Favor of a Balanced Training Curriculum.* Once the civilian dailies got it, though, they put a better name to it: *The Hate Concept.*"

In the article, Coder maintained that the Army mass training program then in progress was based on teaching the foot soldier to "respect the enemy's capability." Coder said that, if given a choice, he would rather lead a group of men who went into battle with an arrogant self-assurance based on underestimating the enemy's capability. "The soldier who respects the enemy is too cautious in battle," said Coder. "On the other hand, an overconfidence based on ignorance leads to chaos if the ignorance is suddenly shattered." Coder theorized that the curriculum that permitted optimum gain from the training program was one in which hate was substituted for ignorance. "Teach the soldier not only to respect the enemy's capability but also to hate the enemy. And to hate him all the more for any remarkable capability."

England at the time was a country overrun with sensitive parents watching their precious sons march off to training camps. The publicizing of Coder's article, which had appeared initially in an in-house military organ, the semi-official Cavalry magazine *Charge!*, did little to reassure the shaken parents. Letters condemning the Hate Concept flooded the dailies. ("I did not raise my son to have the Government turn him into an American gangster.") Major Keith Coder was condemned up and down the land.

Ahh, but Coder had actually achieved success. The military has a way of folding a special protective wing about one of its own when he is being criticized for his military judgment by those who know nothing about military judgements.

Colonel (acting Brigadier) Laben Kinkaid, old "Mortar-Fist" Kinkaid, snapped Major Coder up for his staff. Colonel Kinkaid shortly discovered that he had found a gem.

The same qualities that had held Keith Coder immobilized in the lower ranks for so long, his ill-concealed intelligence and a reservoir of pragmatic toughness, now became the young major's weapons in the political infighting within Colonel Kinkaid's staff. Coder detected quickly that his status on the staff was not that of the "lucky devil who'd gotten a break," as was the estimate of his immediate superiors, a lieutenant colonel and a colonel. Coder saw that he was a lad who had the Co's tolerant eye on his brow.

Good Generals, like good sales managers, like to see a clever, irreverent young monkey back in the pack, stirring up dust and distressing his superiors with his lack of orthodoxy.

"Sir, this Major Coder has gone too far, by heaven," Colonel Williamson reported to Kinkaid. Colonel Williamson was on Staff and was Coder's superior officer. "Do you know what time he picked to inspect Camp Ventura? 0300! Hardly a senior officer about. Colonel Raines didn't even know Major Coder was on the base."

"Yes, and if Raines had known Coder was about," Kinkaid growled, "you can bet we'd not have discovered that Raines has 63 per cent of his vehicles down for repair. Not the 37 per cent he's been reporting."

Major Coder, in other words, became General Kinkaid's favorite. The CO demanded only one form of payment for this affection—results. And Coder, the man of action who had been held prisoner for so long in routine assignments and junior rank, wanted nothing so much as a ring in which to display his brilliant cape work. Theirs then was an ideal union. Coder and Kinkaid. The rebel and the matured rebel.

Coder became the lad one sent off to deliver quaint military condolences to an old and loved Army friend, a colonel: "Very sorry, old man, but we are replacing you with colonel so-and-so," Kinkaid's unofficial note, hand-carried by Coder, would inform the "old friend."

It was Major Coder also who commanded the unscheduled Inspection Team that came out of the night and fell upon a lax commanding officer with the shock of a punch and the odor of a plague. It was Coder who signed the "totally unsatisfactory" report. (Which in many cases had been written prior to the inspection.) His Majesty's Royal Army was girding for war with Hitler. A first move was to trim out the fat of incompetence that had been tolerable during peacetime. So many old drinking companions had to be packed off where they could do little harm. Coder packed them off, dry-eyed and smartly.

By 1940 it was Lieutenant Colonel Coder, and with his first battle in his craw—the evacuation through Dunkirk. Coder had enjoyed the battle: the big command maps, that gradually lost their smell of clean print and became soiled by the stains of sweaty fists leaned on their surface; the tactical decisions made in low-intensity voices by the "professionals"; and, most of all, the sight of a general in action, making crisp judgments involving the lives of thousands of soldiers.

"There is just absolutely no question about it," Coder once told me, "the job of the general in battle is the supreme employment that a human can aspire to. There is no willy-nilly involved, no hit or miss, no 'back to the drawing board.' You are right there on the mark. You make a decision and five thousand men tumble into their graves. You make a decision and the form of government under which children not yet born will live is changed. The power of the general is the most pagan authority still permitted by civilized man."

Coder loved the smell of Dunkirk. He loved the slashing up and down the beach, improvising every step of the way. (The War College is somewhat reluctant to drill students on the techniques of retreat.) One took terrible risks in such a situation.

For instance, Coder was asked by Kinkaid to find some way to get a certain General Henri LaCorte down to the beach from LaCorte's hiding place on the perimeter of the German encirclement. General LaCorte, French Army, was an old friend of Kinkaid's. Coder somehow found a lorry that could be diverted from the critical task of moving British soldiers to the boats and routed it to LaCorte's quarters. The episode could have cost both Coder and Kinkaid their careers had the incident been reported. Particularly since the French general had elected to flee to Paris instead, so he could be in on the capitulation of the French government to the Germans.

Then there are drawbacks to being the general's right arm. Following Dunkirk, Coder wanted a field assignment, his own command. Kinkaid, his promotion to brigadier now confirmed, was reluctant to release his star. After all there was a certain satisfaction in having the excellence of one's staff recognized by other generals.

Take for example the following conversation that took place in the officers club at Fort Gypsy:

"I tell you, Labon, don't let them hold you here at home any longer than you have to," a General Neson "Buffy" Colburn was telling Brigadier Kinkaid. "Don't let them chain you to a logistics desk."

"Come off it, Buffy," Brigadier Kinkaid joshed. "You were always getting a runny nose in the trenches anyway."

"It's worse back here," Colburn said. "Take this bloody 'machine tool' flap. There was a time I didn't know a machine tool from a boar's tit. Now they're like my reserve division and I don't have the damn things. Can't make any fifty-fives without them, the gun factories tell me. And there's a bastard up in Sheffield who has a shipload of them hidden away. We can't get them from him. Some Hague Convention bind or other. Ships of foreign registry, and all that."

"I have a light colonel on my staff I'll wager can get them," Kinkaid slyly boasted.

"Is that this lad Keith Coder I've heard about? How would he like a fortnight's leave in Sheffield?"

Coder lived up to the billing. He retrieved the shipload of machine tools somehow or other. Shortly after, Coder became a full colonel. Brigadier Kinkaid reluctantly agreed to release his workhorse to a field assignment.

Coder received a lovely bit of a command. He led a group of nine demolition experts on a parachute drop behind German lines in Yugoslavia. It was after the drop that Coder discovered that only two of his men were qualified demolition people, and one of these was drowned during the first month of operations. That's the sort of assignment one draws when one goes about issuing "goodby" chits to incompetent senior officers and one of the officers ends up on an evaluation board and has your name fall into his withered claw:

"Now this chap Coder, I chance to know him. I think he'd be ideal in underground work. Sneaky sort. And I notice he did some time with Colonial Intelligence in '32. Was actually inside Negbit Dag. Don't we have a little operation coming up in Yugoslavia?"

So Coder and his band ran themselves breathless about the Dinaric Alps for eight months. Coder blew up a few bridges here and there, but mostly he concentrated on an activity at which he was conspicuously more capable—assessing the quality of the German occupation forces, in particular the mental balance and military acumen of the colonels and lieutenant colonels.

"This is damn fine data we're getting back from Colonel Coder," was an evaluation made back at Coder's headquarters. "Will be invaluable someday, when we have to go in there and fight those swine. This dossier on Ludwig Kelp is remarkable, as though Coder knew the man personally. Better bring him home. He's done a splendid bit of work."

Less than a year after his return from Yugoslavia, Colonel

Keith Coder was seated across from me in my office requesting that I secure the demise of his American mistress.

During the years while Keith Coder advanced from captain to colonel, '32 to '42, Mr. Ralph Dankers increased his number of grocery stores from two to fourteen throughout the midwest of the U.S. The stores were by this time identified as supermarkets, to give a name to the process in which the proprietor makes drudges of his own customers.

Ralph Dankers became chairman of a county political organization in Indiana. He ran for the state attorney general nomination a bit later and was defeated. When the war came to the U.S., Ralph Dankers went to Washington as a minor administrator with the War Production Board.

Dankers' face appeared abruptly one day in the nation's newspapers. He had punched a man named Wilkerson in the nose in a hallway of the Capitol building in full view of an ecstatic newspaper photographer. Wilkerson, who manufactured uniforms for the Women's Army Corps, was one of the first of that ignoble breed—the "war profiteer." (The photograph, with its caption: HOOSIER HANDCUFFS HEMLINE HUSTLER, eventually won several awards for George Schmidt the photographer.)

The publicity catapulted Ralph Dankers into assistant chairmanship of a committee investigating chicanery at all levels of government contracting.

While in Washington, Ralph's wife divorced him. Ralph then up and married the young lady with whom he had been sharing a bed when his wife's detectives had broken into a quiet motel room in Alexandria, Virginia.

While Keith Coder was becoming a colonel and Ralph Dankers was working his way to Washington, Sally Hickey took to herself the first of what was to total six husbands. She married a Dr. Sherrock in Liverpool. Sally was 19. (An account of the marriage of Sally and Dr. Sherrock, a shockingly brief union, is to be found in a reminiscence of mine titled: *The Dr. Sherrock Commission.*)

Sally moved on to wifehood with a General Von Ritterdorf, German military; a Mr. Wakamatsu, Japanese industrialist who, for reasons of his own, claimed to be Chinese; and a Mr. Gerald Ordalt, member of the British Trade Commission, who, years later, was revealed as being overly sympathetic to the Communist cause: as you may recall, all that microfilm business.

As Mrs. Gerald Ordalt, Sally went to Washington, D.C. in 1942. While in that frantic citadel, Sally one evening chanced into a motel room in Alexandria, Virginia. While the shortage of accommodations in wartime Washington was accepted reality, the wife of the gentleman who had contracted for Sally's motel room was not quick to dismiss the joint occupation of the room as a venture in either frugality or an exercise in conservation of resources. The photographs obtained by the intruding detectives tended to reinforce the wife's skepticism. The photos are still in the possession of the Pine Detective Agency. To this day the PIs of the agency still pull the file out every now and again. Sally was that sort of a female.

Following the motel room notoriety, Sally quickly divorced Gerald Ordalt. Mental cruelty was the deciding issue. "He spends more time in his darkroom than he does in our bedroom," Sally testified; a habit of Mr. Ordalt's recalled ruefully by British Intelligence many years too late. Sally's motel room companion, Mr. Ralph Dankers, for those of you who have not been paying attention, also obtained his divorce. He and Sally were married in some remote locale named Reno, Nevada.

Shortly after, Dankers, pursuing his duties as scrutinizer of war-contract malfeasance, decided a trip to England was in order. Possibly he thought to see if the war goods leaving the U.S. east coast were actually reaching the U.K., were not being diverted to some South American municipality for resale. Thus Dankers and his bride arrived in the land of her birth.

A month later the Dankers were house guests at Cornflower, home of Mr. Nigel Cornflower and his niece Hope. At Cornflower Mr. and Mrs. Dankers met Colonel Keith Coder, somewhat of a celebrated military figure since his return from inside occupied Yugoslavia a few months earlier.

As I have already mentioned, Colonel Keith Coder eventu-

ally stopped by my office and requested that I rid him of his
American mistress—a Mrs. Sally Dankers.

"I had one hell of a time working my way through your
lines, Mandrell," Colonel Coder told me. "One of your people, that verbose chap in Mayfair, the one that acts as though
he should be wearing a skirt instead of trousers, I had to see
him three times before he sent me on to you."

"As a military man," I replied, "you must have an appreci-
ation of enemy infiltration. The gentlemen you met have but
one assignment. To ensure the legitimacy of your quest for
the firm of Mandrell, Limited. To ensure that you are not of
the enemy—the police."

"And to ensure that I have the proper amount of money in
my kit," Coder observed, with rancor. "I never heard so
many questions about my financial reserves."

"The thing is that you military chaps are very difficult to
assess financially," I said. "I have always been rather shocked
at the Crown's estimate of a soldier's value. The paltry
reimbursement provided monthly to those whose assignment
is the protecting of the nation might lead one to conclude
that the government places a rather miserly estimate on the
value of the country."

"If you think you're shocked, you can damn well imagine
how the soldiers feel. A chap has to keep his nose about to
pick up a few extra bob."

"Which you apparently do rather well, Colonel," I said.
"Our research confirmed the resources you quoted to my
advisers. Actually, you rather understated your assets. Take
for instance Harte Castle, the estate in County Mayo in The
Irish Free State. You failed to mention your ownership of
those fine lands."

His coldly disciplined stare, aimed at the inside of my
skull, would have done an offended general credit. This asset
of Coder's cannot have gone unnoticed by his superiors, for
Colonel Coder did indeed achieve the rank of general before
the war was over.

"Damn it, Mandrell. I feel you could have dispensed with
the paperwork in my case. Your fee was produced on schedule the last time, wasn't it?"

"Actually it was not the financial aspect of your petition that caused the delay," I admitted. "The item that intrigues me is your motivation; why you are so keen on securing the demise of Sally Dankers."

"That's not quite your business, now is it?" he said. "It's not the fact that she's a woman that's bothering you? I thought Mandrell, Limited placed little distinction on sex?"

"The firm tries not to become preoccupied with it," I said. "There are certainly enough people about attending to that. Once again, your military experience must have exposed you to the factor of Intelligence. Prior to battle don't you people devote some man-hours to determining the enemy's—"

"There's no confusion about motives in a war," he snapped. "The enemy is out to kill you and you are out to kill him."

"And Mrs. Sally Dankers is out to kill you?"

"She sure as hell is!"

We have all, I presume, heard the term "lover's quarrel," normally within an embroidery of adolescent egos. Colonel Coder and Sally Dankers had evidently brought to their particular spat a more mature embellishment.

The colonel mentioned that Mrs. Dankers and her husband ("that dollar-counting idiot"—Coder) would be guests at Cornflower the following week. The location appealed to Coder as an ideal area in which to accomplish the commission.

"Of course you may know more about that than I do," he conceded. "But there's acres of wooded bridle paths. And the estate runs to the edge of Belmont Lake which is miles across and the devil's own deep. I'd rather the thing looked like an accident . . . if not, at least make it quick, and no mess."

He asked then if I wanted him to arrange for my presence at Cornflower. "Perhaps I could get you in as a gardener or footman or such."

I declined the offer. "If the commission does not work out as planned," I explained, "I don't want the authorities tracing my presence back to you."

"Bloody decent of you, I'm sure," he said, sarcastically. "Then how are you going to get to Cornflower? After the Royal Estates, Cornflower is one of the most exclusive homes in the west. Almost as difficult to get to as Bullrusher. It'll be a hell of a long while before the likes of Augustus Mandrell is invited to Cornflower."

"I have a theory," I commented. "I believe that an Army officer cannot achieve the rank of colonel without becoming infected with the trappings, the snobbery of gentry thinking."

He laughed. Coder had a good masculine, whiskey-in-the-billiard-room laugh. A handsome sound. He said, "You're a tough muck, aren't you Mandrell? I remember that."

Shortly after, once we had clarified the financial arrangements, Coder left my office. His departure was not marked by any high degree of amicability. Disclosure of the Mandrell, Limited fee frequently dictates the language of the customer's departure. "Outrageous," was Colonel Coder's final word. But, as ever, he had little choice but to agree to the fee. The firms catering to the same market as Mandrell, Limited are not of sufficient number to encourage "shopping about" for the best price.

There had appeared no pressing need to mention to Colonel Coder the real reason why his application to Mandrell, Limited had been delayed several days. It was not an examination of his finances that had induced the delay, but rather my wish to complete negotiations on another commission, one requested by a Mr. Ralph Dankers. There existed a degree of similarity in the Coder and Dankers commissions. Coder wished to secure the demise of Mrs. Dankers. Mr. Dankers, oddly, wished Colonel Coder removed from this earth.

With so much war and killing going on in the world, one would have thought that personal intervention to secure an even greater total of deceased would be rather the last of popular pursuits. Ah well, like so many old fashioned business firms, Mandrell, Limited but serves an existing market. Mandrell does not, as is the new business approach, create the market and then sustain it.

I met with Ralph Dankers at the Islip Club to discuss the ingredients of his commission. He and an American Air Force general had just completed lunch as I arrived. The general, one-star variety, excused himself as soon as the maitre d' delivered me to Dankers' table.

"Do you know General Starkey?" Dankers said to me, nodding at the departing officer. I said I didn't. "You will," Dankers explained with pleasure. "The whole world will. William 'Geronimo' Starkey is going to be President of the United States before I'm finished with him. He's got everything it takes: An old pro contract man like myself to steer him through the rough-house. Plenty of money. The youth. The drive. A hell of a war record. Still flies missions with his boys in the B-17's. And wait until the women voters get a look at that profile."

*"Ya,"* I commented. "Dot make a difference." I was puzzled by the irrelevance of his conversation. Evasion is normally the refuge of those who are nervous or embarrassed. Ralph Dankers was neither. He was a thin harsh man with hard brown freckles on his forehead above the wrinkles.

"What are you, Mandrell, German?" he asked.

*"Nein,"* I said. "On passport it say Norwegian. But, who is knowing?"

"Yeah, I figured it would take the cold Nordic type to be in the business you're in. You sure keep yourself protected. Took me three weeks to get through to you; through all those middle men. That guy I met in the beauty shop in Mayfair, is he a fairy or something?"

I shrugged and said, "Now I am here. We do business. Colonel Keith Coder, he will not be easy man to eliminate."

Mr. Dankers immediately launched an enumeration of the grevous misdeeds that had made Colonel Coder so eligible for an early grave. The colonel was identified by Dankers as: a wife-stealer; a collaborator with the enemy (" . . . when he was in Yugoslavia doing underground work he was actually dealing with the Germans. Buddy-buddy with that Gestapo killer Ludwig Kelp. . . ."); a wife-stealer; a war profiteer (". . . military version. He's bought this estate in Ireland, God only knows where he stole the money. Probably the black market. . . ."); wife-stealer; and, of course, ". . . disgrace to the uniform. . . ."

"But Coder is goodt soldier," I said.

"We've plenty of good soldiers," Dankers snapped. "And more of them coming from the States on every boat. Like General Geronimo Starkey. There's a man who owns 87 per cent of one of the biggest corporations in the world, Uni-Coffee. He could have had himself posted safe in Washington for the war. But he's a natural born leader, so he's over here leading men. By choice he's here in the thick of it, like myself."

"Mine reference about Colonel Coder being goodt soldier," I said patiently, "mean he is hard man to subtract from population."

"Not as hard as you think, Mandrell. Coder will be at Cornflower this weekend. There's plenty of thick woods and a deep lake on the grounds. Of course Cornflower is pretty damn exclusive. But myself and the missus have been invited down and I think I can get you in as, say, my assistant just in from Washington, or something."

"*Nein*, dot is not subtle. Mandrell he will get to Cornflower. I make point again: goodt soldier like Colonel Coder is difficult target. Difficult target, dot make commission expensive."

The point finally penetrated to Mr. Dankers' cold mind. The remainder of our discussion at the Islip Club centered about the ethereal subject of economics. Mr. Dankers proved an able negotiator; his grocery business background, I presume. He eventually obtained a contract superior to that obtained by Colonel Coder. It was to cost Mr. Dankers less to obtain the demise of Colonel Coder than it was costing the colonel to secure the shedding of his American mistress, Mrs. Dankers.

I was actually preparing for my trip to Cornflower when a message pertinent to the assignment reached me. A certain young lady wished to commission Mandrell, Limited. There was no need to winnow her petition through the normal network of contact men. She had been to Mandrell, Limited previously with similar requests. And, as ever, the discriminating purchaser, seeking quality service, remains loyal to the business establishment that provides same.

During her short life the young lady had tracked through a

cross-hatched pattern of experience in matrimony. She had been known as Mrs. Sherrock, Mrs. Von Ritterdorf, Mrs. Wakamatsu, Mrs. Ordalt, and finally as Mrs. Dankers. But the firm always remembered her sentimentally by her original name: Sally Hickey.

Sally had called Mandrell once more, and Mandrell responded. I sent to her side Mr. Frenchy Cortez, one of my most trusted representatives. The degree of my trust in the debonair Monsieur Cortez, who carried his fifty odd years with a light Gallic shrug, was influenced to some extent by the fact that "Frenchy" was actually myself.

My rendezvous with Sally Hickey (Mrs. Dankers) took place at the Haymarket Branch of the House of LeRoy. Madam LeRoy had somehow secured delivery of a shipment of chapeaux and lingerie made in Central America (shipped in, so some whispered, through filed teeth, hidden in the captain's cabin on the S.S. *Haleakala*.) Choice customers were permitted to paw through the collection at the Haymarket Branch prior to the general merchandising cycle which would take place at the House of LeRoy main salon in Mayfair.

Madam Varady of the House of LeRoy led me to Sally's fitting-room on the second floor, showing a vibrant calf of some forty-five years of beneficial aging as she preceded me up the grand staircase. "Monsieur has an eye for the female figure, I see," Madam Varaday remarked, her warm brown eyes fully approving.

"The humble connoisseur," I said in French, "grasps with delight the few fine objects that come before his senses in this arid life."

"One hopes the gentleman uses the word 'grasps' in the figurative sense," Madam said, playfully but yet with a rueful undertone, as she walked beside me, head bent, along the carpeted corridor.

"I use the word only with discretion," I said. "Nothing less."

Her head swung up with a smile, the warmth of which branded us as lovers.

Madam Varaday opened a white, scrolled door constructed with a center panel of blue quilt. "Madam Dankers' fitting room, Monsieur," she said quietly. After a quick glance within to ensure Sally was presentable, Madam left me, her eyes leaving two vivid tracks across my face.

The world is still too huge a place in truth, for Madam Varaday and Frenchy Cortez never met again.

Sally was alone in the fitting room, seated before a mirror trying on hats. I introduced myself.

"Oh bother," Sally said. "I was so hoping Mr. Mandrell himself would come. I met him once, did you know? Several years ago. Absolutely the most self assured, yet the most charming man I've ever met. Do you have a cigarette, luv?"

Ahhh, dear Sally. The meeting she referred to had taken place shortly following the demise of Sally's first husband Dr. Sherrock. Sally had come round to my offices to pay the fee associated with the Dr. Sherrock Commission. With her had been a Mr. Ben Nett, her late husband's chauffeur (fairly good driver) and bodyguard (a profession he never again pursued). Mr. Nett was still in the employ of the family and had consented to attend the young widow during her period of bereavement.

Sally and I sat in the fitting room then, smoking my cigarettes and discussing her latest need for the services of Mandrell, Limited. Sally continued fitting the oddly configured chapeaux to her head and indeed, the hats engaged a good deal more of her attention than did our discussion. Basically, I suppose, the degree of interest she allocated to the two subjects was understandable. The hats, after all, were new. Her problem was rather an old one to her, weather-beaten actually.

She wanted Mandrell, Limited to shed her of her present husband, Mr. Ralph Dankers.

"He won't hear of a divorce," Sally complained. "His political career, he says, can withstand the weight of one divorce but not two. He divorced this American girl with her hair in those terrible ringlets to marry me, you see? 'Political career!' It's not his political career. He's not running for anything. It's poor General Geronimo Starkey who's going to be elected President. Not Ralph. Oh men! Sometimes, I swear, they aren't worth the—"

We were interrupted—charmingly interrupted—by a young woman who popped in a little side door of the fitting room.

"Sally, have you ever seen such a dreadful thing!" the delightful intruder exclaimed. She was referring to a shift of some sort that she wore. The garment was made of lace and hung by thin straps at her shoulders and came down to nearly the tops of her stockings. The lace was held together with delicate net fibers through which generous portions of the young lady's anatomy could be seen with startling clarity. The exposed areas had a rather familiar turn to them, I found. Ah yes, as my eye traveled upward I discovered the face of Miss Hope Cornflower, a young woman I had encountered about a year previous.

"Now really," Miss Cornflower said, giggling. "How far are they going to go?" She had not yet noticed the pop-eyed Frenchman seated in the corner.

"Best watch out," Sally said, smiling. "If Bertie Roche ever sees you in that thing he'll rape you on the spot."

"Bertie Roche would rape any girl, on the spot, anywhere," Hope said. "Did I tell you he's forced his way into my trip to Cornflower Friday? He had Aunt Cis ring me, knowing I couldn't refuse her. All I could do was insist we lunch at the Poe Park Tavern first, where I will spell out the ground rules to dear Bert. Hands in pockets."

"A lot of good it will do," Sally said. "I'm still black and blue from the Landers' party. Keith heard of it and actually knocked Bert down in the driveway later. So I wouldn't wear that, my dear."

"Oh, sweet, I wouldn't even buy this thing," Hope said, turning and looking at herself in Sally's mirror. "I was thinking of it for Angela Millins. She's been about lately with the younger Roche boy, Bert's brother Tommy. Poor Tommy. Imagine if Angela ever came in on him with this on? He'd die!"

The two charming ladies laughed over the hypothetical predicament of "Poor Tommy." I found that envy, not humor, was my legacy to the lad.

It was during the general laughter that Hope's eye met mine. Sally was saying, "And knowing Angela that's just what she would do. They tell me her bathing costume at Carter's last summer was—"

A squeal from Hope, rather over zestful, stopped Sally's sentence. The dear child spun toward me, to ensure that the ogling gentleman she had detected in the mirror was real. Then she flew out of the room. Sally shook her head and murmured a remark about "the young." Somebody knocked at the main door and a voice inquired if "... madam is all right?" Sally reassured the house and she and I returned to a discussion of the Ralph Dankers Commission.

"The idiotic man insists on holding on to me," Sally commented at one point, "even when he knows my heart belongs to another man. This is the only way out. I'm depending on Mandrell, Limited. Incidentally, do you still have a Señor Antonio Casalou with the firm?"

"Oui," I answered. "Zee Madrid office. You know heem?"

"Slightly. A bit too mercenary for my taste. But that's neither here nor there. Tell Mr. Mandrell that my husband will be at Cornflower this weekend—" (Ah, my dear, who will *not* be there?) "—It's rather an ideal place for ... for ... well, you know what I mean. The difficult part will be getting Mr. Mandrell to the estate. I mean, it's not that all exclusive. But the Cornflowers do have their position and it isn't just anyone who can visit the place."

So I have heard.

I assured Sally that Augustus Mandrell would find some way to visit Cornflower. He had better. Cornflower had become an absolute cornucopia of commercial ventures!

A bit later Sally and I got down to discussing the most interesting ingredient of the commission, the nuts and bolts that held Mandrell, Limited together, the fee. Oddly enough Sally's reaction to the initial figure I mentioned was quite placid. But then, as I recalled, her reaction in similar discussions in years past had always been the same genial acceptance. It was her behavior at the time of actually parting with the pound notes that left an awkward scar on the memory.

As I departed the House of LeRoy I encountered Miss Hope Cornflower waiting in the lower foyer. The maid turned her eyes from Monsieur Cortez's courtly bow and sat rigidly with inflamed cheeks of embarrassment.

When next I saw Miss Cornflower there were again red spots on her cheeks. This time anger had put them there. She was seated at one of the small tables at the Poe Park Tavern, one of the tables in the rear area so popular with MPs on their way back to their constituencies on a weekend. The cause of the maid's anger was seated, or slumped would be more accurate, in the chair across from her. Bertie Roche, grinning like a panting boar, and well into his cups.

Hope spoke low and fiercely to the young man. He laughed and said loudly, "Oh no, my lass. You promised Aunt Cis. Nobody ever breaks a promise to Aunt Cis. The family queen. You'll take me down to Cornflower all right."

The men at several tables adjacent to the ill-matched couple were obviously in sympathy with the besieged girl. They did not intervene however. Some were intimidated by Bertie Roche's identity: fighter pilot extraordinary. Or Mr. Spitfire, as one of the publications (American, of course) had named Bertie. Others held back in deference to the row of ribbons on Bert's tunic; a stunning display for a British military man. Nearly the equivalent in number of that sported by American servicemen arriving in England on their way to their first battle. But let's not get into that.

I viewed Bertie from a somewhat different point of view. To me he was merely a transport ticket to Cornflower.

I made my way clumsily with my attaché case through the closely planted tables. I practically tripped over Hope Cornflower and was in the act of tipping my military cap in apology when my eye spotted of all people, Bertie Roche!

"Bertie!" I cried. "Bertie, you old mutt! How in blazes are you?"

Major Roche's eye, bleary, yet still functioning like a gunsight, zeroed in on the grinning complete stranger. "Who the muck are you?" Bert greeted me.

"Gregg. Dan Lee Gregg," I said, groping for his hand to shake it. He yanked the hand from my grasp. "Come off it, Bert," I said, looking about embarrassed but still with optimism. "I was just behind you at Ox. Between you and Tommy. Last year, who was it you dragged through every pub in Soho after the Irish Monster had a go at your neck? Old Dan Lee Gregg!"

"Oh, get the hell out of here, Smegg or Gregg or whatever your name is," he growled, turning his shoulder to me and concentrating his stare on a bosomy Wren seated by the wall. My dear chap, this will never do.

I glanced bewildered at Bert's beautiful companion. "He's been like that for the past hour. ... I'm Hope Cornflower," she said.

"Oh, that's a bit of a relief," I said. "For a moment I thought perhaps you were his wife. Something I wouldn't wish on any girl. Eh, Bert!" I slapped old Bert's shoulder. He nearly fell out of his chair. In assisting him back to an upright position, I quite naturally took the chair next to his. My movements were hampered somewhat by my attache case that was manacled to my wrist by a silver chain.

"I don't know how I'm ever going to get him on the Bay Shore Express," Hope said. "He's practically unconscious."

"Nothing to it," I said, winking at her. "I'm boarding the Bay Shore myself. I'll get Bert on. Least I can do for a man who's made the contribution Bert's made. While some of us just get to run these silly papers about." I patted the attache case and smiled my humble smile under my rather too-neat moustache.

"Get the hell away from the table!" Bert roared. "I don't know you, Gregg. And shouldn't care to either." His hard-muscled arm swept his whiskey glass from the table, continued outward and rammed against my chest, very nearly throwing me over backwards. The fool had much too deep a reservoir of strength yet in his clutches.

As I wrestled him back to his seat, I stabbed a surgeon's finger in under the name tag of his shirt. The finger sunk in and touched a nerve. Bertie slumped in his chair, head collapsed on his chest.

"Ah well, the bottle's done what Jerry can't do," I said brightly to Hope. "Don't worry. I'll get him to the railway. It's a short pull up the road. Why don't you go on ahead? I mean, this will be a rather mannish business. Oh here, I'd best get the bill first."

"No, no," she said, picking up the odious bit of paper from the tray. "I'll take care of that."

Why, thank you, my dear. She walked out in search of the waiter.

"How about lending a hand here, lieutenant," I said to a young chap at an adjacent table. He rose instantly to assist me with Bert. I choose to believe that it was some Christian urge that actuated him rather than the sight of my first lieutenant's insignia that outranked his lieutenancy.

We hauled Bertie down the road to the railway depot. There was a train about ready to depart, God knows where. "Hurry, Lieutenant. That's his train."

"I thought the young lady said the Bay Shore Express?" the idiot said.

"That's his train!" I snarled. I'll brook no mutiny on this patrol, you insolent beggar.

We managed to get Bertie out to the platform and poured him into a compartment filled with a clutch of young naval cadets who stared dumbfounded at the unconscious National Hero.

"Yes, lads," I told their startled faces, "it's Bertie Roche all right. He's on a secret mission. Take good care of him. Tell the conductor that the Air Ministry will budget his passage." They returned my salute with unpracticed dexterity.

The lieutenant and I returned past the gate, ignoring completely the cries of the busy ticket collector, as indeed we had in our entrance. I then dismissed my surly subordinate.

I waited until the train had been out of the station for fifteen minutes before I went looking for Hope Cornflower. According to the ticket I'd filched from Bertie's pocket, he and Hope had reserved seats. I found her and dropped in beside her.

"Bit of bad news, I'm afraid," I said. "Bert, damn his strength, woke up and broke away from me. He jumped aboard the Southampton train before I could catch him."

We spent an uncomfortable two hours rolling west. Aside from a reluctance to discuss our private lives in the crowded compartment, there was the realization in the girl that she had been cut off from a known, if boorish, companion and been coupled to this ill-at-ease young lieutenant about whom she knew very little. She was somewhat amused and therefore less apprehensive, as she noted the lieutenant's preoccupation with the attache case, his obvious awareness of the romantic implication (Top Secret, Q-security, Guard With Your Life) associated with the lock, chain, and wrist manacle. Miss Cornflower came quite close to outright laughter when, for the third time in less than an hour, Lieutenant Gregg snapped up his wrist for a look at his timepiece, thus actuating the steel jingling of the silver chain, and remarked, "Making ruddy good time."

During the ride I did divulge to the maid some of the details of my mission, in a more or less guarded whisper, of course. I was to deliver the contents of my case to ". . . a certain military officer. Let's call him General 'X'. . . ." at Montalvo before 0800 Monday morning.

"Oh, Montalvo?" Hope said. "That's just across the lake from Cornflower."

Why, yes, so it is, my dear.

"I'd heard they had some military thing or other over there," she continued. "I suppose you'll be staying at End-of-Lake then until Monday?"

Well, I had rather hoped you might have some other suggestion. Ahhh, well.

"I'm not certain," I said, shifting the attache case from between my feet to my lap, for approximately the twelfth time. "There's a vehicle picking me up at Leonardo. Where it will deposit me is rather in the hands of the High Command." I could feel her relax. She had already mentioned that her auto, a two-seater, was awaiting her at Leonardo for the hour's drive to Cornflower. The fact that I already had transportation removed the embarrassment of the obvious solution to my travel needs. A solution she was reluctant to offer. As yet.

At Leonardo we were two of five passengers to detrain. Hope was headed up the road to the little garage that housed her Riley. I walked to the end of the railway platform.

"Goodby," I said. "Oh yes, give my regards to Ira Loftwood if you see him."

"Oh, do you know Ira?" Yes, my dear. My credentials are actually impeccable, if you would care to pursue them.

"Just a few rounds of golf together," I said. "He told me a good deal about you and your Uncle Nigel. Particularly about the Irish Monster. Well, tallyho. Got to locate my transport."

I waited until she had walked down to the garage and entered. Then I followed. When she drove her Riley out she found me standing dejectedly by the petrol pump out front. Since she was that sort of person, she stopped her auto.

"Don't know what's happened," I explained. "There was a message at the depot from Montalvo saying they couldn't get any transport out to me."

"Oh, that is too bad," she said. "But the petrol situation is rather ghastly. We have a bit only because of the farm machinery. And we cheat whenever I can manage leave. I ... I think you might find a taxi for hire here at the garage."

I nodded bravely and turned away, taking care however not to remove my hand from her door sill. I took a deep breath, summoned the last ounce of my courage and spun my face back to her.

"Look here," I said, shakily, "you may not believe this but this is my first courier assignment. I may look like I know what I'm about, but I'll tell you I'm damn near frightened to death I'm going to botch the thing."

Ahhh, she'd have had to have been constructed of chromium steel to stand up to such an artless confession. Yes, Hope, those are near tears you see in the poor lieutenant's eyes.

"Nothing of the sort," she said. "You'll make it. Look, why not come over to Cornflower with me? Then you can ring Montalvo and see what arrangements they wish to make."

Cornflower? You mean the place where Colonel Keith Coder is for the weekend? Relaxing on the tennis courts and waiting for the demise of his American mistress, Mrs. Ralph Dankers? The place where Mr. Ralph Dankers is brooding while he waits to hear of the sudden death of Colonel Keith

Coder? The place where Sally Hickey (Mrs. Dankers) flits about in her new hat looking forward to a new period of widowhood by Monday?

"By God, that's damn decent of you, Miss Cornflower," I said as I slid into the seat next to her.

The drive to Cornflower was charming. The magic of the green countryside, the cocoon confines of the Riley, and the whip of the fresh earth-scented air washing over Miss Cornflower and myself. In just twenty minutes of driving we were chatting away like a couple of west country neighbors. Naturally I took advantage.

I would be involved in a rather complex exercise at Cornflower; a judicious pruning, so to speak. I had faced up to the fact that I could not possibly conclude all three commissions. That is, I could think of no way to accomplish all three and still collect the fee associated with each. Who, for instance, would pay for the demise of Colonel Coder if Mr. Ralph Dankers were eliminated. Conversely, could I approach the executor of Colonel Coder's estate demanding payment for the demise of Sally Dankers? I was determined, however, to collect at least two of the fees. My course of action would to a degree depend on the activities of the Cornflower guests. And seated next to me in the Riley was a young woman who knew the guests.

The art of interrogation lies in no interrogation. The human voice was designed to be heard. Thus, effective interrogation of a person is simply the unleashing and quantitative guiding of that which Nature has already provided the person.

"I suppose you will have a quiet weekend at home?" I remarked to my pretty pawn.

"Heavens no. The house will be rather packed. Let me see, I'm not even certain I can remember everybody. . . ."

There would be a Colonel Keith Coder; very businesslike military type, cold and professional. ". . . He'll spend most of his weekend on the telephone with his command. . . ."

And speaking of cold, businesslike individuals, there was an American named Ralph Dankers. " . . . You'll find him continually twisting the conversation to things like: 'Who's making a buck out of the North African campaign?' That's exactly the way he talks and thinks. 'Somebody in the Iranian Royal Family got a bundle for insisting that the Russians be given the same rights in the occupation as the British.' And so on. I always have the impression that Mr. Dankers' interest in the corrupt side of the war is not so much in exposing it but rather in getting the evidence, or the 'goods,' on the people involved. You know, so he can go back later and blackmail them. At the political level, of course. He's big in American politics."

"Dankers?" I said. "Isn't he married to a British girl?" (You see what I mean?)

"Now there's a true heart," Hope exclaimed. "Yes, he's married to Sally Hickey. What a terrible life she's had. Husbands galore. Each worse than the last. But she's like . . . like a grand dame of the theatre. A dream world person. She concerns herself with only the present. Live each day to the fullest. I believe she hardly realizes there's a war on. I suppose you call it self-centered, but she's the only gay thing about in a fixed atmosphere of grey depression. The rest of us are so frightfully conscious of showing the proper sense of gravity. Sally is the only butterfly left in a world of moths."

"She and Ralph Dankers sound oddly matched," I commented shrewdly.

"Sally has finally realized it," Hope sighed. "She has her gentleman friend. But of course Ralph Dankers won't hear of divorce. His political career. And I'm afraid he knows about the 'other man.' "

Yes, I received the same impression.

"I really don't know what Sally will do," Hope said.

"I'm certain she'll think of something," I said. "You ladies are very inventive."

The other guests were of less interest to me but I heard about them. This interrogation issue is not without a degree of waste motion. There was a guest named Angela Millins (". . . I must admit, she's awfully pretty. All that flaming red hair. . . .") and her latest "young officer." In this case, Bertie Roche's younger brother Tommy was Angela's target. (". . . Poor Tommy. . . .")

"I'm looking forward to seeing Tom again," I said enthusiastically. "Haven't laid eyes on him since Oxford. Probably won't even recognize me."

Yes, one could win some wagers on that. I would have to avoid Thomas Roche so as not to put him in the awkward position of having to denounce me. I had, after all, nothing against the lad.

Then there was an American baseball player, temporarily a captain in the U.S. Army, named Luke Lawless. He was to some degree Hope's escort for the weekend.

The final guest was General William Geronimo Starkey. "If he can make it," Hope said. "His B-17 unit is very 'operational' just now. Very striking man. Certain to be President of the United States one of these days, according to Ralph Dankers. He's more or less Dankers' protege, or lackey is more like it. Rather a shallow person. I heard him say one night that the war is really over. Can you imagine? He claimed that Hitler being stopped in Russia and being stopped crossing the Channel marked the beginning of the end. That from now on it will be just a case of bringing the resources of the Allies to bear. The 'grind them down and mop them up' as General Starkey puts it. The 'interesting,' that was his word, the interesting part of the war, the 'who will win' part is over according to General Starkey. You know. the sort of talk you'd expect from a civilian. God help the American voters."

We arrived at Cornflower in time for tea. The estate was in remarkably good condition despite the wartime shortage of menials; an unpruned berry bush here and there and an occasional bit of unkempt lawn, but all in all rather well attended. The heat of course was appalling. It preserved and deadened every sound.

"My uncle spends most of his time on the grounds now. Poor dear," Hope responded when I commented on the notable neatness. "He hasn't been able to get back to his work at the museum. Oh, there he is now."

We approached a spare, grey-haired gentleman who was standing in the side garden adjacent to the solarium staring at the trunk of a sapling that had been snapped off about two feet from its base. As we neared, Hope whispered to me,

"You mentioned the Irish Monster to Bert in the Poe Park Tavern. Do you know the story?"

"Only from hearsay. What was it really?"

"A Gaelic aborigine we had here at the house last year. Uncle Nigel found him. The thing ran off following an awful row. It's never been seen since. Uncle Nigel can't seem to forget it."

We interrupted Uncle Nigel's bewildered contemplation of the tree stump. "You really should have that pulled out by the roots, darling," Hope said as we joined the gentleman.

Uncle Nigel permitted his niece to kiss his cheek. As Hope started to introduce me, Uncle Nigel returned to staring at the tree. "But it's the only mark he left behind, my dear," he said. "He may even have injured himself when he jumped from the window and hit the tree."

"I wish it were the only mark he left behind," Hope said, with what sounded like deep bitterness.

"Eh?" Uncle Nigel said looking at her with interest. "He left something else?"

"Yes," Hope said. "Some very bad memories. You will have to try and forget him, dear. Chances are he was really a fraud just as Ira says."

Hope introduced me then and we went in to tea. Sally Dankers and the American baseball player joined us. Sally's husband Ralph was confining himself to his room. He had received a spot of bad news just hours before. Ralph's presidential nominee General Geronimo Starkey had been lost in a bombing raid.

Hope and Sally were suitably shocked by the news.

"Really a dreadful thing," Sally told us. "He fell out of the plane on the way back. Attending a wounder gunner, or something, and fell out the door, or hatch, or whatever they call it."

"How awful," Hope said. "Did he have any family?"

"Just his wife," Sally said. "That undernourished American cinema actress, what's her name? Lulubelle Courage. They were on the verge of divorce I hear, so I suppose she won't care."

"You can say that again," Captain Lawless, the American baseball player said. "Not as long as she's in line to inherit all of Geronimo's business interests. That whole Uni-Coffee operation. It's worth millions. She can retire from the movies if she wants. Except I don't know what the boys in the foxholes will do for pin-up pictures if she does. Her studio puts out some real pips."

Colonel Keith Coder's aide, a Lieutenant Paulson, interrupted us to fetch a cup of tea for the colonel. Coder was closeted in an old unused library room at the other end of the great house receiving telephone communications from God knows where. As he left the room with his tray, Paulson gave my chained attaché case a rather disapproving look. I quite agree, old man, my refusal to part with the case is laying it on a bit thick.

Lieutenant Commander Thomas Roche, Royal Navy, arrived about an hour later. A rather lovely red-haired girl, Angela Millins, brought him in her Bentley. I chanced to see them arrive in the driveway and, since I would have the lad's ear alone for a moment, I rushed out and perpetrated an old-school reunion on poor Thomas. He was too much a gentleman to hurt the eager lieutenant who ran up and pumped his hand so warmly.

"Sorry to ... ah ... have lost track of you ... er ... Dan," he stammered. "Here, Miss Angela Millins, this is an old Oxford chum Dan Gregg." Angela was the type of girl who offered her hand; physical contact. I shook it with pleasure.

"Who are you with in Army?" Thomas asked, as I helped him carry Miss Millins' three suitcases to the house. So, that was out of the way.

Ralph Dankers and Colonel Keith Coder both appeared at dinner, which was served buffet style at one side of the living room. The war, you know.

Coder spoke to me for a moment. Who was I with? Could he lock away my attaché case for me in the house safe with his classified papers? "Very kind of you, but I may have to be off at a moment's notice," I said.

Gradually I worked my way around to Ralph Dankers. He was in a discussion with Luke Lawless regarding the baseball situation, "back home."

"Disgraceful," said Ralph. "They should suspend it until

after the war. It's a hideout for 4-Fs. If that fellow Latta can bat .403, he can carry a gun. The club owners have put the pressure on Washington. When I get back I'm going to find out who's getting a buck out of it."

"Glenn Latta wouldn't bat no .403 if me and the rest of the decent pitchers weren't over here," Luke Lawless said. "There's nobody left back there can throw a curve. That's why—"

At this point in their discussion I knocked over Mr. Dankers' whiskey and gingerale with my attaché case. There followed a few minutes of confused repair.

"Why the hell do you carry that thing every place?" Dankers said as he angrily brushed off his wet trousers.

"Have to," I whispered, my voice thick with alcoholic indiscretion. "Too many reputations at stake. Lot of very important people be very embarrassed if deesh papers get into wrong hands." I winked and patted my attaché case.

It was like walking a sheep past a wolf pack. The crafty eyes that had learned their trade over a cash register in the middle of the Depression came to a shocked stop on my face. "Er, .. my boy, how about a round of billiards? Come right along with me." He gripped my arm strongly and maintained his tone of lavish friendliness as he steered me to isolation in the billiard room.

Once in the room, with two potent whiskies in attendance, Ralph stood very straight and alert chalking his cue stick and watching me fumble about trying to manipulate my own cue despite the restrictive chain from the attaché case. My lack of dexterity mattered little. The gentleman appeared much more interested in conversation than in billiards.

"Yesh," I admitted, "I've read the papers in the attaché case.'"

"Oh well," he said, shrugging, "the information can't be all that damaging. I mean, you're overplaying your courier role a little, aren't you?" Another able interrogator.

"Oh dash what you think, ish it?" I said, staggering as my hand slipped from the edge of the table. "Well, how about dish? Last February 13 Senator Ogden Ruffini of your country spent the night in the Bloomsbury Hotel, Room 322 with Miss Cynthia Korb-Soda. When he returned to America

Senator Ruffini recommended that your M-1 rifles be replaced by the Korb-Soda P-5 Repeater."

"Hmmm," Dankers commented, knocking the tip completely from his cue with over-zealous chalking. "February 13th is traditionally the birthdate of beautiful women, but Senator Ruffini seems to have carried it too far. And twenty-two electoral votes in his state. I take it then that's all you have in your case?"

My dear sir, do you take me for a piker?

I told him about the giant Negress who had been sent to General Franco by the President of Mexico via the American embassy in Madrid. "Yes, I believe I heard something about that," Ralph lied. "Don't you have anything new?"

How about the case of the S.S. *Haleakala?* A cargo ship registered in Panama and owned by English citizen Sir Marvin Hook. Guess who stole that ship and its load of machine tools? None other than Colonel Keith Coder, " . . . a guest right here in this same house with us."

"Hell, I can't use that, buddy," Dankers said irritated. "Everybody who's anybody knows about that deal. In fact it was my friend General Geronimo Starkey, the late General Starkey I'm sorry to report, who gave you people the *Haleakala*. His firm Uni-Coffee got the ship after Sir Marvin Hook's death. If Colonel Coder was in on that, it makes him a hero, not a louse."

"Yes, I know," I said excitedly, trying to win back his respect. "But you see you can't just dock a ship and unload a million pounds worth of machine tools. Some corporation has to distribute the things. And of course they're entitled to a spot of profits. I know several firms that would pay handsomely if some military man ensured that they receive the distribution contract."

"By God," Dankers said. "And I thought I knew all the dirty deals Coder's been mixed up in. Well, don't worry, that bastard's number is coming up."

"Now you see why I must keep this beauty chained to my wrist," I said. "I'm responsible for it until I deliver it to General Cleveland Russell at Montalvo. Dash just across the lake."

"General Russell. Old Russ Russell?" Dankers said. "I

know him——" (yes, so I heard) "——That's who's getting all this dope? Why that old son of a bitch owes me plenty of favors. Well, well, well. Senator Ruffini and his twenty-two electoral votes."

About nine o'clock we were sitting about the screened veranda. A very slight breeze could be felt from the lake but the main body of heat that had been trapped by the surrounding green hills during the day still lay just above the grass like a cloying gas. Ralph had not left my side since we vacated the billiard room. We sat in garden chairs on the veranda. I nodded off to sleep now and again. Thomas Roche and the red-headed Angela Millins were at the far end chatting away in a conversation spattered by Angela's pleasant laugh. Piano music drifted out the open doors behind us from the semi-talented fingers of Mrs. Sally Dankers. Nigel Cornflower, Hope's befuddled uncle, our host, was in his study. Colonel Coder and his staff were at their occupations in some other part of the house.

Hope Cornflower had evidently tired of the sweet earned-run averages that Captain Luke Lawless had been whispering in her ear. She was not about. Captain Lawless, with his never-empty whiskey in his hand, sat on the other side of Ralph Dankers. The captain and Ralph were involved in a discussion of Captain Lawless' post-war career.

"Let's face it, Luke," Dankers said at one point, "this war is cutting your playing days. Now look, you're well known to the public. No reason why you shouldn't think of politics. You'd be a cinch for governor or senator. I can practically guarantee it. But let's think about the big apple for a minute. If the war goes another three years, you'll be old enough. Those will be a busy three years for us though. Gotta move you up in rank for one thing. You'll be competing with guys like MacArthur. . . ."

Margaret, the overworked maid at Cornflower, came to tell me there was a telephone call for me. (I had asked the operator to ring me at 9:12.) I returned to the veranda from the telephone with an excited step, my inebriation shattered by a frightening call to duty.

I slid in next to Ralph Dankers and told him that General

Russell had ordered the attaché case delivered to the command post across the lake immediately. I was rather unnerved because, as I explained to Ralph, I had no vehicle. My telephone request to the nearest town, End-of-Lake, for a taxi had produced only a bitter chuckle from a man who had asked me if I knew there was a war on and no damn petrol about for long taxi rides. "As it is, it will take several hours to drive around the lake to General Russell's," I gasped.

"Nothing to it, Dan," Dankers told me. "And it won't take several hours. The Cornflowers have a motor launch. They have the gas too since the launch is listed officially with the Royal Navy as a government patrol boat for Belmont Lake. As a matter of fact I'll drive you across myself. I have my own boat in Virginia about the same size. Well, mine is a little bigger actually. I want to be there when old Russ Russell opens that bucket of worms of yours. I'll get the keys from Nigel and meet you at the dock."

He rose from his chair and was about to dash off. I said, "Why don't you ask your wife if she'd care to join us. This heat appears to bother her."

"Sally?" he said. "Oh, I don't know. This is men's business. I don't think—"

"Can't be much to distract her around here," I remarked, nodding at Luke Lawless who had succumbed to an alcoholic stupor. "Unless of course Colonel Coder can find time to entertain her." Presumably the Colonel has had a bit of practice.

"Ah, yes, good idea to have Sally along," Dankers said. "She loves to sail, and it will be cool on the lake." Yes, particularly in the water.

He went in to the piano and asked his wife. She was delighted. She said she would join us as soon as she fetched a sweater. I followed the Dankers toward the front of the house. When they turned off to their rooms I proceeded down the main stairs. Just as I reached the front door a voice behind me called, "Just a minute, Lieutenant. Can I have a word with you?"

Lieutenant Paulson, Colonel Coder's aide, was standing in a doorway off to my left. His request was rather academic for in his fist he held his service revolver. It was pointed more or less directly at my left eye.

I expressed my dismay to Lieutenant Paulson rather articulately. He paid not the slightest attention. He prodded me along a side corridor to a room at the back of the house. I was ordered inside and brought up before Colonel Keith Coder.

Coder remained seated at an old desk that had been located in the otherwise empty room. He looked at me and said, "I want to see some ID papers, Lieutenant. General Paulk, whose staff you claim to belong to, was reassigned two weeks ago. You're wearing the old insignia. I know John Paulk. That's the sort of thing he doesn't let happen. Let's see some papers and be damn quick!"

"As a matter of fact you are correct," I answered. "I've been reassigned too. I'm with a General Mandrell now. Augustus Mandrell."

Coder covered his surprise very well. He said, "That accounts for the mix-up. I know Mandrell. Or Old Mercenary Mandy as he's called. Lieutenant Paulson, wait outside for a moment please."

When Paulson had left, Coder said, "So you got to Cornflower all right? I should have known you would."

"Yes sir," I said, maintaining my stiff military posture. "Mr. Mandrell made all the arrangements for me."

"Come off it!" Coder snapped. "Don't give me that 'Mr. Mandrell' business. You're Mandrell. Do you think I haven't seen you enough times to recognize you through the disguise?"

I relaxed and spoke in my normal voice. "I thought I'd give it a try. One hears so much regarding the blind stupidity of the military."

Coder chuckled, a good healthy sound as I believe I have mentioned. "When's it to be?" he asked.

"In approximately—" I glanced at my watch "—thirty-eight minutes. Would you care to come along as an observer?"

"Don't get flippant with me. I told you she is out to kill me. This is what she deserves."

"Mrs. Dankers appeared very civil to you at dinner," I said. "Not the least homicidal."

"You know damn well I don't mean kill me physically," he said. "I mean kill my career as a soldier. While we were sleeping together she saw some things she shouldn't have. Some jewelry given to me as a present by a lady in Yugoslavia. When I told her that I wouldn't marry her, she got a bit wild and said she'd start telling what she knew."

"You mean regarding Yugoslavia and Ludwig Kelp?"

He stared at me with his most lethal parade ground stare. "Yes," he said slowly, still watching me close, "about Kelp and a few other things. For instance the fact that the jewelry I got is part of the loot stolen from the museums by Kelp. I didn't think she'd do it. Then one night at Bellinggames I met her and Dankers. Dankers says to me, 'My wife tells me you are rather a good friend of Ludwig Kelp. Strange friend for a British officer.' The stupid bastard didn't realize what she was doing to him; setting him up for a divorce. By showing me that she could tell people about me and Kelp she hoped to get me to change my mind about the marriage. And Sally gets around in circles where the wrong word can ruin an officer. Like King Peter's Yugoslavia exile court here in England. And they'd be likely to believe her. A lot of them know that Sally and I have been good friends."

"Doesn't that affect your career?" I asked. "Your association with a married woman?"

He smiled and said, "Dankers is an American."

"And you feel Mrs. Dankers has told no one about Yugoslavia except her husband?"

"I'd have heard about it if she had. There's only the two of them that know."

"Are you suggesting an additional commission?" I asked slyly.

"Hell no. Even if I was worried about Dankers, I can't afford your services."

"I could perhaps be persuaded to reduce the fee," I said, "seeing that the same customer is involved. I believe the American merchandising people call it a 'package deal.'"

"Or how about 'family plan'?" he snapped. "No. Dankers is a muckraking idiot. And all the people he might talk to know it. Plus his being an American. I'm not worried about that ass."

I wonder, Colonel, if you would take the gentleman so docilely if you knew that he had commissioned Mandrell, Limited to eliminate Keith Coder the Wife Stealer?

I left Coder and ran across the lawns to the dock. Dankers was already in the motor launch. He started it up as soon as he saw me coming. I jumped aboard. Sally was on the bow. She cast us off.

Ten minutes later we tooled into some fog in the middle of the lake. "Don't worry, I know these waters," Ralph shouted from the wheel. "Nigel lets me take the boat out when I'm down. And I see to it he gets his petrol deliveries. She's not as big as my boat. I've got three staterooms to his two. And she doesn't handle as well as mine, but—"

The sharp explosion below decks interrupted him. The motor immediately stopped and we heard a rush of water where there should have been no water.

I dashed below to investigate. A minute later I dragged myself back topside and brought the captain the bitter news. "She's a goner sir. Keel blown open. Must have been a mine. Those filthy Hun!"

"A mine in Belmont Lake?" Dankers boggled. Just then the boat listed over several degrees.

"There's a rubber raft up forward," Sally said, her voice showing quiet courage. "Perhaps we'd best be prepared just in case."

Reluctantly Ralph assisted me in inflating the rubber boat and pushing it over the side. "I don't get it," he kept muttering. "How'd they get a mine in here?"

I leaned over the side to move the rubber boat in closer. I must have underestimated the current or something for I found myself pulled off balance and into the water. My attaché case fortunately fell into the rubber boat.

Ralph came down into the rubber boat to assist me. "C'mon, Lieutenant, this is no time to get clumsy. If those papers get wet—" He was cut off by the discovery he'd made. "Why you're bleeding!" he exclaimed.

"Didn't want to mention it," I said through the blood trickling from my mouth. "Bit of shrapnel from the mine.

Must have come up through the deck. . . . I'm afraid I've had it." I sunk under the water.

Ralph pulled me up by the attaché case chain. "C'mon you jerk," he cried. "You can't drown with those papers tied to you."

"Key," I sputtered. "Here's key . . . unlock. . . ." I handed him the key. He grabbed it and started unlocking the steel bracelet from my wrist. I tried to help him by pulling myself partway up on the rubber boat. "Hold still!" he snapped.

I flailed my arm around the inside of the boat attempting to find something to hold onto. My hand gripped the handle of the attaché case. But the effort had been too strenuous. I slipped back into the water. The attaché case came with me. I barely managed to keep it out of the water by gripping a rope strung along the side of the rubber boat with the same hand that held the case.

"Hold still damn it," Ralph said. "There I've got it now. Let go of the case and I'll pull it in."

"No, no," I said weakly. "I must know it's in safe hands."

"Whose hands could be safer," he said, reasoning with me. "I'm a representative of the United States Government."

"Good, good man," I stammered. "Lock . . . lock it on your wrist. Lock. . . ."

"Oh for God's sake, all right, all right." He snapped the steel manacle to his wrist. "There, it's locked on. Now let go of the case. Senator Ruffini and twenty-two electoral votes. . . ."

I released the attaché case. It contained seventy-two pounds of lead weights, six bars of twelve pounds weight each. I had installed them in the otherwise empty case when I went below decks to inspect the "mine" damage. The attaché case sank immediately to the bottom of Belmont Lake.

I spit the red dye from my mouth and hopped aboard the rubber boat and from there to the wooden boat. I walked forward to the cockpit where Sally stood shivering.

She lifted the lid of a box located under the bench. "Which is which?" she asked, taking two flares from the box.

"This is the red," I said as I selected one of the flares. "I'll light it for you then you hold it over this side, the port side, of the boat. I'll hold the green one on the starboard side." I ignited the flares and we stood in their eerie light waiting.

After a minute Sally said, "Is the fog too thick?"

"No, it's only seven or eight feet high. Don't worry," I said. "We have a good half hour before the boat goes down."

A moment later we heard the cough of an engine somewhere above us. Then came a wooshing sound as the small aircraft glided over us about fifty feet up.

The pilot did a very neat bank which we could barely see against the stars and came back to drop the airplane in astern of us. He turned his propeller over a bit to bring the plane closer. Then he left her idling and jumped out on the pontoon to throw me a line. I pulled him alongside and secured the plane to the launch.

He jumped aboard and took Sally in his arms. "It's all arranged, darling," he said. "I'll have us in Ireland by morning." He turned to me. "All set on this end, Mandrell?"

"Per the schedule," I said. "Have any trouble in the Channel?"

"Piece of cake as you English say. Nobody saw me bail out of the B-17. The boat was waiting just where it was supposed to be. I damn near landed in it from the parachute. I can always depend on Tarbuck. After he got me to shore he went on ahead to Ireland to check on all the arrangements there."

"You shouldn't have any trouble here either," I said. "Even if they hear your plane on shore they'll assume it's a boat. As I see it General, there remains only the passing over of the fee and you may be on your way."

"No more 'General,' Mandrell," he said smiling, as he reached into his shirt to his money belt. "The General is dead. And don't for God's sake call me Geronimo. I've hated that stupid appellation. Dankers' idea of adding color to his hot political prospect. God, I put up with a lot from him just to be near you, darling." He squeezed Sally to him.

As I counted my fee, crisp pound notes, I said, "I wouldn't linger in the Irish Free State too long. The natives don't have much else to do but snoop into other people's affairs."

"Don't worry," Mr. Starkey said, "we'll be out of there in a few weeks."

"Yes I noticed that the S.S. *Haleakala* was berthed at Cork," I commented. "Headed for Buenos Aires, I believe."

"You don't miss much, do you?" Starkey said. He was not pleased.

"I doubt if anyone else will note the coincidence," I said. "After all you are now officially dead. As Sally will be by morning. You have an interesting life ahead of you, sir. All your own design."

"It's been carefully planned, I feel," he said pleasantly. "Exit General William Starkey leaving widowed movie actress wife. Enter Mr. Hank Van de Erve with beautiful wife."

"And she doesn't get any of Uni-Coffee, does she?" Sally asked. "I mean Lulubelle? She said she'd take half of your company in the divorce."

Starkey laughed. "She'll get nothing but the life insurance, which is considerable. No, I've arranged the paperwork. Mr. Geronimo Starkey took a terrific paper loss in the past few weeks. All of his controlling interest now belongs to a gentleman named Hank Van de Erve. Let's go."

As we went about the tricky business of getting Sally on to the aircraft pontoon, she said, "Darling, do we have to have that smelly Indian on the ship with us?"

"You mean Tarbuck?" the General said. "Don't worry, he won't bother you. He's the most valuable man I have in Uni-Coffee. Besides, he's not an Indian. He's—"

I had stepped back on to the sinking launch. Starkey was in the act of assisting Sally into the cabin of the small seaplane. And at that moment a terrible sound split the quiet night.

A voice behind me said, "Sally? Sally, who is that with you? Isn't that General Starkey?"

By the great hairy gods of Mischance and Absurdity! Hope Cornflower stood in the stairs to the cabin, looking dazed and bracing herself against the list of the boat.

My hand flew out almost of its own command and struck her neck. Hope collapsed forward into my arms.

"What happened!?" Starkey barked at me, jumping back on board. "Where did she come from?"

"I don't know where the devil she came from," I stammered. "She must have been in one of the staterooms."

"Is this the famed guarantee of your damn firm, Mandrell?" he fumed. "Here I've reorganized my whole life, risked my neck jumping out of a B-17, taken Sally into a world where she is no longer legally alive, and you louse it up with this bone head."

"You have received a guarantee from Mandrell, Limited, sir," I said stiffly, "I have accepted your money. You will be delivered that guarantee."

"I know what he means," Sally screeched from the airplane. "He's going to kill her. I know Augustus Mandrell."

"No man knows Augustus Mandrell, madam," I snapped. "Least of all a woman. And I am not about to harm Miss Cornflower. Any ordinary dolt could accomplish that. Get aboard your aircraft, Mr. Van de Erve, and leave. Your venture is still secure."

After a second of consideration, Starkey went to his airplane. "No. Don't leave," Sally cried. "He'll kill her." She was still so protesting as the aircraft taxied away and began its take-off run. Not a very auspicious beginning for a honeymoon.

I slid the unconscious Miss Cornflower over the side on to the rubber boat. After opening some valves below decks, I cast off the rubber boat and joined the young lady. As I rowed us away from the motor launch I could hear the big boat gurgling in its last attempt to stay afloat. After a bit there was no noise but the soft lap of waves against the rubber raft.

The rubber boat was so low in the water that the fog surrounded us completely. The moonlight attempting to penetrate from outside the wispy curtain left a strange, shifting illumination all about us.

I started throwing the contents of the raft over the side: fishing lines, signal mirrors, cans of water, marker dye. It was a military survival raft that had been put on board just the day before through some arrangement made by Sally. She had also arranged for the lead weights and the red and green flares to be on board.

Hope moaned and stirred about. I quickly tied a line to the two oars and let them float off behind the boat.

When Hope's eyes opened she found me seated on the floor of the raft facing her. I was unbuttoning my shirt. She instinctively gripped the front of her night gown and squeezed it closed about her neck.

"Oh, Lieutenant Gregg," she said with relief. "Where are we?"

"It's a bit hard to explain," I said. "What's the last you remember?"

"I was aboard the launch. I'd gone there to sleep. I thought it would be cooler than the house. But even the launch was too warm. So I took a sleeping draught. Finally I was able to—My God! Sally and General Starkey! I saw them. . . . Or did I dream?"

"No, you saw them," I said. "They've already gone on ahead with . . . with the bearded man."

"Gone on ahead? Where in heaven's name are we?" She stared around into the eerie fog. "How could General Starkey be here? They've reported him missing, probably dead."

"I'm afraid I've some bad news for you," I said with an embarrassed laugh. "At least you may think it bad at first, until you talk to the bearded man. You see Mr. and Mrs. Dankers and myself were crossing Belmont Lake in your launch. We didn't know you were aboard. Mr. Dankers did something foolish. I don't quite know what. Anyway the launch blew up and sank."

"And how did we get in this raft? Where did General Starkey come from?"

"The General was here before us," I said, doing my best to explain it. "When I say the launch blew up, I mean it blew up instantly and totally."

"That's silly! I remember waking up. There was water in the stateroom, up to the bunk. I remember going to the deck."

"Yes, the man with the beard explained that that's the way it happens with explosions and the like. You're allowed to come here in whatever you were in just before it happened."

She stared at me for a long moment. Then she said quietly, "Lieutenant, are you trying to tell me I'm . . . I'm dead?"

"We all are, I'm afraid. The only consolation is we are all up here. Except Dankers. He went the other way."

"I'm not surprised. Now just a minute. This is absurd, I'm as alive as I ever was. No damage except for this bruise on my neck."

"I know, I know. Sally—Mrs. Dankers—and I felt the same way when the man with the beard told us we were dead. We didn't believe him until he brought General Starkey over to convince us. They were just leaving again when you arrived. None of us expected you, except the man with the beard. He told us you were here."

"What man with the beard? Do you actually mean Saint . . . Saint? . . ."

"I don't know," I said. "He hasn't mentioned his name. He said he could only take two at a time though. We're to wait here until he returns. And we're to—"

"And we're to what? Why did you stop?"

"It's nothing," I said. "I'd best let him explain."

She was quiet then. She sat staring out at the silent fog. "Poor Uncle Nigel," she murmured after awhile.

Then she sighed and said, "So this is what it's like? You just float around in front of the gate waiting to be let in. Why are you removing your clothes?"

"He said I had to," I said, embarrassed. "He said that's the way we go in. He made Sally and the General do it too. Everybody inside is like that. I don't suppose you have to until we are actually ready to go in."

"I might as well," she said. "This nightie is so thin it's practically no cover anyway." Yes, so I'd noticed, my dear. "At least I'll finally get cool." She removed the wisp.

Gad! but you are strung together with commendable excellence, Miss Cornflower.

I completed my disrobing. We sat quietly then, trying not to stare at each other. She was far more successful than I.

"I suppose we'll get used to it," she suddenly said. "If

everybody in there is this way. I suppose sex becomes the last thing you think of up here."

"I'm afraid not," I said. "According to the man with the beard it's the only thing you think about. That's what the place is all about."

"You mean that's all they do? Everybody?"

"And with anybody you wish," I said. "The reason he explained it was to warn Sally."

"Warn her of what in heaven's . . . er, warn her of what?"

"The way it works is you are sort of on the open market if you come in by yourself. Unescorted."

"Well, Sally is all right. She had General Starkey with her. He may not have been very smart about politics and running the war but he was a fine-looking man."

"That isn't enough, you see. Just because they arrive together doesn't mean anything. They have to have . . . known each other."

"But they knew each other. Oh . . . I see, you mean 'known' like . . . when you really know each other?"

"Yes. The man with the beard left them alone in this—" I patted the side of the raft "—for a half hour before he took them."

She was quiet for a moment. A rather interesting silence. Then she said, "Lieutenant, is that why you and I are here?"

"Only if you want to avoid 'immediate selection' as he called it when you go inside. If you are escorted by someone you've known then you have a period of time in which to make up your own mind, make your own selection inside."

"Well in that case, I . . . ah . . . feel that perhaps we are wasting time. Could you . . . come over to this side?"

The gentleman with the beard was truly a considerate man. He did not return for several hours. At one point Miss Cornflower remarked, "Do you think we really need do it again? Oh, I suppose better safe than sorry. And I do need the practice. Which is more than I can say for you, Lieutenant."

Eventually I looked up and said, "Here he comes now."

Hope struggled up to look. While her head was turned away from me into the fog, I touched my finger to a nerve in her neck. She collapsed rather abruptly. I suspect the unique nature of the evening had something to do with it.

I pulled the oars in, checked my pocket compass, and rowed for shore. I found that happily we were but two hundred yards from a beaching area. Off to my left about a quarter-mile away I saw a dozen or so lights bobbing about in the dark: electric torches. And behind them the lights of the great house of Cornflower.

I took the empty rubber boat out to deep water and scuttled it. After swimming back to shore, I took my clothes, the oars and Hope's nightwear and fled off into the woods. The dear girl would not suffer undue exposure for one of the torches was making its way along the shoreline toward her resting place.

Since the names of the deceased were rather prominent, even the London newspapers carried an account of the TRAGEDY AT CORNFLOWER. Dead in the "boating mishap" were Mr. and Mrs. Ralph Dankers and a Lieutenant Dan Lee Gregg. The only survivor was Miss Hope Cornflower. The girl was "under doctor's care" and had been unable to give any coherent explanation of the "accident."

I availed myself of a reading of the official file at the district constabulary office a few weeks later. I found the following conclusion: ". . . the debris found on shore indicates the launch suffered some sort of explosion. Possibly an accidental discharging of some of the munitions carried aboard (launch was official patrol boat of Belmont Lake); statements obtained from the survivor, Miss Hope Cornflower, while somewhat incoherent, support the theory of 'accidental explosion.' Such an accident would account for Miss Cornflower's mental condition. (See medical report on subject Cornflower, Hope. . . .)"

The medical report referenced in the police report was enclosed in the file. The doctor's portion of the medical report was relatively terse, two pages with a single sentence conclusion: ". . . . no physical damage except contusion on neck."

The psychiatrist's portion of the report went on for twelve pages of mumbo-jumbo. But he too reached a one sentence conclusion: ". . . The subject has obviously suffered what can best be described as: massive hallucinations."

# THE IRISH MONSTER
# COMMISSION (1941)

THE NAVAL INTELLIGENCE people were housed in an unbelievably sleazy building located within a few streets of the London waterfront. The choice of the building must have had something to do with "fooling the enemy," which as you may recall was a full-time sport during 1941. Which German agent would suspect that Intelligence was being dispensed in such blighted surroundings? That's Intelligence.

A young woman, a maid who filled her uniform with soothingly unmilitary projections, greeted me from behind her desk. "Captain Riordan?" she said. "Oh, you must be the gentleman who rang up Lieutenant Butcher this morning. He's waiting to see you. Second door down on your right. Watch the file cabinets as you pass. They're about ready to topple on somebody, I'm afraid. Terribly uneven floor we have here."

Her remark concerning the insecure file cabinets was prompted not so much by the existence of the unstable flooring, but more by my apparent condition. The aroma of alcohol rode on my breath with pungent authority. A similar residue of past dissipation was also indelibly woven into the fabric of my sea captain's uniform. Then of course my bad leg contributed to the general uncertainty of my forward momentum. But the lass's concern had been more for the well-being of the drunken old sea captain than for any damage the filing cabinets might sustain.

She was that sort of a girl. Her name was Hope Cornflower. She was unaware that I knew this.

Lieutenant Butcher spoke to me in a paper-infested little warren of an office. "You reported when you rang up this morning," he said, "that you saw a surfaced U-boat on your voyage in."

"And had her I would too—sunk to the bottom—if I'd any sort of decent gun crew on board the S.S. *Nemisis*. Instead I'm shackled to that pack of near blind landlubbers you people gave me."

"I'm afraid Intelligence has little to do with the assignment of crews." Lieutenant Butcher was a youngish chap, with minimal tolerance for drunken merchant captains who criticized the Royal Navy. "Now this U-boat, you say there was an aircraft sitting on her deck?"

"She wasn't just sitting there," I said. "She was moored to the deck. When the pig boat surfaced, this airship was aboard her. A mother hen and her young."

"And could you describe the . . . ah . . . airship? Would you say the shape was somewhat like a cannon? Some class U-boats carry a deck gun that, at a distance, gives the appearance of—"

"A lovely looking cannon she was," I snapped. "What with wings sticking out the sides about twenty feet, and a tail up behind. Maybe a rooster it was at that."

"All right, it was an aircraft," he said, getting a bit testy himself. "Yours is the first report I know of describing an aircraft carrier U-boat." He opened a notebook to a clean page. Then he took a pen from his pocket and commenced examining the nib, pressing it on the blotter and the like to test its flow; the waste-motion absorption with insignificant detail that is peculiar to those who have never learned how to get a job started and get it done with. Precisely the type chap I'd hoped to encounter.

"I've carried enough airships across the Atlantic the past two years to know the look of them," I said. "This one had two engines, like those B-25s the Yanks have been sending over in their so-called lend-lease program. I wish to hell America would get into this bloody war. It would cut my damn paperwork in half."

"A B-25 is a land-based aircraft," Lieutenant Butcher commented patiently, as he wrote the date neatly at the top of his notebook page.

"So was this, Lieutenant. She had wheels on her. Maybe it's that the Germans have found a way to roll an airplane across a stretch of water, would you think?"

"It had wheels?" he said, surprised. Wheels? My dear chap, you haven't heard the half of it.

"Two of them, one inboard of each engine," I said. "Now the engines ... that's where she didn't look like no airship. There was no propellers on the outsides—"

"Probably stored below until they got her to wherever they were taking her," he said, writing away at an excited clip.

"They weren't stored below," I said, tapping a cracked fingernail on his knee. "If you'll be letting me finish my sentences, you'll be finding out what I come to tell you. . . . The propellers now—they were *inside* the engines."

"Inside? You mean—"

"I mean inside. The engine had a hole in the front and a hole in the back. Inside these holes were all these small propellers, row after row of them. I saw them plain through my glass when the pig boat put her bow to us as she dived. That Hun captain thought I'd be holding the same heading. He—"

The lieutenant had been to a degree speechless. Abruptly he found his voice. "Where, man? Where?" he cried. "Where did you see this? My God, don't you realize what you've described? Haven't you ever heard of. . . ." He shut his mouth. The inherent slyness of his trade slid over his eyes. "Ah . . . can you give me the position of the S.S. *Nemisis* at the time of the sighting, Captain?" he said, carefully.

I gave him the co-ordinates. "That's somewhat south of the normal convoy lane, isn't it?" he asked.

"Now, you're talking some intelligence," I nodded. "I'd wondered where you'd be hiding it. Yes, that's south of the convoy lane. I had me a hot number three bearing so I hauled in closer to the coast. Came down past the Irish Monster Islands. I know those waters the way I know my own bridge. From before this damned war."

"The Irish Monster Islands?" Lieutenant Butcher said, as well he might.

"That's what we called them in those days," I said. "You knew you was going to have a rough crossing if you spotted one of the devils on your way out. The charts call them the Farrell Islands. Off the northwest coast of Ireland."

"Oh, you mean if you saw any of the natives," he said, turning back to his notebook. "I thought those Farrell Islands were uninhabited."

"They're uninhabited all right, if it's humans you're talking about. The things you see on them are monsters as far as I'm concerned, or two-legged apes. Running around with no clothes and the like. I hear there's not any left now but the one. We saw him this trip, standing on the hill and throwing rocks out at us as usual. And us a good half-mile off shore."

Despite himself, Lieutenant Butcher's attention was dragged from his book. "Throwing rocks? No clothes?" he said. "Do you mean some sort of primordial human? A wild man say?"

Miss Hope Cornflower inserted her pert young body into the little office. "Here it is, nice and hot," she said as she leaned between us to place a tea tray on Lieutenant Butcher's desk. "I've brought you a cup too, Captain Riordan," she said. "If you'd want to join us."

I answered the young lady with a cordial grunt of some sort and turned my major attention to scrutinizing her bent-over body. Beneath the tight skirt I detected the classic lines that have, lo these many centuries, so frequently triggered a spot of rape; a superb juncture of thigh and buttock.

Lieutenant Butcher, I noticed, was also absorbed in probing the resilience of the skirt-covered flesh with his eyes. I restrained myself from reaching across the girl's bent back and striking the lecherous swine.

"There now," said Miss Cornflower, straightening up and smiling at the three cups of steaming tea. "I'll just take mine to my desk," she said, "and not disturb your business."

"Captain Riordan has just been telling me something that I think you'll find interesting, Hope," Lieutenant Butcher said to the girl. "Your uncle still has his post at the museum hasn't he?"

"Goodness, yes," she said. "He's there nearly every evening until eight or nine. I keep after him to leave earlier but he refuses. Cook, of course, pretends to be furious with him; having to heat up supper and all. I'm only sorry I can't be there with him. Some fascinating things are coming in. Dug up by the bombs and all."

"That's right, you did work with him a good deal before the war, didn't you?" the lieutenant said. "I was wondering, have you ever heard of a group of primitives living on an island off the Irish coast? The Farrell Islands?"

"The Farrells? There's nobody on them. Daddy has a hunting lodge not far from the coast there. I spent two summers there with the family before the war and I never heard of anyone living on the islands. They're quite a ways off the coast and completely unliveable. Even the fishermen stay away from them because the waters are rather treacherous."

"Aye, the fishermen stay away," I said, "but not because of the sea. It's the monsters they're afraid of."

"Here, I have to rush this information about the jet . . . the airplane off to Commander Johnson," Lieutenant Butcher said rising. "Hope, you sit here and let Captain Riordan tell you about his Irish Monsters. I'll be back before five."

Thus did I introduce into the life of Miss Hope Cornflower her first knowledge of the Irish Monster. I told her of the legends mouthed by the North Atlantic merchant captains, how it was a tradition among them (". . . among them that's a bit weak in the liver, and there's more of them than you might be thinking. . . .") to steer off course to avoid sighting the Farrell Islands. "It's their belief that to be cursed by the monsters, to have them throw a few pebbles at you, means a bad crossing for your ship."

"Do you mean now?" she asked. "These primitives are there now?"

"They're there, and no doubt. At least there's one of them left. Used to be bunches of them, men, women, tykes, when I first started sailing. Now it's down to one; this one fine healthy looking animal we saw on the way in."

"And he's always on a certain island?"

"He moves about a bit. Mostly he's on the one big island, Wilson's Rock, but he knows how to get about in the water. It must be fish he lives on. There's nothing else."

"Why it's unbelievable!" Miss Cornflower said with excitement. "Even if these people have been isolated for only twenty or thirty years—why, they would make fascinating study! I'll have to tell Uncle Nigel about it immediately, tonight. Can you show me which island you last saw the man on, Captain?"

Although I am normally a close man with the secrets of my trade, I melted before the fervor in the lass's young eyes and blabbered to her a rather detailed docket of charting and seamanship directions to the island of the Irish Monster and in particular to an island called Wilson's Rock. Heaven help me.

"And what do you think your uncle might be doing about the monster, miss?" I asked slyly. "Sending a bunch of Royal Navy sailors up to grab the beast?"

"Good heavens, no," she said. "If I know Uncle Nigel, he'll be off in the cutter to Ireland himself, to Kiskame. Then he'll like as not rent some sort of power boat from the Irish. They still have them and the petrol to run them, you know. Uncle Nigel will go out for a look himself before he reports anything official to the museum people. Oh, I do hope he finds your Irish Monster!"

I feel certain, somehow, that he will, my dear.

Miss Cornflower removed the tea tray from Lieutenant Butcher's office. I accepted her period of absence as an opportune moment for my own departure. I had no stomach for hanging about awaiting the return of Lieutenant Butcher and his absurd questions about jet aircraft.

I taxied to a small hotel along the waterfront. Limping through the threadbare lobby, I paused long enough to snarl a vicious complaint to the aged clerk who was busily spilling some sort of porridge substance down on to his grey beard from a tarnished spoon. In reply to my complaint, the clerk spit a bit of the porridge after me. He would, I felt, recall my return to the hotel should any snooping employee of the Crown, a lieutenant from Naval Intelligence say, inquire after me.

In a room on the second floor I found a sleeping sea captain. His mouth was open and there emanated from this tunnel beneath his nose the fumes of the brewmaster's revenge. I returned the good captain's uniform to the wardrobe and retrieved my own tasteful garments. Before taking my anonymous leave from the hotel, I slipped into the arms of the sleeping man a full bottle of inexpensive whiskey. This bottle contained only whiskey, whereas the bottle the captain and I had shared that morning had contained a further ingredient; at least, the captain's portion had contained the added ingredient.

Let us hope, Captain Riordan, that you have regained your stability by 7:30 this evening. Seven bells, as you may recall, is departure time for the S.S. *Nemisis*. It appears it would befit your position as master of the vessel to be aboard at sailing.

Three days later I loafed about the docks and watched while the cutter, *Cornflower II,* was prepared for sailing. The *Cornflower II* was the property of Nigel Cornflower, uncle, as you may have guessed, of Hope Cornflower. Uncle Nigel was the energetic director of the Municipal Museum.

After dark, I slipped aboard the *Cornflower II* and examined her charts. A route to Kiskame on the northeast coast of Ireland had been laid out. I copied from the charts a few pertinent facts regarding the area about the Farrell Islands. My knowledge of the islands was somewhat less voluminous than I would have liked. I knew only that they were uninhabited, marginally conducive to rendering support to human life, uninviting in both appearance and accessibility, and endowed with a wispy, half-remembered history by the adjacent coastal natives as the site of terrible deeds in centuries past. Rather one of the few areas left in the British Isles where one might stumble upon a race of monsters; unspoiled, uninhibited, and most attractive of all, unrepentant throwbacks to another age. What a find for Nigel Cornflower!

The last lap of my journey to the Farrell Islands was accomplished in a rubber boat. For a patient man, the islands were not too inaccessible. A current from a point some fifty miles from shore brought me within rowing distance of the first of the island chain. Two further days of rowing during the favorable high tide periods brought me to the largest of the islands, the one identified as Wilson's Rock. A patient man can do it. Yet, patience is not the only virtue required. One must know, too, a chap possessing a rather over-powered, sea-going craft. A craft, say, in which many cases of whiskey and other products which are normally disfigured by duty can be moved from port to port without the bother of imposing upon the poor overworked chaps at Customs a further chore of senseless paperwork.

This boat owner, a man dedicated to true free enterprise, must then be cajoled into navigating his vessel to a point fifty miles off the coast. He must also be ready to forget that he lost a passenger and a rubber boat overboard during his outbound journey. "Lost at sea" is a risk engaged in by any passenger who goes to sea, and any master worth his salt is only too willing to dismiss such an embarrassing incident from his mind.

I spent two days by myself on that desolate, mist-shrouded stone called Wilson's Rock. I was kept busy. I scurried about the ugly place depositing a small collection of artifacts here and there; broken bits of pottery, stone axheads, a bone or two of some odd animals (a rib from an adult yak; a splintered tusk from a wild boar; a piece of plate from the back of an armadillo).

I seined several fish from the local waters. As I cut them into pieces with a stone knife, it appeared that the eyes of the dumb brutes leveled reproach at me for having delivered to their previously peaceful waters the eccentricities of Man. I scattered the fish about also, residue presumably, of my incompleted meals. I tramped the island, setting my bare feet into the sparse soil wherever an imprint would take. I built a shelter of sorts with some sea-rotted wood I'd brought with me. I labored mostly without the comfort of clothing. After a bit I came to appreciate the utilitarian aspects of nakedness, once I'd lost my, very civilized, fear of being seen. I had been preparing my epidermis over the previous several weeks to achieve that overall surface effect known as weatherbeaten.

Happily I had never been plumbed by the surgeon's scalpel, therefore exhibited no rents of overly neat repair. My only outward disfigurement, the bullet hole in my back, had been forced to heal at its own discretion. I recall that I had felt somewhat put upon during my convalescence from the ballistic abuse, lying beneath several inches of loose soil while Mr. Gamal Risshor and the Egyptian Secret Police searched the area about the Aswan Dam for my body. But had I obtained any medical service at the time, I could not have considered the solution to the Irish Monster Commission I was in the act of executing on Wilson's Rock. (As to the steel filling in one of my upper molars, well, I'd just have to keep my mouth shut.)

About noon of the third day, I heard the far roar of a power boat coming through the mist that separated me from sight of land. I felt I was ready. I ran to my mooring site, pushed the rubber raft into deeper water, and sank it. It bubbled to the bottom with all of my worldly possessions, with the exception, that is, of my guile. By the time I had again reached Wilson's Rock, the motor boat had beached, and Nigel Cornflower and a rifle-carrying companion were ashore. I watched them as they treaded carefully over the rocks to the center plateau of the island. They wore heavy rain gear, for the spray on the trip out must have been tiresome. The Farrell Islands are perpetually shrouded in a cocoon of mist. Ahhh, all the better to grow your queer fruit.

Nigel was the first to stumble on one of my treasured heirlooms. When he and the short man noted that the object was a stone axhead, their original jubilation turned to wise apprehension. The small man brought the rifle to "port arms" and held it in this readiness grip while their search continued. They next found some of my inimitable footprints. Nigel's enthusiasm returned. The ancient axhead and a new footprint—how his dusty museum heart must have pumped. Poor mutt. The other chap, more practical, less the poet, took one look at the size of the imprint and swung the ugly nose of the rifle in an arc covering all of the island. WANTED; PRIM-ITIVE MAN, DEAD OR ALIVE.

The distrust of civilized man, a distrust fiercely bred in my tribe (we threw rocks at their ships), appears to have been quite within reason.

The time had arrived for the taming of the savage.

I waited until their backs were turned, then stepped from behind my rock. They were but twenty paces from me, well within earshot of the series of ferocious grunts I emitted. They spun to face me. Ahhh, can the craftsman's satisfaction ever be measured with accuracy? Isn't it really too nebulous a quantity for any calibration instrument?

The mouths of my audience literally dropped open at the sight of the Irish Monster. There he stood, on two wide-spread legs; arms out to the side, fingers tensed like claws; head and lower face covered with hair that had been chopped to irregular lengths with a broken seashell; eyes ablaze with the indignation of the trespassed homeowner; mouth open to expose the rows of white daggers, his most personal weapon of combat; chest bare of all but several smears of fish blood running like lizards through the matted hair; the rest of the carcass bare also, except for a normal compliment of dirt and sand.

Welcome, sirs, welcome to my unpretentious isle. And what brings you out this way?

The man with the rifle had immediately aimed the weapon at my theatrical body, causing me to drop from my act the bit of business wherein I was to fire several stones at the audience. Should the gentleman's dedication to anthropology be of a fleeting consistency, I for one had no wish to force his secret from him. Speech came slowly to Uncle Nigel. Eventually he was able to throw out his arms toward me and screech, "My God—he's here . . . it's true! . . ."

I growled at his enthusiasm, not menacingly, more that I was embarrassed by his outburst and wished he would exhibit more aplomb. For God's sake, pull yourself together, man. The other man took note of my superficial docility and relaxed somewhat the rifle's rigid alignment. This action freed one of his hands and permitted him to push back his rubberized headgear.

By the great sweaty god Preposterous! The gunbearer was Hope Cornflower!

Now, it is quite true that my training for my profession has caused me to attain a number of skills not enjoyed by the average chap. But, I must admit that I am still in many instances the victim of my Western environment. I am no more immune to certain Victorian concessions than the next man. Thus: it requires just as much nerve on my part for me to prance about in the buff in front of an attractive young lady as would be required by any lad of Christian upbringing; to do it with any degree of agility at any rate. Ach, but we are the pawns of our conventions.

Nor was I alone in my social dilemma. Once the initial bonanza of sweet accomplishment had drained through Uncle Nigel's senses, he turned to the girl. "Well now," he said, "we'll have to see about making friends with him. And . . . er . . . of course get him into something to wear."

"Oh don't be silly, Uncle Nigel," the girl chided with a smile. "It's going to be difficult enough making friends without trying to force him into a pair of trousers." She was being a bit more sensible than I for one thought to be quite proper. "Besides," she added, "it's not as though he were a real young man, I mean like one's acquaintence. He's more . . . well, an animal, or a specimen."

How quickly one descends the social scale. Perhaps I have underestimated your civility, Miss Cornflower. You certainly appear to have underestimated mine.

For the next hour, the three people on Wilson's Rock played a fascinating game. The Cornflowers attempted to ingratiate themselves with the Monster. The Monster attempted to expand his narrow world to accommodate the existence of these strange invaders. The Monster, of course, was in the driver's seat. When events did not meet with his satisfaction, he would scream and throw himself into a belligerent crouch, ready to spring upon the offender. If the Monster chose to examine Uncle Nigel's eyeglasses, why then Uncle Nigel had to stand by and watch helplessly as the Monster smelled and then chewed on the spectacles. Miss Cornflower did not go unscarred in the encounter. She too bore with stoic patience the several minutes of inspection that ensued when the Monster discovered beneath her headgear a mane of fine blond hair. The fish-stained and broken-nailed hands of the "specimen" became fully entangled in the golden mass. The Monster produced a surprisingly civilized ability to laugh once he discovered that, by yanking on the girl's hair and running several paces back and forth, he could force the young miss to follow him, spinning and turning in her clumsy raingear to maintain her balance.

"He . . . er . . . appears to have somewhat of a sense of humor," Uncle Nigel commented helplessly.

"I wish he'd bloody well find himself another game to play," she cried. "Owwww. . . !" Well, perhaps not too stoically.

I complied with her wish though. I released her and picked up the rifle she had dropped. This evidently was not the "other game" she had had in mind. Both of my *captors* became rather wide-eyed cautious. They circled about me slowly and called their fearful observations to each other.

"Watch now, Hope, he's pointing it your way."

"Oh look, the damn fool's found the trigger!"

"Don't frighten him now, he might shoot himself."

"And he might just shoot you," Hope said. "As for frightening him, it occurs to me he's the one doing all the frightening."

Rather astute of you, my dear. You see, I have discovered, in operations similiar to this, that I cannot always depend on those who are being flummoxed to do what I want done. Quite frequently they must be led. A disguise has two parts; the physical (the identity) and the personality. Of the two, the first is of primary importance only for the initial contact with the "Patsy," as the Americans call him. Once the identity is established, the manufactured personality becomes all. In what has popularly become known as the Cloak and Dagger business, the cloak serves but to get one past the door. It is the dagger that leaves the vivid memory. For my purposes, the dagger, the weapon, must be considered to be the personality. In the Irish Monster Commission, I wielded the Monster's personality with the skill of a Cyrano, if I do say so myself.

For instance, when Uncle Nigel started roaming the island

in search of further evidence I noted his flagrant curiosity and determined to impair it. (I had by this time lost interest in the rifle and had discarded the ugly instrument without inflicting remorse on the owners.)

My two days of preparations on Wilson's Rock had not been quite sufficient time to allow me to seed the evidence of a residence of several centuries. The graves, or the bones at least, of my ancestors were, for one thing, noticeably absent.

Therefore, when I saw Uncle Nigel on the scent, I judged it time for my return to civilization. I ran down to the motor launch and ferociously inspected it with a great beating of the sides and other projections with my fists.

"Come on, Uncle Nigel, come on," Hope called. "We might never get him near the boat again."

The man from the museum was reluctant to leave the treasure island. He did not come running until I had smashed the windscreen and was pounding on the engine hatch cover with a rock.

"Quick, let's cast off while he's aboard," Hope cried as she scrambled over the bulwark, showing a pretty turn of derriere, I might mention, even through the rain gear.

The noise of the engine exploding to life was the first phenomenon of the day to intimidate the Monster. He grunted wildly and cowered in the forward corner of the small cabin as far away from the engine as he could get without going overboard.

"Lord, look at the poor thing," came the comforting cooing from Miss Cornflower. "I'm afraid he's going to have a bad time of it from now on."

I could not afford, however, to become completely docile. My followers would then attempt to lead. When we were about a mile from the island, I gradually crept from the cabin and worked myself reluctantly aft toward the engine housing. I finally brought myself to placing both hands on the hatch cover and, with clenched teeth, dared the beast to confront me.

"Aye, he's a plucky one right enough," Uncle Nigel observed. "I just hope he doesn't want to take the helm. These are terrible waters."

"I'll start something cooking," Hope said. "Perhaps the smell will draw him to the cabin."

"I doubt that he'll eat anything, Hope. Didn't you notice? There wasn't a sign of fire on the island. He's likely never seen fire. Can you imagine! We are certainly indebted to your friend Captain Riordan."

"What a blooming uproar that Captain Riordan has started," Hope said. "Commander Johnson is ready to skin poor Harry Butcher alive because Harry let Captain Riordan get away. You know how Harry is. He waited until next morning before he went to Captain Riordan's hotel looking for him. By then the S.S. *Nemisis* was out to sea and her rather inebriated captain with her. They even considered sending a destroyer after him—oh, don't go up there!" she cried at me.

I had climbed on the bulwark and was walking the bouncing railing toward the forward deck. I snarled at her and continued forward until I had reached the pitching deck. I stood on the bow then with fists on hips staring defiantly out at the oncoming waves.

"A remarkable sense of balance," Uncle Nigel commented. "I can see we're going to be up to our necks in the old argument about heredity versus environment when they get to see him. He does move like an animal. Just wait until Ira Loftwood gets a look at him!"

The view through the broken windscreen evidently prompted a different consideration for the young miss. She said, "I think we'd best put him directly on board the *Cornflower*. Not take him ashore when you return the motor launch."

Uncle Nigel stared for a moment at the somewhat unorthodox bowsprit on the motor launch. He said, "I suppose there might be a bit of commotion dockside at that. The Irish are not the most scientific-minded people in the world. I'll put you aboard the *Cornflower* with him, but mind, keep Jerry with you at all times. I'm just sorry we didn't bring one of the dogs."

Dogs? Good Lord, I hadn't thought of dogs!

Hope went to the cabin and cooked coffee and bacon (the acquisition of these staples being one of the joys of visiting

Ireland in wartime; not the only one, as has so often been announced, there was also the joy of departing). The cooking was, in part, designed to entice the savage from his perch. I refused to budge, much to the shock of my stomach which had been without hot gruel for five days. Instead I lay on the heaving deck and attempted to pluck a meal from the passing waters. During one short lapse of attention I very nearly came up with some crustacean or other. Fortunately I was able to release the damned thing before Uncle Nigel noted my success.

We came alongside the cutter *Cornflower II* and I willingly hopped aboard her. Before Uncle Nigel was clear of us on his way to return the launch, I was halfway up the mast shaking my fist at a few circling seagulls. (They appeared to be more or less accustomed to the gesture.) Eventually I allowed Hope and an old sailor named Jerry to cajole me to the main cabin. Jerry and I got along famously. I crouched in a corner and glared at him. He sat on the stairs with a club in his hands and glared back.

Hope was somewhat at a loss wondering how to communicate with the animal. After a while she removed a piece of raw beef from the larder and laid it tentatively on the table. I bounded up, snatched the meat, and ran back to my corner. I gripped the food in two hands, gnawing on it and daring them with my eyes to take it from me.

"He's a fine set of teeth, now hasn't he, Miss?" Jerry commented.

"You'd best bring him another piece from the locker," she said. "He must be starved."

Reluctantly, friend Jerry did as he'd been told.

As soon as he had left, I lumbered to my feet and approached the girl. She had removed her raingear by this time, revealing a pair of denim work trousers lashed tightly about some of her major working parts. Gad, but she was put together with the soundness of lapstreak. A bulky, high-necked sweater covered her further collection of interesting mechanisms.

I grunted at her and pointed at the larder from which she had removed the piece of meat. "I'm sorry," she said. "There is no more." She tried to indicate with her open palms the void beyond the cupboard door. My grunting became more insistent. I grabbed her sweater by the shoulder and jerked her toward the cupboard. She was glad to open the door for me.

There were stacks of tinned fruits and fish in the small area, which I knocked about with a rude hand but otherwise paid no heed. I quickly satisfied myself that there was indeed no meat to be had, accepting the privation with the grace of a man who has seen many a meal elude his ambitions. I then turned my attention to fields that were obviously more ripe.

I stared at the fistful of sweater in my hand and became absorbed in the feel of the garment as my clutching fingers kneaded it. This action pulled the fabric taut across the dame's delightful bosom. I grunted with confusion as I stared at this unexpected contour.

"Good Lord," Hope murmured, "I suppose you've never seen a woman before, have you? Well, at least you've not got your mind cluttered up with the sex thing and all, like some young men I know. Perhaps you're better off in the end. Although I've no doubt Ira Loftwood will be wanting to teach you the whole silly game when he sees you. No, no—mustn't touch!"

She attempted to twist away from my inquisitive hand. I released her. A carnal escapade with the delightful Miss Cornflower was not the objective of the Irish Monster Commission. Should a seduction of the maid become essential to the success of the program, I felt that the Irish Monster might possibly exhibit a roaring aptitude for clearing the undergrowth of ignorance that presently overlay his lechery. The direct cause of my unclutching of the girl was the sound of Jerry, and his club, returning to the cabin.

Hope took the section of beef Jerry had brought from the locker and severed several filets for her charge. I spent the next half-hour attempting to answer the indignant communiques reaching me from my digestive tract as my gullet forced upon it the raw cow. Come, come my tubular friend, are you so spoiled by the English chefs?

Uncle Nigel returned on board and we set sail for England. "I've no idea what the immigration people will think of this,"

Uncle Nigel remarked at one point in the trip. Nor do I, sir. Then too, perhaps one should give a bit of thought to the laws which define the crime of kidnaping.

During the three-day voyage, Miss Cornflower took time from her nautical duties to attempt friendship with the wild man. He proved surprisingly receptive. By the time we docked in the south of England, the young lady was able to take the rough hand of the Monster in her own and lead him all about the ship.

"You've certainly worked wonders with him, my dear," her uncle complimented her. "We may have to revise many of our theories regarding primitive man's independence of his women folk. He may have been quite as henpecked as any today."

"Don't forget," the girl said, "I'm not his women folk to him. He obviously hasn't seen a woman for years. Captain Riordan said that the merchant captains have seen only men on the islands for the past twenty years at least. Besides I have the impression that he's not as attached to me as he seems. It's more that he's using me as a shield; between him and all these frightening new events in his life. I think he'd still pitch me overboard should he set his mind to something and I got in the way."

The opportunity to test Miss Cornflower's observation came when we docked. We still had a further leg of our journey to negotiate, several miles of inland travel to Cornflower, the family estate. Hope brought me a pair of denim trousers, my travel wardrobe. When she attempted to insert my calloused foot into the garment, I growled and snatched the offending cloth from her and threw it across the cabin. My dear, you do not appear to realize that my role as a primitive would be compromised by such a concession. Show me a naked man, an aloof naked man, and I'll show you a chap who is free to spout any number of absurdities for which there is certain to be an attentive audience. "Image," I believe the Americans call it.

Uncle Nigel glanced at the crumpled trousers and said, "We'll just have to wait until dark before moving him to the auto." For the short moonlit walk to the Bentley I again permitted Hope to lead me by the hand. But she had to grasp my full arm and press it against one of those mysterious bulges beneath her sweater before I would consent to enter the strange machine. My arm remained thus trapped once we were seated. Therefore I was unable to reach out and smite the elderly chauffeur who had suggested that he spread some newspaper on the rear cushions prior to my being seated. The fastidious driver soon learned that soiled upholstery was the least irritant he would suffer during the memorable drive.

For instance, the initial forward motion of the Bentley was distinguished by a ferocious snarl from the Monster. The grey-haired driver stiffened and very nearly drove us off the edge of the dock. The same response erupted in the driver's ear every time he applied the brakes. The Monster apparently knew little of the laws of motion. Each time he felt his body jerked forward with no visible enemy about doing the jerking, he could retaliate with but this vocal hostility. The only entreaty capable of reducing the poor chap's trepidation was the security imparted by Miss Cornflower's soft palm wandering, however reluctantly, over the tensed and fish-stained chest of the aroused immigrant.

My docility endured until we had parked before the great house. I rushed from the machine as soon as the chauffeur opened the door on my side. I brushed him aside and attacked the offending metal beast. Two of the doors gave easily to my wrath, snapping their hinges once I forced them beyond their normal operating arc. The rest of the auto was too well anchored and without a gripping surface to provide me sufficient leverage to impart any further dramatic evidence of my displeasure. I could have disassembled the bonnet but unlocking the halves would have meant demonstrating a knowledge of mechanical devices rather beyond my station. The Cornflower family was saved the expense of a new roof for the auto only by the quick thinking of the disorganized chauffeur. He drove the vehicle out from under my pounding fists and in the process threw me to the driveway from my perch on the running board.

The minor lacerations suffered by my hide were, I felt, well invested. During the following days any suggestion that I be transported from the Cornflower estate was rebutted by a reference to the scene in the driveway and my apparent distaste for motoring.

Organizing sleeping quarters for the night in the house became something of a problem. As we entered past the front door I clutched Miss Cornflower's arm, and no entreaty by the Cornflower family (Uncle Nigel and Hope were the only members in residence) or their staff could persuade me to release the dear thing. A suggestion that the police be summoned drew, I am relieved to report, immediate rejection by Hope.

It was Hope too who finally settled the dilemma. She escorted me to a guest room and closed the door so that we were alone in the bed-chamber. She had told Uncle Nigel that I would most likely fall off to sleep shortly, giving her the opportunity then to retire to her own rooms. It was not that simple. I released her arm all right, once I ensured that we were truly alone, but I was certainly much too overwrought by my catapult into the twentieth century to think of sleep. It was eventually necessary for the young lady to sit by my reclining figure stroking my forehead before I succumbed to Orpheus.

The next morning I was awake at dawn. That appeared a sensible hour for a chap of my background to be up and about.

I took a few minutes to shake off the luxurious euphoria of my rest on the carpeted floor of the Cornflower guest room, an improvement over the two nights in the wet embrace of Wilson's Rock that did not go undetected by my sulking ligaments. I then sent a cheerful announcement of my arising echoing about the house.

As Uncle Nigel came running up the corridor I heard him cry worriedly, "Listen to that scream. He must have impaled himself on some piece of furniture or other."

He and Hope and a couple of the staff, all in nightclothes, burst into my room. I crouched in the center of the rug ready to attack. They froze in the doorway.

"Oh, I hope he hasn't forgotten everything that has happened the last few days," Hope remarked. "What sort of memory is a man like this likely to have?"

"He'd have to remember some things, obviously," Uncle Nigel said. "There, see he's recognized us now. Or you at least. He appears far more tense than he was aboard the cutter. Must have something to do with removing him from his element, the sea."

"Ugh, but he's an ugly sight before breakfast," the dear girl said. "We'll have to find some way to clean him up. Perhaps the garden hose."

"We may as well remain up," Uncle Nigel said. "I imagine Ira Loftwood will be here as fast as his Jag can carry him."

"Let's try some food on our guest," Hope said. "We have that in common anyway. I'm starved."

I permitted the young lady to introduce into my life the joy of munching cold cabbage and raw potatoes for breakfast. I sniffed at the proffered bread but decided to put off my triumph over that staple until the following day. A bath was drawn in my room and Hope tried to induce me into the tub. I'm sorry, my dear. Short of yourself entering the water and then inviting me in, I must decline all forms of hygiene, at least until the visitors have had a look at the Monster in all of his glory. The image, you see, must be sustained at all cost.

About nine, a Jaguar containing three men came pell mell up the driveway. The driver was Ira Loftwood, a fellow anthropology enthusiast. He was dressed in the uniform of a Royal Navy captain. The other two men were twenty years Loftwood's junior. One wore a Royal Air Force captain's uniform, the other a Navy lieutenant's. I recognized the RAF captain from his newspaper pictures. He was Bertie Roche; fourteen German fighters had tasted his marksmanship.

Hope had been sitting on the floor of the main hall with me showing me pictures in a magazine. When she heard the Jaguar she jumped up and went to the front door. As her uncle joined her she said, "Damn, he's brought the Roches. I suppose I'll spend the morning keeping two running steps ahead of Bert and his clutching paws."

"Young Tom has certainly grown up," Uncle Nigel said. "Looking more like his father every day, particularly in the uniform. I hadn't known he was in the service."

The three men entered the hall. Bertie Roche imprisoned

Hope in a hug that was more an animal grappling than a greeting.

"Well, where is he, man, where is he?" Ira Loftwood cried to Uncle Nigel. "Good God!" He caught sight of me as I rose from the floor. His eyes very nearly dropped from his head.

"I say," Bertie sputtered, "can't we get him dressed a bit? Anthropology and all that is bloody all right but Hope shouldn't have to put up with this."

It was explained that the Monster showed a fierce preference for his natural state.

"Get me a pair of trousers," Bertie snapped. "Tom and I should be able to convince the old boy that he's out of uniform." A butler was sent off for the garment.

"Let me get a look at him first," Ira Loftwood said. He walked about me, his arms folded and head cocked. "Nasty wound there in his back," he remarked. "Must be several years old at least. I've seen bullet wounds looked like that after healing."

"I don't doubt that some drunken seaman must have fired on the island," Hope said with heat. "From the safety of his ship, of course."

"Well there's no doubting that he's still in fine condition," Loftwood said. "Look at him, up on his toes when I come near. A ruddy good specimen. All we have to determine now is: a specimen of what. Milesian, Firbolg, or just some misplaced castaway."

"I don't know what to make of him," Uncle Nigel said. "He has no language that we know of. Of course we've only tried English and French. We'll have to try Spanish, Portuguese—"

"And German," young Tom Roche said. "Could easily be a U-boat survivor. Though he doesn't look too German."

"How'll we know until we take that mess of hair from his face?" Bertie Roche said to his younger brother.

"Oh, we're going to have some fun with this," Ira Loftwood chortled. "I can't believe that he could have been on those islands for very long without us knowing it. And a whole colony of them out there for years is ridiculous. I don't care what that fellow Riordan said."

"Then how do you account for him?" Hope snapped, for

Loftwood was trampling in the dreams that her uncle had been hatching since he found me on Wilson's Rock. "He's no U-boat survivor, I'll tell you that. Why, the thing eats raw meat and, I'm quite certain, has never seen a woman before in his life."

"Hatched out of an egg, Snookie?" Bertie said to her. "And how do you know he's never seen a woman? What have you and the distinguished gentleman been at?"

"Oh shut up, Bertie!" the girl flashed. Bertie laughed. His brother Tom withdrew into a red mantle of embarrassment.

"You appear to have left your manners in the cockpit of your Spitfire," Ira Loftwood said to Bertie, with a touch of the sternness befitting a senior officer upbraiding a junior.

"No, Uncle Ira," Bertie said, with a quick flash of his own anger. "I didn't leave them in the Spit—I lost them there."

The butler arrived with a pair of tweed trousers. Bertie grabbed them and said, "Come along, Tom, let's make this chap decent. Watch him now, he's starting to growl. If you get in back of him and grab his arms. . . ." Bertie was a somewhat husky lad, dissipated, I suspect, but still young enough to easily throw off the backlash of the wild life. His brother Tom was on the frail side.

I darted between them and ran over to stand behind Hope.

"What sort of a wild man is this?" Bertie said circling after me, as after a Messerschmitt. "He knows enough about women to get himself behind their skirts. C'mon, Hope, move away from him." He took her arm and tried to pull her out of the way. I had hold of her other arm and pulled her just as hard to retain her between us.

"Come along, my timid lad," Bertie said and grabbed my wrist to jerk my hand from Hope. He had the good grip of a fighter pilot. His brother moved in to get behind me.

I deliberately bumped against Hope just as I released my hold on her arm. She staggered to the side nearly falling. I looked at Hope and then screeched at Bertie, accusing him of having hurt her.

"Here, let's stop that bloody sound," he snapped, "or it's my fist I'll—"

I leapt at Bertie. My soiled fingers snapped about his throat and my knee in his chest carried both of us backwards and on to the cold tile floor. My attention was rather explicitly directed to avoiding Bertie's thrashing legs as he attempted to place his knees in a position to take advantage of my lack of protective cover. I was, therefore, unaware that Thomas Roche had come charging to alleviate his brother's embarrassment. I first detected Tom's arrival when the edge of his hand struck the side of my neck, leaving in its wake a rather impressive welter of damaged sinew. My grip on Bertie's neck grew fragile for a moment, and the young fighter pilot heaved me from his chest with startling ease. Had I lost weight, or was this opponent constructed of a somewhat greater meat density than I had estimated? While I mulled this riddle, young Tom struck me another palm-edge blow just adjacent to the kidney. My nervous system was sufficiently impressed by the agility of the young gladiator so as to deliver upon my body a second of complete immobility. In that fraction of time Tom snatched both of my wrists and bent my arms up behind my back to the rotational limits of my elbow sockets. Rather grubby advantage to take of the disoriented traveller from Wilson's Rock. Ahhh, but you have seen nothing yet of the Roche family's incivility, my naked friend.

Bertie came to his feet and rammed his fist into my stomach, rather lower on the intestines than is generally thought sporting. My shocked muscles attempted to bend me forward from the waist in an effort to somewhat centralize their area of discontent. But Thomas remained at his post and held me upright with my own bulging arms.

A sweet scream of protest issued from Hope as Bertie drew back his vengeful fist for another whack. Bertie, his eyes filled with a stout disregard for compassion, released the fist as though he were being paid to disable me. His knuckles struck my jaw with a little less speed than that generated by a railway train.

It was coming to me that I had allowed myself to be overmatched. I was familiar with the use of the human fist as a weapon of offense. I had also been rather well tutored in the infighting technique delivered to Western man by the

Orientals, the chopping with the palm, that Thomas Roche was utilizing so effectively on my carcass. (Not that I am that in favor of having the Royal Navy involving its young officers in this form of reprisal. Rather a step backwards. I mean, all those sixteen-inch guns that the poor taxpayer is financing, aren't they being utilized at all?)

I was, as I said, versed in both of these combative measures, but I had become aware too late that the Irish Monster was of course without said knowledge. He had to pretty much stand his ground while dear Bertie exercised a passable left cross that terminated somewhere in my beard.

The division of combatants was decidedly without my full sanction. Aside from the abuse of my continued good health, there was a more pressing consideration—the loss of prestige. There were certain activities that would be disastrous to my intentions, should they be allowed to occur. A complete physical examination of my body, for instance. It would be rather difficult to sustain my role should anyone encounter say: the steel filling in my molar, or the residue of even the infrequent cigarette smoking I had indulged in, the tarnished lungs. And what trace of modern man's medical mania would a blood sample reveal? Those anti-bodies injected during childhood to impede certain diseases, are they ever without their internal scar?

My one defense in the prevention of such an intrusion into my personal statistics was my ferocity. Yet here I was grappling with two gentlemen who were doing rather a good job of proving that my intractableness was not without its limitations.

Hope cried out again and tried to run toward the brutal fray. Ira Loftwood restrained her. "Hold on, Hope," he said. "Obviously if we're going to get anyplace with your wild man we must teach him some discipline. This will do him a world of good. We're going to have to insist on a great deal of co-operation from this fellow: Medical exams, x-rays, blood tests—" (Ah-ha, what did I tell you?) "—If we don't— Damn it, Bert, there's no need to be that brutal!"

I quite agree with you, Mr. Loftwood. Your nephew shows a shocking aptness for barbarism.

"Maybe you could just slap him about a bit," young Tom

Roche said to his brother, over my shoulder. "He appears to have the idea."

"I'm not taking orders from Uncle Ira anymore, my lad," Bertie said to his brother, as he prepared to unleash a fist from somewhere in the vicinity of his ear. "Or from you either."

Bertie's fist came like a spear straight for the point of my chin. All right, my boy, I shall ride out this one last blow with you. You had best make full use of my generosity. From this time hence I will insist you demonstrate a good deal more imagination in your mayhem.

During my period of privation I had been feeling out the location of Tom Roche's foot behind me. As Bertie's fist struck, I threw my weight backwards and at the same moment stamped my bare foot on Tom's polished shoe, pinning it to the floor. Tom and I, linked by bone and muscle, both fell in a dead straight line for the tile floor. The younger Roche had his choice. Retain his grip on my wrists and absorb the velocity of my weight as we struck, or release me. Happily he chose the second alternative. Had he ridden down with me, there is a good chance he'd have broken at least one of my elbow sockets. They are not, to any practical degree, replaceable, as you may be aware.

I was free.

Now, Bert, my lad, let us have a peek at the other side of the coin.

The Monster could not launch an offensive employing either the civilized fist nor the Oriental palm edge. But the fellow was not completely without weapons, else how had he survived his tenure on the wild Irish coast?

With a great, perhaps overly candid, scream of vindictiveness, the animal rushed upon Bertie.

I wrapped my arms about him pinning his arms to his sides. Then I unsheathed *my* weapon. My open mouth darted at his neck and hungry teeth sunk into his flesh. The scream this time emanated from Mr. B. Roche.

I had been careful to catch a bit of the collar of his uniform in my bite, and was thus spared the messy business of actually breaking through the skin of his neck in my carnivorous retaliation. But the lad was not unimpressed. He would carry a black and blue memento for several days, a reminder of what might have been had not the collar impeded my bicuspids.

Once again brother Thomas launched a relief column. He charged at Bertie and me, his eye ablaze and his arm cocked for another lethal blow. The Monster proved a quick student in this new indoor sport so recently introduced into his life. Just as Thomas committed his reflexes to delivering the blow, the snarling primate jerked himself to the side. Thomas' hand struck Bertie in the forehead driving the head back until it was arrested by the tile floor with an unpleasant sound. Bert succumbed to total relaxation.

Immediately I leapt astride Tom's back and, by trapping his legs with one of my own legs, I brought him crashing to the floor belly down. From the edge of my eye I saw Ira Loftwood and Hope Cornflower rush toward us, their posture obviously that of appeasement. With a great growl, I unpeeled my teeth once more and, to all appearances, was about to separate about three pounds of grizzle from the back of Tom Roche's neck. Ira Loftwood grasped one of my arms and Hope the other.

"No, no!" Ira screeched. "Good God man, let him be!" I allowed myself to be dragged off, but not before sinking a finger into Tom's vertebrae complex and jabbing a certain nerve, thus inducing tranquility in his writhing body.

Ira Loftwood examined the inert Roche brothers and pronounced them unconscious but otherwise of apparent good health. Loftwood then stared, with a mounting respect, I feel, at myself. I stood next to Hope, her arm still holding mine, and allowed her to unwrinkle from my exterior the firm ridges of belligerency.

"You know, Nigel," Loftwood said. "you may actually have something here. Just imagine it, a genuine throwback. A man from another century, and God only knows which century." Loftwood became quite brisk, very much the Royal Navy Captain. "We must establish a program immediately. We'll get Hollyer and Anspach, and I believe John Klein is back from Africa. We'll set up a series of tests. The thing will have to be rigidly controlled. He's already been exposed to much too much of the comtemporary environment, your home here for example. We will have to determine some method for measuring that factor. I'll get my leave extended. Not much on now anyway since the invasion scare is over. Damn good bit of luck having their expert General Von Ritterdorf get himself killed. And Hope, you too. I'll arrange for you to be free. You are obviously the one person our friend responds to." I relaxed against the girl and purred a bit. "By George, this is going to be exciting."

Uncle Nigel said, "You know who would be terribly interested in this, Ira? Sir Marvin Hook."

"To hell with him," Loftwood said. "He won't allow anybody access to that library of his, so we won't let him near our Monster."

"Come on, Ira," Uncle Nigel said, "now you're being as selfish as he."

"Well damn it, I intend to be. When I think of the data he has locked up in that castle, I say the hell with him. You know what he'd want done. He'd ask that our naked friend be brought up to him on a silver platter. And we'd probably never see him again."

"That's out of the question," Hope said. "There's no way to transport the Monster—oh, we have to have a better name than Monster for him. Anyway we can't move him except on foot. You should have seen what he did to the auto yesterday."

"I don't know what we'll do then," Uncle Nigel said. "I doubt if Sir Marvin will leave his castle. He's still deathly afraid of the labor union people. Well anyway I'll notify him of our find and leave it up to him."

"And you can tell him that if he wants to see the Monster," Loftwood said, "he'll damn well have to come down out of his castle to see him."

Uncle Nigel turned to Hope and asked, "Do you happen to know where I've put Sir Marvin's private number?"

The girl said she did and started off with her uncle to his study. I padded along behind them. Ira Loftwood ordered me to remain with him. He did not insist however, once I uncovered my teeth and delivered a particularly ugly bit of noise from the rear of my throat. In Uncle Nigel's study, Hope went through the complex business of ringing Sheffield and from thence the very private castle maintained by Sir Marvin Hook. I busied myself nibbling on the bindings of several old books pulled from the hundreds that were cased in the walls.

At one point in her telephone labors Hope put her hand over the mouthpiece and made known her feelings regarding Sir Marvin. "I'm afraid I agree with Ira," she told her uncle. "Sir Marvin is as nasty a person as I know of. He probably has the greatest following of impatient mourners in England. There will be dancing at his graveside. Involving him with your Monster will somehow be costly. He'll see to that."

Uncle Nigel shook his head and said, "Every scholar in the country is dying to get at Sir Marvin's private library. Thus far we have all treated him with the same scorn he has shown for us. The result is he permits no one access to the library. Perhaps he will relent if we show him some kindness. Do you realize that he has in that castle the only remaining copy of Captain Nyburg's African Journals? The original Simon Redwool letters, including the one with the Jesse James blood stains? We must find some way to get at Sir Marvin's library. He obviously is not—"

Uncle Nigel's plea was interrupted by a voice on the telephone. Hope had reached Sir Marvin Hook. She identified herself to him, then listened to some reply. Whatever it was the gentleman said brought bright red embarrassment to the girl's cheeks. She snapped, "Here is my uncle," and handed over the receiver to Nigel. As her uncle took up the conversation, Hope came over to me muttering. ". . . bloody lecher . . ." were the only words I could isolate out of her indignation.

Hope tried to take me from the room. She discovered that the Monster was oddly intrigued by the environment. He had never been in Uncle Nigel's study and, once in, was evidently reluctant to leave. As Uncle Nigel reported to Sir Marvin the "miraculous find," the Monster prowled the room sniffing and tasting various unanchored items: pencils, inkwells, open letters. Gradually the primitive's interest centered upon the telephone. It was obvious that his keen ear had detected a third voice in the room, but he was having difficulty locating its source. He searched the wastepaper basket and the area beneath the desk blotter with predictable success.

Eventually the Monster's highly tuned senses brought him to the device held at Uncle Nigel's ear. A perplexed grunt left the brute's lips as he froze stock still next to Uncle Nigel and pressed his weather-beaten ear against the ear of the older man. Uncle Nigel was delighted. He tilted the receiver in order to make the voice of Sir Marvin more accessible to the Monster, and at the same time gestured to Hope to point out the remarkable behavior of their guest.

Thus did I hear one of the most fascinating conversations of my life. Sir Marvin had a deep controlled voice, not unlike that possessed by that American entertainer who a few years previous had convinced his countrymen that invaders from the planet Mars were busily dispensing several unique forms of carnage about the streets of New York City.

As I attached myself to the conversation Sir Marvin was saying: ". . . and all the more unbelievable finding such an item here in the British Isles. What I cannot understand though, Cornflower, is your refusal to permit me to conduct the "authenticity evaluation" here at the castle. I will determine quick enough if the creature is fraudulent. Not that I do not have a high regard for Ira Loftwood's competence. I have in my library, for instance, the original manuscript of Loftwood's book *Goidels, Brythons, and All That*. But Loftwood must be rather occupied with his naval assignments."

"As I said, Sir Marvin," Uncle Nigel replied, "we cannot transport the . . . er . . . chap anywhere. Besides, Ira and I have definitely decided to conduct the verification here at Cornflower. I'm going to invite every sound anthropologist I know of to participate. Incidentally, I'd like you to know that I did not endorse the Crown's ban on your book: *The Scottish People, A Race of Bastards*. I thought your evidence a bit flimsy but I—"

"Never mind my book," Sir Marvin interrupted. "We'll talk about your Monster. You may not be aware, sir, that I do not leave my castle. I am surrounded by a hoard of enemies. Therefore I maintain electric fences and a few carnivorous creatures prowling the area between the castle and the outside world. Have you any concept, Cornflower, how much meat a full grown Bengal tiger eats in one day? And, what with this meat rationing thing, it's a bloody bother keeping the damn cats fed. We're experimenting now with raising our own food supply, packs of hounds. Labrador retrievers for the most part, since they give one a good return factor. Their weight-gain and tissue-density curves plot somewhat higher than those of the German shepherd even on a cornmeal diet. Great sport watching the tigers run down the retrievers. The old cat-versus-dog conflict."

Uncle Nigel's hand holding the receiver between his ear and mine trembled a bit. He said, "If you don't mind my saying, Sir Marvin, you have certainly earned the animosity of your workers. The conditions in your woolen mills are rather a disgrace to the industry. The report in the *Times* said that even the Welsh coal miners fare better."

"My dear chap, did the report also mention that my mills return the highest profit per pound invested? I am not maintaining a seaside resort for the illiterate of Birmingham and Sheffield. When those people come to my mill they know they are going to produce. If they start a row they know they will be attended to by my security force. They are totally treacherous. Despite all my warnings they have gone crying like babies to the jackal of the industry—the labor union people. They are attempting to organize. I have been forced to retaliate. The wage reduction was actually good for the country. Can't have inflation, you know."

"But you are paying a terrible price," Uncle Nigel pointed out. "Your isolation in your castle cannot be a pleasant way to live."

"Ahhh, but you would be surprised, sir. I am quite content here. I would voluntarily leave my shelter now only to go and witness the public execution of a dozen labor union officials. In particular, a leech named Stephen Hunt. Beheading would be my choice. Yet I find myself intrigued by this Irish Monster of yours. I would like to see the fellow."

"You will have to come to Cornflower in that case. We will not move him."

"That appears to be your final word." Sir Marvin's voice, one that contained the hum of a large electric generator, slipped into a deeper vibration; as though an unexpected load had been placed on the generator and the mighty inner windings were tightening to overcome the invader by sheer power. "Let me clarify my position, Cornflower," he said. "I am not unaware of the activity of my enemies. I have learned that some firebrands in the labor union ranks have actually hired a man to kill me. A very clever man I am told. Obviously the man cannot gain entry to my castle. He must therefore attempt to lure me out."

"Sir Marvin!" Uncle Nigel sputtered. "I would never be a party to any such—"

"Come, come, old man. I am well aware of that. Of all the people in anthropology you are the one man whose motives I have never questioned. You are a pure scientist, my dear Nigel. But, you see, this assassin might be aware of the esteem I hold for you. That the whole field holds for you. But even in your case I cannot let sentiment blur my judgment. Should this prove a plot against me I must regard all equally guilty."

"Damn it, sir," Uncle Nigel said, "you have my permission to remain in your castle for the rest of your life!"

From the other side of the desk Hope said firmly, "Here, here. That's telling him."

"Let me put it this way," Sir Marvin's implacable voice said. "Your call came to me here in my laboratory. I am at my work desk. On the board before me is a lovely Monarch butterfly, Damais Archippas. A particularly succulent example. His wings flutter and his body pulses foolishly, as though he perhaps knows what's coming. I take up now a gold pin, four inches in length. The incision will be behind the head. Going in over the horns, so to speak. Ready, Cornflower? There! ... Did you hear him scream, old man?"

Uncle Nigel actually dropped the telephone. I snatched it up and growled my own opinion to Sir Marvin. The line was dead, also.

In the days following the visit of Ira Loftwood and the Roche brothers, all activity at Cornflower swung like a magnet needle to the unwashed creature from Wilson's Rock. Gentlemen from all the nooks and crannies of anthropology: museums, university libraries, catacomb labyrinths, grave excavations, rock quarries, scroll caves, they all descended upon the house. They examined the "Cornflower specimen," as I had come to be known (or "Willie," as Hope and Uncle Nigel called me, after Wilson's Rock). The experts then voiced carefully worded estimates of just who and what I might be. Their guesses had to be forced from them, for to a man they feared the ridicule of being identified with an incorrect supposition. And yet (for even an anthropologist is human, after all) each wanted the glory of being the first to guess right. I said that all of them proved woefully engrossed in their reputations, but there was one exception. A Doctor Innis from the University of Edinburgh looked me over for half an hour on the afternoon of the third day and then turned and silently picked up his beret. As he stomped for the door, Ira Loftwood pressed him for an evaluation.

"I'll not be wasting my time, Mr. Lockwood," Innis said fiercely. "You've dragged me here from my desk at the university, at incalculable expense to my government, to look at nothing at all. That—" he raised a walking stick and pointed to me "—that ... thing! is a fake. It hasn't an honest breath in it. Aye, Irish it is, I've no doubt. And as lacking in legitimacy as the whole of that land. I'll bid you good day, and don't bother to see me out."

Since you choose to become personal, Dr. Innis, have you ever, perchance, read Sir Marvin Hook's book, regarding the origins of the Scottish race? The indignant doctor from Edinburgh did not obtain immediate release from association with the "fake." War time rail travel was not so simple to come by. Dr. Innis remained with us for two days awaiting a railway reservation. Each time he and I passed in the great house, the good doctor would rear back his great bearded head and cry, "Remove the creature from me sight or I'll take my stick to him!"

Happily, Dr. Innis' was a minority report. The doctor himself was rated, in a field that is rather overrun with eccentrics, as a man with a very elusive grasp on reason.

But the doctor did little to entrench the validity of my claim. On the occasion of the initial denunciation, Ira Loftwood watched the departure of the stormy Scot and then turned to stare at me. Dr. Innis' remarks had triggered an ugly trail of speculation in Loftwood's mind and his brain slithered slowly toward an unwholesome conclusion.

"I don't know," Loftwood said thoughtfully to a Dr. Giral who was drawing sketches of my skull structure. "Suppose this creature is a fake. Suppose, for instance, Sir Marvin Hook wanted a bit of sport with us. Make fools of us. Suppose he hired an actor to sit on Wilson's Rock waiting for one of us to find him. Hook certainly has money enough and a mind twisted enough to pull it off."

Monsieur Giral, a wartime exile from the French Academy, smiled and said, "No, no, no, Ira. Do not be absurd. Sir Marvin, he ees not zee mun-stair you think. I have speak with heem this very morning. He ees full of zee ques-choons regarding our Cornflower Specimen. To heem I say again, of course, zat zee Specimen he cannot be moved. He had asked me, you see, to encourage zis move. Sir Marvin—ho, ho—he say 'Giral, I sink of you as a Monarch butterfly and someday I weel hear you scream.' Zen he slam down zee telephone. So you see it cannot be a plot."

"I wish I could be as sure as you, Joseph," Loftwood said.

This Navy captain, Loftwood, had become the major puppeteer in the exhibition of the Irish Monster. He was the impresario marketing the property of the retiring Uncle Nigel. As such, Loftwood was the man upon whom the Monster lavished the major portion of his peculiar charm.

His dangerous ruminating on this occasion, for instance, demanded distraction. I therefore released a startling wild bellow and launched a running attack upon a Dr. Santean who had arrived that afternoon and had followed me about for two hours attempting to plant the receiving end of a stethoscope against my carcass. This sneak Santean was lurking at the other end of the drawing room (the main exhibition room) and had his back to me when I attacked. As I came upon him I discovered in his hands a half-filled hypodermic needle. The fiend!

I hurtled Santean's little black bag through the window into the garden. I was about to send the shaken medical man after his satchel of insidious mumbo-jumbo, but Ira Loftwood and Hope Cornflower restrained me. They were getting rather good at it, what with all the practice. I permitted myself to be hustled off to my room. It was about closing time at the zoo anyway.

And shortly my bed time, my favorite part of the day, as you shall see, arrived. Hope Cornflower remained with me to tuck me in, as had become the accepted regimen. We had a special training exercise to go through first though. Each evening as we entered the boudoir Hope had to consult the log book. Therein were inscribed the daily instructions from Ira Loftwood and Uncle Nigel. It had been discovered, within a few days of my arrival, that the one person who had any influence at all over the Monster was Miss Cornflower. With her gentle direction, the wild man had been trained in the following accomplishments: 1. he accepted the wearing of a pair of trousers—(but only after the garment had been cut down to a length that reached just above the knee) 2. adjusted to submerging himself in a tub of hot water every evening (but could be restrained from splashing the complete contents of the tub onto the floor only when Miss Cornflower took a piece of soap in one hand and ran its smooth contour over the exterior of the primitive) and 3. settled docilely while his chin whiskers were removed by scissors (he would not consent to the clean finish imparted by a razor).

It was decided by the learned directors of the Cornflower Specimen project that all attempts at rehabilitation of the Monster would be handled by Hope. Thus, each evening a list of recommended areas of enlightenment were scribbled in the log. The list was comprised primarily from suggestions delivered by that day's visitors. "See if you can get him to eat cooked meat." The Specimen did.

"Observe his reaction to music. A recording of Beethoven's Sixth is on the gramophone, also a Rimsky-Korsakov's Scheherazade." "Willie" showed no reaction to the former. Upon listening to two minutes worth of the latter, however, he ripped apart the gramophone with his bare hands. This was considered very significant.

In the evening following Dr. Innis' denouncement, Hope found in the log the suggestion that she attempt to induce her charge into a sleeping garment consisting of a pair of cotton trousers and a jacket of like material. I believe the Americans call them pajamas.

When my bath was concluded, Hope led me to my bed where the nightwear was laid out. We started with the jacket portion. It required twenty minutes of instruction in that quiet secluded bedroom before the Monster grasped the fundamentals of enclosing himself in the garment. It was not until Hope had slipped in and out of the jacket several times that the dull chap finally sensed the intricacies of filling the sleeves with his arms. Oddly, the old boy absolutely refused any help from the young lady, aside from her personal demonstration, in acquiring mastery over the art.

Then came the trousers. For some reason the Specimen's mind could not make the transition from his normal wear, the short-legged trousers, to the pajama bottoms. The clod, for some reason, could not fathom the similarity in engineering principle. His major triumph—and he was obviously trying to succeed, to comprehend, to the limit of his imagination—was the installation of both feet in one leg of the garment, through the bottom opening of the leg.

"But, don't you see, Willie," Hope said in exasperation, "they can't *both possibly* go in there. Here now, this one goes—oh why won't you let me *help* you!?"

The poor brute held out to the girl the crumpled trousers, his eyes showing something very akin to shame at having to concede defeat.

"No, we're not going to give up now," she said briskly. She put her hands behind her head and unbuttoned her dress. "I can't understand it," she added. "You were doing so well with the other things: hammering the nail into the table, tying the knot in the rope, putting the square blocks in the holes." She had removed the dress. After a moment's hesitation, she walked over and closed the drapes over the French window. Then she slipped out of her petticoat.

The befuddled Monster, of course, stared at the elastic and strap contraption which surrounded approximately one-fourth of her marvelous body with unseeing eyes, so absorbed was he in the flickering realization that he had failed this his one friend in the civilized world.

"Now don't you worry," Hope said, sitting her neatly

girdled derriere on the edge of the bed next to her pupil. "See, now this is how we do it." She took the trousers and inserted one silk-stockinged leg into the garment. "And now this other one . . . see?"

My dear young lady, I see only that the two hundred and six bones comprising your basic framework have been sheathed in a cabinet of masterful craftsmanship. A small miracle of structural integrity. One is tempted to research even further, to discover if any misalignment developed in the artisan's skillful matching of the yet uncovered areas of the masterpiece.

The instructor found it necessary to perform the entering and exiting of the pajama bottoms several times before her dull charge exhibited even a glimmering of comprehension. He eventually learned to hold the garment open for the teacher so that she could demonstrate the technique. This procedure though resulted in a slight accident.

The Monster, sitting on the edge of the bed, held the pajamas open. The teacher inserted one spectacular leg into the trousers successfully. As she attempted to shelter the other leg similarly, the heel of her shoe caught in the fabric. The Monster evidently grew confused and tried to jerk the garment upward into place. This caused the girl to topple forward on top of poor Willie with a squeal that was not quite fright. There ensued an embarrassing jumble of colliding parts, an abrasive grinding of soft flesh and thin elastic against rigid muscle. The confused scramble on the bed was not easily resolved, for the participants shortly discovered that Willie had somehow gotten one of his legs fully inserted into the portion of the trousers already occupied by the girl's leg.

At one point in the awkward grappling the two pairs of eyes involved reached opposite ends of the same exact plane, a plane measuring just the length of a cigarette. For a split second the two sets of eyes stared at each other in a naked communication that startled both owners.

Miss Cornflower finally was able to roll free of her shackle, except for her arm which was pinned beneath the invader's back. She lay beside the confused "Willie" for a moment, regaining her dedication.

"That was a very silly thing to have happen, Willie," she said, her voice touched with a thin, comforting, coat of lust.

"I hadn't realized you were so big, so . . . mannish. It's a shame there aren't some of your own people available, some girls. Really an awful waste. The more time I spend with you, I'm afraid— No, no, mustn't play with that. . . !"

The Monster's attention had become centered on the straps that formed the connecting link between the lady's silk stockings and her elastic shorts. He discovered, quite on his own, that when he pulled the strap and released it, it immediately returned to its original position, and returned with a playful little slapping noise. The old boy was greatly intrigued by this phenomenon.

Hope jerked her arm free of the Monster's weight and attempted to increase the distance between the fumbling hands of the primitive and the new plaything. She had not reckoned with Willie's simple mind. He pursued the fleeing elastic bands, grunting his delight as he discovered in his pursuit that there were more of these objects located at various intervals about the lady's scurrying thighs.

Following a scramble that took them from one end of the bed to the other, Hope realized that she could not deter the gentleman by combating him at his own level. He was far stronger and faster, and he was immune to her anger. She therefore applied a supplication that of late had proved effective with inducing Willie to do her bidding. She wrapped her arms around his head and pulled his face against her neck, then she crooned to him while stroking his long hair. On this occasion she found a bit disconcerting the fact that his beard and warm breath were, because of her dress, in contact with her bare skin.

Willie responded as he had in the past. He gradually relaxed and his hands slowly released the elastic bands. "Here now," she said, "You move right over here on the—oh! No, no, no, you must keep your head up. Now you lie here and I'll bring you something nice. That's it, over on your side, facing toward the wall. Now, eyes closed and be a good boy and I'll bring you something very nice." There were small licks of flame in her voice and her hands that pushed Willie into position trembled.

She left the bed and I heard her steps move across the room. The next sound fell upon my ear like a stunning promising chord. The sound of elastic being moved over some soft surface. Then came a small metallic click that reminded me of the small metal contraptions on the ends of her garters; two of them loose and striking together. Then the footsteps returned to the bed.

"Have you your eyes still closed, you naughty boy?" she said as she kneeled on the bed. The licks of flame were brighter and starting to eat into her breathing.

Her fingernail touched my upper arm and her passion drove it into my skin. I tensed impatiently waiting for her to throw herself upon me.

The fingernail in my arm went deeper—too deep!

I snapped my eyes around! It stuck from my arm like a great, sterilized serpent's fang. A polished nail driven into a coffin in which they would bury the Irish Monster. A stainless steel tube through which would leak insidious truth.

I snatched the hypodermic needle from her hand and jerked its terrible snout from out of my flesh. But even in the instant that I had reached for the devil's tool I had seen its contents diminish by half as Hope forced the plunger downward producing a noise that I had mistaken for the sound of elastic moving over a soft surface.

"Now, now, Willie, be nice," Hope said as I threw the hypodermic across the room. She attempted to encircle my head with her arms. You damned wellspring of deceit, woman! I threw her from the bed. I jumped to the middle of the bedroom floor and crouched there.

The contents of the hypodermic were unknown to me, but there was too much coincidence in seeing two such needles in one evening. Obviously the vile juices let loose in my body would soon attack and fell my consciousness. My keepers had evidently tired of my aloofness and were determined to gain a greater familiarity with me. They had instructed Hope to choose an auspicious moment and then plunge into me the grappling hook that would draw them within striking distance with their kit of foul instruments.

I had not absorbed the full dosage of their force-fed congeniality. There was but one way to maintain my isolation. I had to find a shelter in which I could nest unmolested until the perfidious brew drained from my senses.

I dashed for the bedroom window. My legs took me two strides and then collapsed beneath my weight. I lay helpless on the floor and through a cotton mist watched Hope slip into her dress and run from the room. Carry your triumph in a tight grasp, my girl; squeeze from it an abundance of comfort, for you will need comfort when next I have risen.

The following hours were lived in a gray spectrum, punctured here and there, always without warning, by daggers of high-pitched violin music. I sensed and saw four faces over me; Hope, Uncle Nigel, Ira Loftwood, and Dr. Santean. There was a discussion that revolved around my heart beat and respiration. I was rolled over and then back again as a cold piece of metal ran over my exterior. "Let's try his eyes, ears, and throat, now," Dr. Santean said.

A great flash struck my eyes, one at a time, driving the violin music even higher. My head was levered about by a hand gripping my hair and some unknown intruder slid into my ears.

A flat wooden snake worked my teeth apart and gradually forced itself inward. "He's fighting the depressor," Dr. Santean said, vexed. "He's not totally unconscious."

"Which means there's a good chance he could swallow his tongue," somebody, Loftwood I think, said. "Here let me get it in. I'd better just set it crossways like this to protect him." My teeth bit eagerly on the wooden probe locking it in place.

"Why not give him the remainder of the injection," Hope said. "I was able to give him only half."

"I'd rather not," Dr. Santean said. "You see, ha-ha, we're not dealing with a human of normal immunities here. Goodness knows what a full dose for an average twentieth-century man would do to him."

"Why that's ghastly!" Hope cried. "The needle you handed me had a full dose in it. Suppose I'd given all of it to him? He might be dead."

"Well ... er ... perhaps," Dr. Madman conceded. "But at

least we'd have salvaged the knowledge that a primitive cannot survive 20c.c.'s of the drug, you see?"

"All right, Santean," Ira Loftwood snarled, "get on with the goddamn examination. And when you report back to Sir Marvin Hook, you can tell him we've no fake here. You tell him the Cornflower specimen is the real goods."

"Oh, Sir Marvin is quite convinced of that," Santean simpered. "He said that if I found no contradicting evidence, no fraud, he would be down to see the specimen in person. In fact he is motoring down tomorrow, unless I call him and tell him that your prize is nothing but a vengeful member of the woolen mill guild. Purposely planted here to draw Sir Marvin from the castle."

I had the impression that I forced myself to stay conscious for the whole of the medical examination. A scaly creature, a flickering tongue, bile-eyed reptile, came clawing through cracks in my skull attempting to nest in my brain. His name was sleep. For hours I fought him back, forcing him to withdraw from the cracks, my only weapon a raging scream that I crashed about his ears. But he always found another crack and if my attention wandered for a second, I would then turn and find his slimy green body slithered halfway into my skull. His terrible eyes pointed lustfully at the warm dynamo throbbing in the center of my head.

I must have turned my back to him once too often. When I opened my eyes I was in my own bed and the sunlight told me it was after 10 A.M.

There was a small bandage on my biceps and a small purple incision beneath it. Dr. Santean had sucked a sample of my blood. Another gauze patch on my thigh marked the area from which a piece of my skin had been stolen. A tasty morsel, Doctor? Ahhh, but the wooden depressor was still locked in my teeth.

I was still bustling about gathering my wits when Hope Cornflower opened the bedroom door and stuck her head in. Enter Delilah.

I scampered away from her and sat in the corner with a rigid mask of unforgiveness on my face. She attempted to placate me, her voice sweet and soothing. I refused all offers of emotional involvement. When at last we left the room to go to breakfast, Miss Cornflower's lips were locked in that white thinness that in women denotes the pressure of a guilt that is slowly being rationalized by some female logic to something other than guilt, duty perhaps. Ladies, bless them, are very good at that sort of thing.

At breakfast we were joined by young Thomas Roche. His belligerent brother, Bert, happily was not with him. (I had no taste for a chunk of raw Spitfire pilot for breakfast.) I could not determine if Hope was aware of Thomas' attitude toward her, but even the primitive brain of Willie detected that the young man was "smitten," as I believe the word is. He could hardly keep his eyes from her. Beware, lad. She is somewhat treacherous.

The two young people chatted away ignoring completely poor disfigured Willie. Following the meal I was put on exhibition for two gentlemen from Dublin University. They appeared less than enthusiastic with regard to claiming me as a fellow countryman. In the afternoon I set myself to prowling about for a sight of Dr. Santean. I hoped to find the distinguished physician in some isolated area for a few minutes. In my wandering I came upon Hope and Thomas Roche sitting in the garden.

Hope patted a chair next to her and asked me to sit. I chose the chair located furthest from her. Her lips drew thin again. I sat silently for the most part, except that every few minutes I would peek under the bandage on my leg at my epidermal loss and let out a little whimper. After about the fourth time Hope snapped, "Oh for God's sake stop doing that. You'd think we took your complete leg."

Uncle Nigel wandered into the garden. "And how's the lad today?" he said to me, patting my shoulder as he passed. To Hope he said, "Do you remember that sea captain Riordan who first told you about Willie? He's down in the village. A Lieutenant Butcher from your office brought him out. Seems Riordan is reneging on his story, the jet aircraft thing. Lieutenant Butcher is all in a flap. Captain Riordan also claims he never heard of an Irish Monster, so Lieutenant Butcher wants to show him Willie. Ira went down to fetch them."

At that moment the driveway was abruptly filled with the

frantic sound of charging motorcycles. While Thomas Roche and Uncle Nigel peered over the hedge at the motorized invasion, I edged over to stand timidly beside Hope.

"By George, it's Sir Marvin Hook!" Uncle Nigel shouted. "He's actually here!" He scampered off to welcome the butterfly killer.

"So Sir Marvin really came down out of his castle," Hope said to Thomas Roche. "And in grand style—an Army motorcycle escort. How does he rate that?"

"I suspect the Army chaps are being nice to Sir Marvin just now," Thomas said. "Something to do with a shipload of industrial machine tools he's supposed to have hidden away in South America. I heard a bit of gossip about it from a chap in supply."

"They don't know much about Sir Marvin if they believe he's going to hand them over," Hope said.

A few minutes later Uncle Nigel appeared on the terrace and called for Hope to bring me in. "Hurry, child," he said in an excited voice. "Sir Marvin wants to see Willie!"

I looked at Hope and said, "Food?" one of the two words she taught me during my residence at Cornflower.

She did not answer, but led the way to Uncle Nigel. The poor brute from Wilson's Rock followed her, thinking he was being led to food. In a sense, he was correct. The firm of Mandrell, Limited is indeed nourished by the likes of Sir Marvin Hook.

"Sir Marvin is in the old library," Uncle Nigel said. "He wants to see Willie in there. I don't know why he selected that room. Come along. Sir Marvin is waiting."

In the main hall we met a familiar chap, familiar to me at any rate; a hulking bull of a man named Jason Cole. Mr. Cole wore a turban of white bandage on his head, a memento of our previous meeting. He was Sir Marvin's bodyguard. And he fulfilled his assignment with skill. At least he had the dark night a month before when I had attempted to negotiate the elaborate security barrier surrounding Sir Marvin's castle. Mr. Cole had very nearly thrown me into the moat wherein the tigers roamed. As it turned out he succeeded only in convincing me that Sir Marvin could not be reached in the castle.

"Sir Marvin wants me to bring along your specimen," Mr. Cole told Hope, Uncle Nigel, and Thomas Roche. "You folks wait here."

"Well, I suppose that's all right," Uncle Nigel conceded.

"I don't know that it's all right," Hope said. "Is Ira Loftwood back yet?"

"Not yet, my dear," Uncle Nigel said. "I can't see that Ira would object to the arrangement either. After all. . . ."

While the Cornflowers enmeshed themselves in establishing house rules, the straightforward Mr. Cole grabbed my arm and started pushing me down the corridor toward the old library, a room at the far end of the house. Willie permitted himself to be herded along with surprising docility for a man of his temperament.

Mr. Cole opened the library door and thrust me inside. "Here's the silly thing," he said to the man in the room, Sir Marvin Hook.

Sir Marvin was also a big man like Cole. His dark hair was well marked with the grey that had probably started attacking him at about age forty, say five years previous.

"Leave him here," Sir Marvin said. "Get back down the hall and keep all those fools away from this room." The voice, with its strong low register hum was the same voice that had described to Uncle Nigel and myself the demise of the butterfly a few nights previous.

When Cole left, Sir Marvin locked the door behind him and pocketed the key. He never took his eyes from me as he did this. "Even if you are not what you seem to be," he said, "you at least cannot be concealing any weapon with which to do me harm, not in that rag," He nodded at my pair of cut-down trousers. "And if it comes to physical combat, I think I could show you a thing or two despite our difference in age."

I gave him a low growl, and crouched a bit, a warning that he had thus far failed to enchant me. "Ah, you recognize the voice of belligerency, do you?" he laughed. "You are at least then from fighting stock. So are many of the hands in my woolen mills. I have managed to tame them. I believe I can do you the same service."

He had walked to a door at the side of the room. He

opened it, grabbed a bright chain that had been anchored to something just inside the door, and he called, "C'mon Blissful. C'mon Repentance. Come out and meet an Irish Monster."

He pulled from the adjoining room two dogs, a pair of chows. The animals were a matched set, at least with respect to incivility. They entered the room snarling on the ends of their chains.

I crouched further and snarled back at them. They were quite unintimidated. They practically strangled themselves in an effort to break their chains to get at me.

I suddenly became rather more aware of the decor of the room we were in, the old library. There wasn't a stick of furniture in the room. The walls were lined with built-in book racks all of which were empty. There was a fireplace in one wall in which was laid a slow burning fire. The windows were small and, I suspected, locked. Sir Marvin held his vicious charges with one straining hand and locked the door through which they had entered.

A man is entitled to a normal dosage of fear for his life, but to my thinking Sir Marvin was exceeding any rational limit.

"Now let's have a good look at you, Monster," Sir Marvin said, as he advanced toward me, his salivating dogs preceding him by three paces. "They tell me you have proved most uncooperative to your hosts. The trouble was they didn't know how to handle you."

I held my ground and tried once more the defense of snarling and clawing at the noses of his animals. It served only to further antagonize the creatures. One of them, Repentance I think, lunged dramatically and snapped at my clawing hand. I felt her wet lip brush the back of my hand and heard the terrible crunch of her teeth.

Sir Marvin, his eyes lit with a mania frequently observed in wounded buffalo, allowed the lunging animals to proceed toward me. I made one more attempt to subdue them. I reached quickly and caught Repentance a sharp clap along the side of her head. She became only more infuriated and honed her yelping with an agonized undertone that encouraged Blissful to a higher rage. Their zestful combined lunging very nearly jerked Sir Marvin from his feet squeezing a distasteful laugh from his chest.

"One at a time," he cried. "One at a time. Here Blissful, you first." He manipulated the chains in his hands. Somehow Blissful's arresting gear was extended while Repentance's was subtracted. Blissful lunged closer to me and at the same time her lunge pulled Repentence backwards. They were evidently secured to opposite ends of a single chain. The chain was routed through a ring held by Sir Marvin's large meaty fist.

Blissful's increased combat range brought her well within reach of the frightened Monster. I leaped back from her snarling mouth. I had attacked Bertie Roche a few days previous with those primitive weapons that nature has planted in my gums. As I stared with fascinated horror at the wet fangs planted in Blissful's jaws, I realized that Man clearly had not survived his jungle growth period by reasoning with his four-footed neighbors on their terms.

As I gave ground to Blissful, screeching my indignation at every step, kindly Sir Marvin and the restrained Repentance also advanced toward me thus allowing Blissful to back me fully to the wall.

I slid along the wall, crouched and becoming a bit sore in the throat with my retaliatory screeching. What is your pleasure, Sir Marvin? How long do you intend for this barbarity to continue? It must be obvious that we are evenly matched. I can outrun your dogs (as long as the chains remain in place, you swine) and your dogs are well equipped to preserve your carcass from my fury.

We circled the room completely. As I slid past the hot fireplace, Sir Marvin jumped forward an extra step, permitting Repentance an additional two feet of striking distance. In my scramble to escape the ambush, the back of my leg struck the fire screen and depressed it sufficiently to bring the flame of the fire within eating distance of my calf. Several years growth of leg hair was singed out of existence, its departure heralded only by the ring of Sir Marvin's gross glee.

The next turn around the room was supervised by Repentance, who proved to be only slightly less antagonistic than Blissful, but more agile. She forced me at one point to clamber up on to the empty bookshelves. I was able to scramble back to the floor only because Sir Marvin was so overcome with sympathetic laughter that he was momentarily incapable of maintaining his forward pursuit.

That bellowing noise from your gaseous belly offends me, sir. The incivility of your animals gives me little pleasure. You have chosen the battleground and the weapons. So be it.

I waited until it had become Blissful's turn to again lead the attack. She was the more vulnerable of the two dogs, because she was the more insistent on butchery. Her leaps at the defenseless rabbit were more frantic than those of Repentance. I continued to give ground and I waited with the coiled alertness of a hangman's trap.

Blissful sprang. She depleted her allotment of slack chain before quite reaching the peak of her leap. The tautness of the chain jerked her head sideways for a second while she dropped back to all fours. In that second, the treacherous rabbit turned and struck.

My hand darted into the coarse fur of Blissful's neck. My fingers sank with laudable greed into the oily flesh that housed the snarl. My timing had been off by a fraction. Had I grasped but another half-ounce of that tubing throbbing beneath the skin I'd have been able to disengage the plumbing of her throat from its anchorage. As it was I was able only to dramatically impair her breathing.

I held her off the floor with my tightened fist. Her purple lips stretched in a crooked grin that for an instant appeared almost rakish (as though she knew what was coming, or was she possibly a masochist?). She lashed her body about furiously fighting for air. Her dull claws grappled the skin of my forearm and removed several strips before I was able to restrain her forepaws with my other hand.

Sir Marvin bellowed something, some frightful curse and the chains in his hands sang through the ring he was holding. The portion of the chain that had restrained Repentance to a non-combative status abruptly became elongated. The great chow hurtled toward me with all of her teeth extended before her. Her yellow eyes flashed not with a dedication toward rescuing her struggling sister, but rather with the worry that the quarry was in position for the kill and she, Repentance, would arrive too late.

I had to relinquish my hard-won ground. Repentance charged in beneath the acrobatics of Blissful. I released Blissful and dropped her on Repentance rather than sustain a fanged invasion of my soft underbelly. At that, one leg was tardy in its withdrawal and Repentance placed on it a reminder of her rancor, a red incision that quickly welled with free-running corpuscles.

Sir Marvin, the rear echelon general, had regained the advantage. He had rescued his front line with a timely disbursal of reinforcements. Ahh, but the master puppeteer had entended too many strings into the arena. He controlled the length of the chains but if the fox were agile it was the fox who would control the horizontal manipulation of the chains.

I left the sanctuary of the wall and bounded more into the middle of the floor. Repentance was instantly after me, charging past the sluggish Blissful. (A bit winded, my dear? Insufficient exercise perhaps.) Repentance's chain crossed over Blissful's chain. Sir Marvin, who wished to reset the battlelines along the same configuration that had in the past given him such delight, was attempting to reel in the subdued Blissful and allow Repentance to carry the battle.

I dodged back in the other direction, drawing Repentance into a snarling collision with Blissful. The dogs scrambled to their feet, barking their impatience at each other for a second before they both resumed the chase of the elusive animal before them.

Sir Marvin frantically rotated the ring in his hands, attempting to alleviate the double twist that had by this time overtaken the chain. While he worked with his snarled lines, I danced about the dogs in an apparent illogical sequence of movements, and jeered at them with a taunting, inhuman sound that evoked from them a madness of temper that was beyond reason. And the chain continued to whip and cross upon itself. Blissful was back into the battle by this time and, although she had suffered somewhat a depletion of her energies during the hand to hand engagement and was thus somewhat slower afoot than Repentance, she exhibited what appeared to me to be a rather base appetite for pure revenge.

I continued to maneuver the slow dog against the fast dog. Sir Marvin's increased concentration on the tangled chain was marked by a series of guttural outbursts that might well have given pause to the English dons who had been overseers of his fundamental grasp of the mother tongue.

The tide of battle, as they say, had turned.

The distinguishing characteristic of the competent general is his ability to identify this point of fluctuation in his fortunes. The hallmark of the great general is his ability to exploit the shift in tide.

Once more I enticed Repentance to launch herself at me just a split second before Blissful made the same lunging commitment. And once more their collision resulted in a snarling pile-up of reddish fur in which might be glimpsed slashing paws and thickets of teeth.

But this time the gibbering primitive did not back off to savor his mundane triumph. Instead he leapt across the entangled animals and bounded upon the startled puppeteer. The look in Sir Marvin's eye changed quickly from perplexity to something that went beyond pure rage. He raised both of his huge arms and set himself to crush this witless amoeba that had dared trifle with his amusement. One of his hands held the apex of the chain complex, the ring.

I smiled at him then; a large, warm, quite human smile. I said, "But you see, old man, you should never have killed my butterfly."

The shock sank past even his rage. His mind ... boggled, I believe is the best word we have around. During his moment of distraction I wrenched the chain ring from his grasp. There was considerable slack in the fetters by this time for Blissful and Repentance had regained the scent and were charging neck and neck along my back trail.

I dodged behind Sir Marvin, ducking the arm that reached out for me. As I went by him, I slipped a loop of the chain about his neck. His chows came past him, one on each side of their master. Sir Marvin started to come about also. No, no, sir, you have had your turn.

I threw my full weight on the chain. Sir Marvin staggered

wildly to one side, his hands clawing at the tightened steel loop sinking into his neck. But he was equal to my attack, he retained his feet. And the chows were upon me before I could again yank the chain. It is illogically true: wickedness, a wickedness such as Sir Marvin possessed, requires a man of an odd allotment of strength. The strength is not a physical strength, such as Sir Marvin also possessed (he had friends among the gods). It is more a strength of will. Chaps with it are ruddy hard to kill.

I managed to kick Repentance one alongside the withers, breaking her stride and forcing her to momentarily block Blissful's charge. But I could no longer retain my grip on my portion of the chain. It led the brutes to me like some silver beacon, and its possession located me always between the chows and Sir Marvin, inside their perimeter of aggression.

As I relinquished the chain and jumped out of reach of the chows, Sir Marvin, who had been fighting against the tautness of the steel cord, abruptly found his center of equilibrium shift some 180 degrees. He staggered away from me. Blissful and Repentance continued toward me. The two opposing forces quickly dissipated all the slack from the chain and it snapped to tautness with a vibration that was not lacking in musical content. The chows accomplished what I had not been able to accomplish.

Sir Marvin was jerked backwards and slammed against the floor. His flight was remarkable for its complete lack of agility, particularly the enjoining of his cranium and the thinly covered oak flooring.

After that we did naught but circle the room. The fleet-footed wanderer from Wilson's Rock set the pace. The chows followed him with as great an enthusiasm as before. Their progress however was not quite what it had once been. The gentleman they dragged along behind them scaled out at better than fifteen stone. Even blind fury loses a bit of its vigor under such a burden.

Following the tenth or twelfth circuit, the chows were obviously beginning to wonder if the prize were worth the toil. I suspect they pressed on only because each was reluctant to be first to admit the loss of passion. Sir Marvin exhibited little interest in the outcome. He slid placidly along behind his charges, his hands and feet bouncing occasionally as they encountered some ridges in the nap of the rug. He offered neither encouragement nor conciliation; only loyalty. He remained in attendance, always the same distance behind the chows, the chain linking all three of their necks. He was there for consultation should any be required.

The noise of a key being turned in the lock of the main door disrupted the simplicity of our march. I charged the door as it started to swing open. The chows sensed immediately the change in tactics and, on the assumption, I suppose, that anything was better than what they had, they roused themselves to one last pursuit.

Jason Cole was the visitor stopping by to see if Sir Marvin had possibly grown weary of the entertainment. He had.

My shoulder caught Mr. Cole at the belt buckle, throwing the startled man back against the far wall of the corridor, clearing him from the path of the caravan. I galloped into the corridor. My new-found friends, dredging up a few good barks from their laboring chests, galloped after me.

The chows found the polished tile of the corridor rather sticky footing for a few seconds, but once they had induced Sir Marvin on to the tile they were able to set a smart pace down the corridor toward the group staring at us from the center hall of the house.

I heard Mr. Cole gasp out his employer's name as the tail end of the parade swept by his glaring eye. The gasp was a salute of sorts for the old warrior passing in review. Sir Marvin did not return the courtesy.

It was a bleeding, frightened, gibbering primitive who stumbled into the group in the main hall. I fell rather helplessly into the arms of Hope Cornflower. At the sight of me, there rose out of the remainder of the group a universal condemnation of Sir Marvin Hook's bestiality, plus a few cries here and there of "I told you so."

I detected also one whiskey voice that croaked, "That's an Irish Monster? Never seen one in me life." Captain Riordan was aboard.

The chorus of censure continued only until it was noted that the suspiciously relaxed lump dangling from the end of the dog chain was maintaining a very unvillain-like posture.

The chows had been brought to a halt when their burden had struck the step that one mounts to reach the level of the main hall. Blissful and Repentance had negotiated the step on the run. Sir Marvin was beyond such dexterity.

One of the first to reach Sir Marvin was his lackey Jason Cole. It required only a second for Mr. Cole to determine that his pay checks would never again be signed by those huge hands. Cole's loyalty evidently extended beyond the grave. He removed a pistol from beneath his coat and his eyes sought out my priceless anatomy. He found me and started walking toward me like some hulking thing from out of a crypt.

"You stupid person," Hope cried at him. "Can't you see he had nothing to do with it. Those terrible dogs did it." She moved herself in front of me, between myself and the rising pistol.

Dr. Innis, the doubting Scot, who was still awaiting rail transport back to his university, stepped forward. Innis, who was of no mean bulk himself, felled Mr. Cole with a bash that distributed its wrath at the exact center of Mr. Cole's chin.

While the general housecleaning took place in the center hall, Hope bundled me off to my quarters for repairs. Her soothing fingers siphoned the pain from the several areas of damage and her feminine cooing restored the Monster's trust in the strange creatures of this new environment. As a matter of fact his trust was so permanently reactivated that the half-naked beast would endure, with no sign of fear, the full embrace of Miss Cornflower's comforting arms. He even appeared to be learning the complexities of this form of communication and showed signs now and again of attempting to return the gestures.

"Now, now, this will not work out at all well," the young lady said, as she wiggled from under my weight on the sofa. "You see, you're much stronger than I and you don't—no, no, naughty, naughty. You're not allowed to put your hand there. You remain here now while I get the medicine kit. That leg of yours needs some salve."

When she returned a few minutes later she stopped by the experiment book. "What did they want to try today," she said idly as she leaned over the book. "Perhaps teach you how to make friends with dogs."

She read the new entry. "Now who in heaven's name thought this one up?" she said crossly. " 'Try and determine the Specimen's appetite for sex, if any.' " Sounds like something Bertie Roche would consider essential ... it's in Ira's handwriting all right." She closed the book and came toward me with the medical kit. "I have no idea how they think I can do that. Anyway, Ira must have written it in before all the excitement. I imagine the last thing on your mind after a day like this would be sex. Even if you had any interest in it at all."

My dear young lady scientist, conclusion without experiment is hardly the route to truth. Where are we headed if we discard research and validation? Perhaps the simple creature from the sea can find some way to revive your scientific discipline.

"Now you lie here," she said pushing me on to the sofa. "And I'll clean that cut."

I tapped a finger against her chest and said, "Food?"

"No that is *not* food—oh, you mean the blood stain on my dress. I guess I am rather a sight from having held on to you."

I tapped again harder, "Food?"

"Oh bother," she said. "I suppose I'd best take it off or you'll have me all bruised."

The drapes were drawn again, as they had been the night before; the better to hide the hypodermic needle. The dress was removed, also the petticoat (keen-eyed Willie had been quick to point out what was possibly a stain on the latter).

The maid deposited these garments on a chair. As she walked back to the patient she saw the direction of his gaze. "Oh, I'd best get rid of this," she said, "or we'll go through that garter snapping business again." She put aside the distracting garment and again approached the sofa. Let me note here that no scientist ever entered her investigation with any finer equipment.

A few minutes later the wound was clean. Hope said, "Come along Willie. Bath time. Then you'll—Willie! I've told you—mustn't put your hands. . . ." She saw the freezing withdrawal creep upon the edge of my face, the eager pupil retreating to his shell as he is rebuffed without explanation.

"Oh you poor thing," the sweet nurse sighed. "I suppose it's all right. You don't know what you're doing, so it can't do any harm. Here, give me your hand."

Several minutes went by before it occurred to the scientist that she had inserted an invalid hypothesis somewhere in the formula. She pulled away from the sofa and said breathlessly, "I'm afraid I was wrong, it can do some harm. How you ever learned to unhook this is beyond me. I'll tell you, Willie, the longer I stay on these islands . . . c'mon now, time for your bath."

She drew the bath. I removed my shortened trousers (by myself, you might be interested to know) and entered the tub. My handmaid remained outside the tub as usual and applied the hygiene lessons.

"I would think, Willie, that you would have learned how to do this by now," she chided. "You've learned to use a fork and a hammer. This should be child's—no, no, now, I can't go in. Let go. I'll have my bath later in my room. That's a good boy. Oh, I see. Since I've no clothes left on except these you must have thought . . . wouldn't I like to see Ira's face if I told him. 'We took a bit of a bath together. Well, you're the one who asked me to evaluate his appetite for sex.' Oh, he'd die. Now, Willie, I told you I'm not going in. Your hands are all wet . . . and warm."

A few minutes later she murmured, "Wait now. Let me go and lock the door. It would be just like some silly ass to want to come up and watch or something. Maybe take pictures for their damned report to the museum."

When she returned she was totally prepared for her bath.

Until now it has gone unrecorded that I was somewhat instrumental in conserving for the Empire that evening the amount of fuel required to heat one tub of water. There's many an unsung contribution that went into winning the war, believe me.

There was still a bit of daylight in the sky when Hope and the Monster parted. As she scampered into her clothes, the charmed Willie sat slowly up from the jumble of sheets on the bed. His lips moved for several seconds attempting to release some thought. Finally he mastered the barrier. He said, "Sex?"

"My God," Hope exclaimed. "Now there's two words you know, food and sex. How am I ever going to explain your mastery of the second to them? I suppose if I could teach you to say 'survival' they'd all celebrate it as some sort of scientific breakthrough or other."

She came over to the bed and patted my cheek. "Ahhh, Willie . . . Isn't it remarkable how little the damned thing has changed over the centuries. You get some sleep now."

About an hour later I took my final leave of the Cornflower estate. I exited through the window and took with me only the pair of abbreviated trousers and of course the page from the experiment book containing the final entry. I could think of no reason for leaving the latter. A comparison of the handwriting to Ira Loftwood's genuine script could only have led to some embarrassing ruminating by the collected scientists.

I took with me from Cornflower one further abrasion on my carcass. The tree I selected for my travel from the second storey to the garden proved unworthy of my trust. It broke under my agility and a sliver at the point of fracture slid into my forearm.

There was happily a cure for the accumulation of abuse that had been so liberally distributed over my carcass. I set myself to collecting the cure.


"You left in a damn hurry, now, didn't you?" my visitor said. "I thought you'd at least be around for the police investigation of Sir Marvin's death. We all sounded a bit witless describing the Irish Monster, and no monster to show."

"I am not fond of the police," I said. "They are rather more thorough in certain pursuits than your scientific friends, if you don't mind my saying. Fingerprint files and the like."

"I'm certain you would have fooled them," he said. "That was you, Mandrell, wasn't it? My God, I've never been so shocked in my life, walking into Cornflower and seeing you there in the main hall."

We were seated in a little office I maintained during that period, just off Bristol Square. We were involved in the logical culmination of the Irish Monster Commission. The "pay off" as the delightfully explicit Americans term it.

"I presume that you obtained your objective?" I said to the gentleman. "Sir Marvin's library will be made available for the rummaging of the scholars?"

"Yes. The executor of the estate is a Brazilian banking firm, Uni-Coffee. I chance to know one of the directors rather well. Incidentally, Hope Cornflower took your departure much harder than I would have thought. She has asked me some strange questions regarding the experiment book."

He stared silently at me for several moments, a probing silence. Finally I shrugged and said, "She is evidently a normal young woman, Captain Loftwood. Given to forming emotional attachments for household pets: cats, dogs, goldfish and the like. I assure you, it is quite healthy."

"Yes, well, let's get on with it," he said, his manner a bit cooler than it had been. "Here's your money. A thousand pounds. I'll have a hell of a time accounting for it to the museum directors when the war is over, but. . . ."

As he was leaving, he said, "You never did explain why you elected to accept the commission. When I first approached you, your rejection of the thousand pounds as inadequate was rather adamant."

"Let us say that I am not without sympathy toward your cause," I said. "Anthropology evidently is here to stay. In fact, it probably represents the science that is closest to perpetual motion. You, I take it, had no difficulty in retrieving your artifacts, the items you lent me for my residence on Wilson's Rock?"

"I grabbed them from Nigel Cornflower's library as soon as I realized you had left. It is assumed that you took them with you. I had a spot of trouble with that idiot sea captain Riordan. Fortunately I was able to immerse him in an alcoholic shell during most of their investigation. Naval Intelligence has bundled him off to God knows where. They're still after him about jet airplanes mounted on submarines, and the like. Disgusting waste of time and manpower," the Royal Navy captain said, "but I can't do anything about it."

I counted the banknotes he had laid on my desk. "Quite correct," I said, holding the money tighter so as to implant the brand of ownership with the heat of my hand. "You understand of course, there is no receipt?"

"Good God, why would I want one?" he said. "Ah yes, one more item. We have discovered that Dr. Innis was an impostor. The real Dr. Innis never left Edinburgh. The University refused to fund his travel. The fake Innis ducked out right after you."

"I am not surprised," I said. "The blow Dr. Innis delivered Jason Cole's chin exhibited much more the skill of the street fighter than a man of science."

"Don't be so cocksure about anthropologists," Loftwood said, with a touch of defensive belligerency. "It's not too well known, but Monsieur Giral who came to inspect you on the second or third day started his career in the Paris sewers as a raker or plugger or some such thing. That's where he made his first valuable discoveries. The Giral Tusk, for instance. It led him into a study of anthropology."

"You are correct," I said, "that fact is not too well known. Bon soir, Captain Loftwood,"

"Yes, goodby," he said. He paused before his exit and stared at the floor. "Damned keen rug you have in here," he said. "Afghan, isn't it?"

I nodded. "But it contains a few bullet holes, unfortunately."

"Nothing's safe from this damn war," he muttered as he left.

A few nights later I sat in the front seat of a private auto on a quiet road in Tilbury. The uniformed gentleman seated in the back seat of the auto was speaking.

"Why'd you insist on this vehicle?" he asked. "I've a nice comfortable staff car up at the crossing."

"For our mutual benefit," I said. "You cannot know a great deal about the firm of Mandrell, Limited, except of course that it does obtain results. You must ensure that the firm is discreet. The success of your assignment hinges on nothing less. Before you now is a display of Mandrell, Limited's talent in this sensitive area."

"You're beyond me," he said. "Just because you didn't let my driver get a look at you . . ."

"Let me put it this way," I said. "You will note our positions; our strategic disbursement, if you wish. You are there, with your hands fully within my sight. I am here, with my hands completely out of your sight. I might be holding a Webley, or a Smith and Wesson .38 for all you know."

"Your point is made," he said disinterestedly. "You won't mind if I reach for the thousand pounds, will you?"

He handed me the money and sat back while I counted it. "You have obtained your shipload of machine tools, I presume?" I said.

"We found them. Tied up at an old pier in Tampico. They're on their way to Liverpool now. The records were with Uni-Coffee, a bank in Brazil that's handling Hook's estate. One of the directors, a chap named Starkey, is chummy with our ambassador there and let us in on it. If that bastard Hook had co-operated, he'd be alive today."

I have my doubts, Colonel.

"But then you would not have had this opportunity to display your talents to your superiors."

"Ha, most of them think it was an act of God," he said. "The dogs and all that specimen thing. It's only the brass who came up with the 1,000 quid who know the story. And I'll tell you this, Mandrell: they are the brass that count in this game. I haven't done my career a bit of harm." He opened his door and prepared to leave.

"One last thing," I said. "There's a sergeant and a lieutenant on a motorcycle in the bushes about ten car lengths to the rear of your staff car. The lieutenant is in the sidecar and is holding a light machine gun. Would you request that they leave with you please? I have an aversion for the inherent inaccuracy of machine-gun fire, not to mention the noise. I assure you I am prepared to retaliate from this vehicle and I am not without a certain skill in these matters. The sergeant and the lieutenant, incidentally, are from your regiment so I don't suppose you'll have any trouble convincing them to move on."

He stared quietly at me for a moment. Then he smiled and said, "You don't miss much, do you? I think perhaps Mandrell, Limited is a reliable firm. I'll accept your word about your defenses. It's not worth risking two good men, and all the uproar, to put it to a test. Who knows, Mandrell, we may do business again someday. It's a funny war."

"And likely to be a hilarious peace, Colonel Coder. Good night."

Steve (Big Steve) Hunt and I met on his home ground in Birmingham, the location of one of the late Sir Marvin Hook's larger mills. (Some of you may remember Mr. Hunt as Dr. Innis, the doubting Scot; others, for reasons that I would not care to ponder, may not.)

"The guild treasury is going to show quite a hole when the damn auditors start looking for this 2,000 pounds," Hunt said to me cheerfully as he tossed a packet of notes into my lap. "We'll just have to muck up the books a bit, spread the increase in wages over several months, or the like."

"The new owners have been reasonable? They will permit you to organize the workers?" I asked.

"They've been absolutely top drawer, old cock, top drawer. Uni-Coffee is managing things now. They've a director, Bill Starkey, over here in England at this very moment. He's a colonel with that Yank air force group, the Eagle Squadron. Believe it or not, he and myself are as chummy as a couple of Liverpool tarts already. He'll give us any raise the government will permit. Fantastic bloke." Our meeting took place in a small beach cottage that was noticeably without heat.

I said, "You do realize by now, don't you, that there never was any necessity for you to be at the Cornflower home? All you really accomplished was to add an ingredient to the case that has activated undue police interest. They know that the real Dr. Innis never left Edinburgh. They are still looking for the impostor."

"And where in hell will they ever find him?" Hunt said. "The only good coppers are off to the war. They've that idiot

Sir Bruce Peak at the Yard who couldn't find Goering in a telephone stall. I wanted to be at Cornflower to get Marvin Hook if you didn't. Two thousand doesn't come easy to a labor union, Mandrell. There's a bit of sweat on every shilling. I hope it didn't bother your wild-man disguise having me call you a fake all the time? Don't forget, it was you told me to do it."

"That was the only logical course," I said. "You had no other credential. You had to play the pig-headed unbeliever. As a matter of fact you achieved a much greater eminence than some of the qualified people there, purely by casting the single minority conclusion. You were remarkably convincing, Mr. Hunt."

"I'll tell you a little secret," he said in a huge whisper. "There isn't a labor union man about worth his pay if he can't stand up in front of the boss and demand the full moon for his people when he knows in his heart they don't deserve no more than a roll of cheese."

I was unaware that this was a secret.

"And now a bit of drink to celebrate," he cried, and pulled a large whiskey bottle from a cabinet. He passed each of us a full tumbler of the brew. It required but a single sniff of the liquid to recognize that it had been tampered with since leaving the distillers.

"Here's to no more of the likes of Marvin Hook," Big Steve said and held up his glass. When he detected my hesitation he said with blatant slyness, "What's the matter, Mandrell, don't you like Big Steve's whiskey? Shall I help pour it into your craw, lad?"

He came slowly to his feet. His sigh indicated that the task before him was a distasteful one, but one also that he was supremely capable of dispatching. "Aye, lad, it's the working blokes that need the 2,000 more than yourself," he said.

He made several mistakes. Two of the most obvious were the locating of the whiskey bottle within my reach and the taking of his eye from me while he set down his full glass. I was calculatingly lenient in applying the force that brought his skull and the bottle into collision; he would rise from the floor within a reasonable period. I am not fond of welchers but I was indebted to Big Steve for his timely assault on the pistol-ladened Jason Cole in the Cornflower hall. I am not a man who forgets a debt. Not at least without considerable forethought.

I must report unhappily, that Mr. Hunt's attitude at the conclusion of our venture was not a unique reaction. Others before him had exhibited a similiar reluctance to opening the final gap between themselves and their pound notes. I have often felt that if Mandrell, Limited's business potential were not so restricted—let us accept the truth: not every chap I meet can be regarded as a possible subscriber, ninety per cent of them, for instance, are fiscally inept—anyway, if the firm were not so restricted, I quite likely would turn away many who come to me who are obviously without honor. But then, I do not mean to carp. If one establishes a commercial venture, one must be prepared to accept the idiosyncrasies of his chosen field. A businessman is, after all, just that—a businessman.

Alfred Pembroke was another kind of man.

I met with Mr. Alfred Pembroke several months after Sir Marvin Hook's demise. I had been to Iran in the meantime on a bit of business and had not had the opportunity to remind Mr. Pembroke of his obligations. The Iranian Farmer Commission had gone very poorly. I use the word "poorly" in its full monetary sense. My return passage to the United Kingdom had cost me even the nice bit of pearl that I had managed to scrape out of the adventure. I did gain a rather remarkable Afghan rug in the sorry affair but the rug was hardly an adequate substitute for financial solvency.

Thus I established communication with Mr. Pembroke and reminded him of an overdraft on my services.

"I assure you, Mr. Mandrell, I've had every intention of paying your thousand," Mr. Pembroke told me. "What is a lepidopterist if not an admirer of beauty. And honesty is certainly a thing of beauty."

"Sir Marvin Hook, was he not a lepidopterist?" I asked.

"Not on your life!" Mr. Pembroke bristled. "That man was a . . . a maniac. Driving steel pins through living butterflies. That's the work of a madman. Believe me, there's not a member of the Lepidopterology Society who did not stand up and cheer when we heard of Sir Marvin Hook's timely death. Ah ... incidentally, a few of the members feel that since Sir Marvin's death was accidental—those awful dogs!—you cannot quite lay legitimate claim to having been responsible. It therefore follows—"

"I have not brought you to this flat to negotiate, but to collect, Mr. Pembroke. Our agreement specified only the demise of Sir Marvin prior to the end of the cocoon season. I did not commit myself to the method of demise."

As he handed over the money, with a reluctant hand, he said, "That's why we feel a little cheated, the method of demise as you call it. We realize now we should have insisted on a more appropriate end for that man."

"Possibly bitten to death by a cage full of butterflies?" I commented idly as I counted the money.

"Have you been talking to Don Ball?" he asked in surprise. "No, I guess you couldn't have. Anyway, of all the suggestions put forth at the general meeting I believe that of Mr. Raymond Reid came closest to expressing what every member felt in his heart."

"You're referring to some method for doing away with Sir Marvin?" I asked.

"Oh yes. You see what we should have asked you to do was to secure Sir Marvin to a large wooden board, alive of course, and squirming about with all his might. And then you should have driven a steel skewer all the way through him, from his head on down. That, I dare say, would have taught him a lesson."

"If you don't mind giving away professional secrets," I said, "just how does one go about preparing a butterfly for mounting?"

"You mean the 'cleansing'? Well, there are several ways. Some use chloroform or ether, but that does run into expense. Personally I prefer the Reid method. I have this tiny little silver hammer ... well, you've seen how they take care of bulls and cows and such at a slaughter house?"

"You mean a poleax?"

"Of course one always closes the eyes first."

Whose eyes, Mr. Pembroke?

I believe I have noted somewhere or other in these chronicles a policy of Mandrell, Limited's regarding the soliciting of business. The firm does not. That is, we do not chase about on the highways and byways gripping complete strangers by the jacket lapels and urging them to enter negotiations.

Yet there have been occasions when a lack of knowledge of the firm's existence has impeded the fermenting of a wholly worthwhile commission. (A dramatic drawback to our dependence on word-of-mouth advertising.) On several such occasions I have taken it upon myself to acquaint the interested party, or parties, with the fact that Mandrell, Limited is at their service. (*The Bullrusher Commission* comes to mind.) From thence, usually, the matter is arranged in a gallop of irrevocable logic.

The Irish Monster Commission is a case in point. Captain Ira Loftwood mentioned the commission to me initially. After analyzing the petition I was forced to refuse the Captain. (His financial resources amounted to 1000 pounds.) Shortly after the breakdown in negotiations, a Colonel Keith Coder came to see me with an offer for the identical commission, the dispatch of Sir Marvin Hook. Unfortunately Colonel Coder presented an identical fee, the rudimentary 1000 pounds.

Despite my ineffectual grasp of basic arithmetical processes, I found a certain charm inherent in the coincidental offers—if two men offer a thousand pounds apiece, then ten men will offer. . . .

I will admit too that the fortunes of Mandrell, Limited at the time tended to tilt my judgement. I had just completed *The English Invasion Commission* and should have been doing rather well. But once again I had encountered the "renege factor"; in this instance employed by the military of my own country. The Special Services people paid me 5,000 pounds prior to flying me into Occupied Europe on the trail of General Von Ritterdorf, the German amphibious invasion expert. But they refused to pay the remainder of the fee, another 5,000, upon my return to England. They claimed that General Von Ritterdorf had fallen into the impellers of the hydro-electric turbine "under his own power." (I felt they could have spared me that.)

Anyway, the loss of half of the Von Ritterdorf fee left me with a lenient attitude toward the promotors of the next commission. Captain Ira Loftwood had offered a thousand for Sir Marvin Hook. So had Colonel Keith Coder. A week of research into the life of Sir Marvin Hook led me naturally to Big Steve Hunt of the woolen mill guild. Another 2,000. And then on to Mr. Alfred Pembroke and his reluctant 1,000.

The total at this point was 5,000. Not quite sufficient a sum to commit me, even considering the value of the pound in those happy times. My research pertinent to Sir Marvin Hook had revealed that securing his demise would be a more or less strenuous endeavor. (I am not partial to Bengal tigers.)

Then I discovered that Sir Marvin retained in his library two of the original Simon Redwool letters. Data describing the activities of Simon Redwool, one of the most mysterious men to participate in the development of the American West in the 1800's, was the rarest of Americana. The man who, at the time, possessed the most complete file on Simon Redwool, was an American himself. It occurred to me that the American collector might be interested in enhancing his Redwool portfolio.

The gentleman was not difficult to reach. He chanced to be in England at the time, a member of the American Eagle Squadron. "If Sir Marvin Hook has the number seven Redwool letter, the one with the bloodstains of Jesse James on it, I'll pay the 5,000 pounds," the gentleman told me. "But if he has only the number nine Redwool, the Butch Cassidy letter, that's not worth any more than 2,000."

By sheer, rare restraint I forced myself to refrain from quibbling. I said, "We must understand the ground rules. I will guarantee the demise of Sir Marvin. But I am afraid that I cannot guarantee that the letters, whatever their numbers, will become your property."

"Don't worry about that," he said. "A Brazilian firm, Uni-Coffee, will execute Sir Marvin's estate. I own controlling interest in Uni-Coffee. I'll get the Simon Redwool letters."

And to the best of my knowledge Colonel (later General) William Starkey did obtain them. When we had our last meeting connected with the Irish Monster Commission (we met again somewhat later in the war) Colonel Starkey said something that I was to remember years later with bitter-sweet outrage. He said, "You handled this deal pretty well, Mandrell. If you're interested in picking a lot more money see me in the United States after the war. I need somebody to run down the rest of the Redwool letters."

And once again, dear reader, it becomes my reluctant task to suspend this journal. Naturally the very process of setting the record of the firm of Mandrell, Limited to paper has generated within me vivid recall of the actual physical structure of the incidents that I have herein described. The actual smell of ancient stone in the security corridors of Greenwood for instance. The sight of the slender wire unwinding on the recorder as Bertie Roche's farewell message to the confused world in which he lived escaped the speaker. The sound Mr. Ralph Dankers made, a "surprised grunt" best describes it, as he started his pursuit of the weighted attaché case to the bottom of Belmont Lake. The feel of the heaving deck of the cutter *Cornflower II* beneath the bare feet of the Monster during his trip from Wilson's Rock to England.

All of these and more come vividly to mind. Of course I have one favorite memory. It has to do with that delightful young lady Hope Cornflower.

Hope provided me with an unbiased estimate of my professionalism, if you will. The craftsman is rarely able to assess the effectiveness of his labor viewed over an extended period. We are not generally accorded a "one man show" by some enterprising impresario. To receive such a judgement then by one qualified to speak is an intriguing experience.

Miss Hope Cornflower delivered her evaluation of my craftsmanship in the year 1947. She was Mrs. Thomas Roche at the time. She and her husband and General Keith Coder were standing in the hall of General Coder's London town house when Hope spoke the treasured words. I was there also, awaiting payment of the fee associated with the Sealed

Tomb Commission. Mr. Thomas Roche had just mentioned the name Augustus Mandrell.

And Hope, lovely Hope, said: "Who in heaven's name is Augustus Mandrell? I've never heard of him."

Thank you, my dear.

AUGUSTUS MANDRELL

## The Shattering Novel
## of a Political Assassination . . .

by
**Vassilis Vassilikos**

"Unique, exciting reading . . . Vassilikos's gifts are dazzling."

—*New York Times Book Review*